Eloisa James is a *New York Times* bestselling author
and professor of English literature, who lives with

We hope you enjoy this book. Please return or
renew it by the due date.

You can renew it at www.norfolk.gov.uk/libraries o
by using our free library app.

Otherwise you can phone 0344 800 8020 -
please have your library card and PIN ready.

You can sign up for email reminders too.

NORFOLK ITEM

30129 087 800 588

NORFOLK COUNTY COUNCIL
LIBRARY AND INFORMATION SERVICE

D1346820

By Eloisa James

*ebook only

Eloisa James

The Reluctant Countess

PIATKUS

PIATKUS

First published in the US in 2022 by Avon Books,
An imprint of HarperCollins Publishers, New York
First published in Great Britain in 2022 by Piatkus

1 3 5 7 9 10 8 6 4 2

A CIP catalogue record for this book
is available from the British Library.

ISBN 978-0-349-43438-4

Printed and bound in Great Britain by Clays Ltd, Elcograf S.p.A.

Papers used by Piatkus are from well-managed forests
and other responsible sources.

MIX
Paper from
responsible sources
FSC® C104740

Piatkus
An imprint of
Little, Brown Book Group
Carmelite House
50 Victoria Embankment
London EC4Y 0DZ

An Hachette UK Company
www.hachette.co.uk

www.littlebrown.co.uk

*For every woman who fell in love with a
scoundrel like Hippolyte Charles
(including Empress Joséphine)*

The Reluctant Countess

PROLOGUE

A cottage on the outskirts of Fontainebleau, France
1807

At the age of sixteen, Lady Yasmin Régnier prided herself on her courage. After all, hadn't she made her debut before the entire French court?

Yasmin had curtsied before the empress, disregarded the curled lips, ignored the giggles. She had held her head high and smiled at everyone who met her eyes. They all knew that her mother was Emperor Napoleon's mistress, but Yasmin held her ground.

But now?

The unease she felt when she woke alone, her husband nowhere to be seen, her personal maid not answering her call, was turning into panic. She started trembling, not only because the cottage was bitterly cold.

She walked slowly down the wooden staircase from her bedchamber, knowing from the echoing sound of her steps that *Mon Repose*, the darling house where her husband brought her after their elopement, was empty. Where was the friendly housekeeper, Mrs. Bernard? Where was the cook, Mrs. Recappé? Her personal maid, Desirée?

More to the point, where was her beloved and loving husband, Hippolyte? Her hand tightened on the railing. Something had happened, something terrible. Even if Hippolyte had returned to Fontainebleau, he wouldn't have left her alone.

Dread clenching in her stomach, she walked into the drawing room. The chamber was small for a lady, hardly large enough for its grand pianoforte, but Hippolyte had assured her that the cottage was merely a place to enjoy their honeymoon, their *voyage de noces*, while staying within reach of the palace. After all, their elopement would be a huge shock to her parents and the court. Soon they would move into their own *manoir*, suitable for the daughter of a *duc*.

But first, Hippolyte had to use his charm to smooth the way for the announcement of their marriage. Yasmin had faith he would succeed. He had a special relationship with Empress Joséphine: anyone could tell that.

She wrapped her arms around her bosom. Without Desirée, she couldn't lace her corset and her breasts were on the point of falling from her gown. The cottage was chilly and getting chillier by the moment.

The drawing room fireplace was empty. Even if she carried wood from the shed, how would she start a fire? Her maid woke the coals in the morning, or lit the fire with a spill from the stove.

She went to the kitchen, but it was still, quiet, and empty, the stove cold to the touch.

Glancing out the front window, she saw that snow had fallen, perhaps three fingers high. No footprints or tracks could be seen. Hippolyte must have left in the middle of the night, taking the others with him. Somewhere in the distance, bells were ringing. But all she could see around the cottage were tall trees, soaring dizzily toward a patch of gray sky.

Where was she?

With a jolt of horror, she realized that she didn't know. She had escaped her family home, running into Hippolyte's carriage and his arms. He had kissed her passionately all the way to a small chapel, where a cheerful abbé had married them.

After that, back in the carriage, Hippolyte had pulled her to him. She had no idea how much time passed, how far they'd traveled. By the time the carriage stopped, they were burning with desire. He kept laughing and kissing her, even when introducing her to the servants.

Now they were all gone.

It felt like a horrid fairy tale. Perhaps a cackling witch would stroll in the door.

Just as that notion presented itself, she heard carriage wheels crunching on snow. With a little cry, she ran to the entry. Hippolyte had come for her. She stopped and composed herself.

She was Madame Charles now.

Hippolyte had said she had new dignity. He had said—

The door flung open, and a man walked in, his fur-lined cape billowing behind him, his face set in lines of rage and disapproval.

Yasmin dropped into a low curtsy. *"Votre Grâce."*

"I knew your mother was an *intrigante* when I married her," her father snarled, advancing a few steps. "An *élégante*, to call a spade a spade. The daughter of a duke mad enough to sell herself for a small emerald."

Fury poured down Yasmin's spine. "You disrespect *ma mère*!" But she stopped there. Could she say aloud that her father owed his title to her mother's *affaire* with Napoleon—which began with that emerald?

No.

"I knew who your mother was when I married her," the *duc* said, ignoring her exclamation. "In truth, who could say *'Non'* to an emperor? God knows your mother was only one of a string of women. I expected more of my daughter. What an *imbécile* I am!" He jerked his head toward the door. *"Vite!* I don't want my horses to take a chill."

Yasmin's mind reeled. "How did you find me? But no, I cannot come with you. I am married!"

His lip curled. "You're disgraced, not married. For God's sake, Yasmin, did no one ever tell you that Hippolyte Charles is a fortune hunter?"

Yasmin's mouth fell open. "No." The word squeaked from her throat.

"The truth is widely known."

"No one will gossip with me," Yasmin said numbly. "Because of . . . of *Maman*."

She thought a trace of sympathy softened her father's face. "Your so-called husband came to the house and informed us that he'd 'had' you for a week, and that you believed yourself a wife."

A sob tore out of Yasmin's chest. "No!"

"He will marry you in truth only if we hand over the Cassan estate. We certainly will not relinquish the estate that your mother *earned* from the emperor." The *duc* gave the word "earned" sardonic emphasis.

"Hippolyte loves me!" Yasmin cried. "This can't be true!"

Her father gave a bark of laughter. "I blame your mother for not watching you more closely."

A sob pressed on the back of her throat. "It can't be! But what—what will I do?"

"You will come home. If you're with babe, I promise you this: I'll force that reprobate to marry you and put a dagger in his back within minutes of the ceremony."

Her darling, handsome Hippolyte. "No!"

"It's in the hands of God. I don't suppose he used a condom?"

Yasmin had no idea what her father was referring to. Tears were pouring down her face, her heart smashed into a thousand pieces.

In future years, she always had trouble remembering the next few months. Yasmin had believed every whispered compliment and deceitful promise that Hippolyte had given her. Without him, the world was airless and dark.

She prayed for a baby, to have something of his, and when her courses began, her heart broke again. Her stomach and her bones and her heart were hollow and empty. Aching.

Every day, the gossip columns detailed Hippolyte's antics at court; he was Empress Joséphine's favorite, with his luxurious black mustaches and exquisite sense of fashion.

And every time Yasmin thought about him, a stone landed in her stomach. Her false marriage taught her a great deal about cruelty and degradation, and she learned more on the rare occasions when she ventured out of the house accompanied by her mother. No one dared snub a *duchesse*, but their savage comments about Yasmin's lack of virtue were always audible.

Somewhat to her own surprise, she kept living, broken heart or no.

It took time, a whole year, but Yasmin decided that she was not a lesser person for being tricked. Hippolyte was. She had only been foolish for falling in love. For tumbling into his embrace with such joy.

After two years, she returned to court, head held high. By then, the stone had moved from her stomach to her heart, and she felt safe from further danger. Not for her, the tempests of emotion that followed love.

Her first evening back in the palace, Hippolyte

Charles sauntered up to her and kissed her hand. "Such an exquisite angel could make a man such as I contemplate marriage." The horrid man smirked at her.

She gave her laugh an edge of mockery, knowing that the court was listening with fascination. "Then allow an angel, monsieur, to assure you that Heaven is unlikely to be your final abode."

CHAPTER ONE

For over a decade, Giles Renwick, Earl of Lilford, had watched with distaste as acquaintances succumbed to lustful impulses that cast their lives into chaos, if not catastrophe. At the age of thirty-two, he prided himself on a private life as disciplined as his estate. He had never made a fool of himself over a woman.

Until now.

Lady Yasmin Régnier was ineligible for his attentions in every way: not as a wife, nor yet a mistress—she was a lady!—nor even as a friend, since they vehemently disliked each other.

Yet here he was, blood pounding as he waited for the first waltz, which she had promised to him. Meanwhile the lady was romping through a country dance with Edwin Turing.

All polite society knew she'd turned down Turing's marriage proposal, along with those of at least eight others. Wasn't it Shakespeare's Juliet who described Romeo as a bird with a string around his leg?

Other ladies dispatched rejected suitors to woo other women. Lady Yasmin blithely kept her wooers on a string, thirsty for a smile or a waltz. It was profoundly irritating to count himself among them—and scant relief that no one in London realized that he was so . . . enchanted?

Was "en-lusted" a word?

No matter his obsession, Giles could never ask her to be his countess. Lady Yasmin's gowns were cut too low, and her skirts were dampened to cling to admittedly lovely thighs. She loved to gossip—and giggle. She smiled and flirted with everyone from new babies to elderly men with a foot in the grave. It was rumored that she carried a small flask of brandy to balls, claiming to hate lemonade.

She wasn't dignified, or polite, or even truly British, given her French upbringing. Not to mention the fact that her mother had been one of Napoleon's mistresses, a fact Yasmin made no effort to hide.

One of her silliest suitors had written a sonnet claiming her hair was the color of cowslips and her eyes as violet as twilight. To Giles's mind, her beauty didn't matter, though he appreciated her low bodices as much as the next man. What caught him was her laugh, the way she shared joy so freely.

Yet asking her to be his wife was unthinkable. Full stop.

He allowed himself to dance with her once an evening, always the first waltz. Thereafter, he courted proper, eligible ladies, forcing himself to avoid Lady Yasmin. Telling himself that he was searching for an appropriate countess, as demanded by custom and tradition.

When the first waltz was finally announced, Giles made his way to her side, bowing and kissing her gloved hand. His whole body relaxed as his arm closed around her, and they moved into the dance.

With a start, he realized that she had burst into speech.

Then again, when wasn't she chattering?

"Your sister is dancing with Lord Pepper," Lady Yasmin told him with an expectant glance.

"Yes?"

"It wouldn't be a terrible match on paper, but you mustn't ignore his penchant for the racetrack. He must find a wife with a large dowry."

If there was one thing Giles loathed, it was gossip. Tittle-tattle of this sort had shattered his family and led to his father's death, though Lady Yasmin would be unaware of that as she grew up in France.

He was the very last person to rebuff anyone on the basis of idle chatter.

"You're giving me that hateful look again," she observed. "I thought perhaps you reserved it for me, but I saw you glowering at Fitz earlier."

Fitz—or the Honorable Fitzgibbon-Foley—was an irritating beetle of a man. The fact that the betting book at White's had identified Fitz as an excellent candidate to win Lady Yasmin's hand in marriage had no bearing on his opinion.

"I prefer to judge a man on his merits, rather than idle gossip," Giles said. "I think a great deal of Lord Pepper." Not that he knew more of the younger man than vague memories from Eton. Pepper hadn't taken up his seat in the House of Lords, which meant that Giles paid him no attention.

"You are responsible for your sister's welfare," Lady Yasmin retorted, as she floated through the dance. "You have chosen to escort her to events yourself, rather than place her in the hands of a reliable chaperone, which means that you *must* pay attention to such details."

It was entirely predictable to find irritation seeping into his veins; it happened whenever they engaged in conversation.

"What gentleman doesn't attend the races at Doncaster and Ascot?" Giles inquired, raising an eyebrow. "No one would question Pepper's place in society."

Lady Yasmin's brows were perfect arches even when she scowled. Giles had a mad impulse to trace them with a finger. A finger that would drop down to touch the sweet flush on her cheek and then caress her lips.

Presumably, those lips were inherited from her French father, because no Englishwoman had lips that plush, let alone tipped up into a near-constant smile.

She wasn't smiling now. "Are you referring to those who question my place in fashionable circles?"

"I—"

"True, my mother's position as one of the emperor's dearest friends precludes her rejoining English society, had she longed for such delight." Lady Yasmin's ironic tone made her mother's feelings clear. "But my grandfather, the Duke of Portbellow, assures me near daily that the English do not visit the sins of parents upon their children. My mother gave me one of Napoleon's hats, and my grandfather perched it on a skeleton he keeps in the drawing room. He considers the family connection, as it were, a jest."

"You are indubitably a lady," Giles stated. "I meant that blather about the racetrack is no reason to discount a suitor for my sister's hand before the man has even proposed."

"So you don't care that your younger sister is dancing with a hardened gambler?" she inquired now. "*I* would, were she my sister. But were she *my* sister, she would have a chaperone."

"Lydia doesn't want a chaperone," Giles said.

She wasn't attending. "I'm not sure I had that right. 'Were she my sister'? That's right, isn't it? Because Lady Lydia couldn't possibly be my sister. 'I would, was she my sister'? No, that definitely doesn't work."

"Your English is improving," Giles said. Instantly, he felt like a condescending ass, because her command of the language was excellent.

Lady Yasmin didn't take offense. "I wish you'd tell my grandfather as much. His Grace corrected me twice at breakfast this morning." She rolled her eyes. "If only he could hear me now, using the subjunctive like an Oxford don."

They were nearing the bottom of the ballroom, so Giles drew her closer and began turning in circles. Lady Yasmin kept talking, effortlessly following his lead. "My point is that it's natural for your sister to refuse a chaperone."

"Why?"

Her mouth tightened. "I suppose you think I'm getting too high for my nut, Lord Lilford. But I know young women."

"I'm not sure what you mean by a reference to your nut." Giles took a deep breath, fighting off the fact that his cock responded to her scent as if . . . He wasn't any good at metaphors. Perhaps all the blood in his body had drained from his head.

Lady Yasmin gave him an impish smile, and he instinctively drew her closer once again. "American slang," she told him. "Getting too high for your nut means that you are overreaching."

Giles cleared his throat. "The phrase applies only to male overreachers."

"His nut," Lady Yasmin said. "Like a—" She broke off, her brows drawing together again. "Not a reference to a squirrel hiding his treasure in a tree?"

"No," Giles said. "I believe we're talking about male anatomy." Not that he had ever discussed male anatomy with a young lady before.

"Bollocks!" she said, with an enchanting giggle.

Giles swallowed hard. The woman he was holding in his arms *was* a lady. Her mother's situation didn't mean . . . Though Lady Yasmin clearly wasn't chaste in the strictest sense . . . His thoughts fogged with a bout of pure lust.

"I find the differences between English and American usage fascinating," Lady Yasmin said. "But I keep tripping over naughty words. English is littered with them, far more so than French."

"Americans and British are fond of bawdy puns," Giles agreed. The smile on her mouth made him want to bite her. Kiss her. Both. The only explanation was that he was losing his mind. It happened to men in middle age, though at thirty-two he hardly considered himself there yet.

"To return to the matter at hand, the fact that your sister doesn't want a chaperone is proof that she needs one."

Giles frowned. "Lydia spent three years at Mrs. Bretton's Seminary, and Mrs. Bretton herself assured me that my sister is a pattern card of excellent behavior. In fact, she said that my sister is innately ladylike."

"Of course she did," Lady Yasmin murmured, rolling her eyes. "I expect your sister was a parlor boarder?"

"She was," Giles confirmed.

"After charging you a king's ransom, Mrs. Bretton could scarcely tell you the truth, could she? Moreover, she hopes you will place your daughters in her care, in time."

He felt his frown turn to a scowl. "What 'truth' are you referring to? More gossip?"

"God forbid. You've made your opinion clear," Lady Yasmin said, glancing at the orchestra. "This waltz must be almost over."

Giles had bribed the orchestra director to play the longest waltz in their repertoire, so he ignored that observation, spinning in a few more circles so their thighs brushed together. He was cursed with a sensitive nose that sent him urgent messages about who had bathed before the ball, and who had not. Even among the washed, there were those whose perfume burned his nose, billowing like an invisible cloud around their bodies.

In contrast, Lady Yasmin's scent clung to her skin, only perceptible during a waltz. In a perfect world, he would back her against a wall, and kiss her until she . . .

He cleared his throat. "You believe that my sister is ill behaved?"

Even to his own ears, his voice sounded unfriendly.

"I am not saying Lady Lydia is wanton. She's scarcely out of the schoolroom. I'm simply telling you that her entire mind is focused on young men. For example, where is she now?"

"She's dancing with—"

"Not any longer."

CHAPTER TWO

At the age of twenty-five, Yasmin considered herself an expert in that species known as "gentlemen." Like a flock of chickens, they often clucked in unison. Like a herd of cows, they could be categorized by breed, or nationality. And like a sleuth of bears, they could be dangerous.

You should never underestimate a bear—or a gentleman.

Take her best friend Cleo's husband, Jake Astor Addison, for example. When he looked at Cleo, his expression was absurdly loving. He crowed his feelings to the world. He came from America, a country that famously produced herds of rough-hewn gentlemen. And finally, he was dangerous. When he walked down a London street, people instinctively moved to the side.

Giles Renwick, Earl of Lilford, was censorious, buttoned down, and unsurprising. In a flock of British aristocrats, he blended right in. True, he was more beautiful than the average English gentleman, given his white-blond hair and eyes that glinted silver by candlelight, but one did occasionally see a particularly handsome Hereford.

Yet there was a steely core to him, a chilly gaze that spoke of power and privilege, but also inner strength.

That wasn't what made him dangerous to *her*, though.

She kept imagining that a different Giles was hidden under his starched exterior: a man who was loyal and thoughtful, whose sense of humor paired with a deep capacity for passion. Who would love a woman all the days of his life. Sometimes she fancied she saw raw desire in his eyes, and she couldn't stop herself from responding like a cat basking in a ray of sunshine.

Consequently, she spent many futile hours attempting to lure out *that* Giles. She tried to amuse him and failing that, to irritate him. Even so, every time he looked at her with antipathy, it hurt her feelings. She was an idiot. She was responsible for her own bruised emotions since she constantly poked at him.

One didn't poke a bear. Everyone knew that.

But she couldn't stop herself. "Lady Lydia is no longer in the ballroom," Yasmin told him now.

"Are you certain?" Giles replied, his voice edging into a growl as he looked about. In her head, she thought of him as Giles, even though he punctiliously addressed her as Lady Yasmin.

Lady Lydia should be easy to spot, as her head resembled a dandelion, but Giles wouldn't find her. In the past few weeks, Yasmin had seen the girl slip away many times, in company with various gentlemen.

"She may be seeking fresh air," she offered. That was one way of describing Lydia's penchant for engaging in passionate kisses with her latest flirt.

"Likely, she ripped her hem and had to retreat to the ladies' sitting room," Giles said, his gaze returning to Yasmin's face. "My sister is prone to accidents."

"I was under the impression that those incidents occurred in her first Season? I was in attendance last year when Lady Lydia fell down the steps at the Vauxhall pavilion. I did not see her debut, but I heard—"

"That's the trouble with society," Giles interrupted. "You heard about it."

She really shouldn't poke the bear. Or, in this case, the hidebound, oh-so-proper peer. Yasmin raised an eyebrow, ignoring her own counsel. "Did your sister not trip over a footstool and fizzle?"

He looked at her blankly.

"Fizzle, fart, foist," Yasmin explained.

"Such an accident could happen to anyone," Giles said, the expected disdain crossing his face.

"Indeed, it *has* happened," Yasmin said. "As I told Lady Lydia after that tittle-tattle reached my ears, the French propensity for rich food has led to many a public foist, including mine before Napoleon's assembled court."

There was a pause. "I suspect you burst into laughter after that mishap," Giles said, a curious expression in his eyes that she couldn't quite read.

"I did," Yasmin confirmed. She had a lifetime's experience negotiating humiliation in the court. One of her favorite rules for survival amongst the aristocracy—whether French or British—was that a show of weakness had to be avoided at all costs.

"My sister is not as . . . audacious as you are, Lady Yasmin." There was no mistaking the disapproval in Giles's voice. Presumably, he thought ladies ought to faint after the disgrace of farting, although men urinated in dining room chamber pots in the full sight of those same ladies.

His opinion shouldn't matter, but it had the wretched effect of making Yasmin's throat burn.

"You may loathe gossip, but I loathe rules that pretend no woman breaks wind," she retorted. "Your sister was shamed for a natural result of the digestive process."

"Gossip can be ruinous, no matter how innocent a mistake."

"I know that," she said. "Believe me, I have experienced the unfortunate consequences of gossip. As I told your sister, one *cannot* allow such unpleasantness to affect one's confidence."

Giles's mouth tightened. "I didn't realize you and my sister were so well acquainted."

It took everything she had not to flinch.

"Well enough to offer unwanted counsel," Yasmin said. "Oh, don't look like that. I shan't infect her with my scandalous ways. Your sister was polite, but no young lady wants advice from a spinster."

"What?"

He bit the word off, as if the idea of her being a spinster was absurd, but Yasmin wasn't foolish enough to take it as a compliment. "The distance between seventeen and twenty-four is insurmountable. What's more, I am not even a female relative. Lady Lydia has taken me in dislike, which should make you happy, shouldn't it?"

His brows drew together. "It does not make me happy. Why would you say such a thing?"

"Because you don't like me either," Yasmin said, impatiently. "Oh, for goodness' sake, can't we just be truthful? You and I have both fizzled on occasion. You and I have low opinions of each other. You would be happy if a scandalously dressed and frivolous lady such as myself had little to no contact with your innocent sister, even if I am looking out for her best interests."

"I do not have a low opinion of you."

"Poppycock," Yasmin countered. "You've made it clear that I don't dress or speak in a manner that you consider worthy of your respect."

The waltz drew to a close before the earl could respond, which was just as well. "Good evening, Lord Lilford." She dropped a curtsy.

The earl's eyes were glacier cold, but he wrapped a hand around her arm. "Lady Yasmin."

"Excuse me?" She narrowed her eyes at him.

"My sister," he said tautly. "You know something about my sister that you are not saying."

Behind his shoulder, one of her suitors was bounding toward them like a puppy with overly large paws.

Yasmin wasn't friends with Lydia. But Giles's sister, headstrong, unmothered, and unchaperoned, was running headlong toward ruination. It didn't sit with her conscience to let it happen, not given her past. She sighed. "I suspect you'll find Lady Lydia in the back garden."

"Alone?" Giles's eyes searched her face when she didn't immediately respond, and his jaw tightened. "You are insinuating that my sister ventured outside with Lord Pepper, unchaperoned. She would never do something so inappropriate."

"I'm certain you're right," Yasmin said. Who was she to destroy his faith in his sister? "If you'll excuse me, I see my next dance partner—"

His hand tightened on her arm. "No, we are going into the garden for a breath of fresh air. You feel faint."

"I do not feel faint."

"We shall prove that you are wrong before you can spread more tittle-tattle about my sister."

Yasmin drew in a sharp breath, and her stomach tensed into a knot. His characterization hurt. She would *never* share unkind gossip about a young lady.

No matter how much she enjoyed waltzing with Giles, this had to be their last. She had tried over and over with the Earl of Lilford. She had tried to make him laugh, and tried to make him cross, and generally tried to get him to *see* her as someone other than frivolous at best and a strumpet at worst.

He never altered his opinion.

That idea she had about a hidden Giles? That was mere foolishness.

"I would never spread rumors about Lady Lydia," she said, keeping her voice calm, although she'd like to shriek. His rudeness stemmed from concern for a younger sibling. Not from his belief that she, Yasmin, was the sort of woman who would gleefully destroy his sister's reputation.

Of course, he apparently *did* believe that she was malicious, but he wasn't the sort of man who would be rude for the sake of it. Just look at the way he always asked her to dance, even though he disapproved of her. Civility was intrinsic to his character.

Though he never danced with her more than once, making it clear to all and sundry that he did so out of punctilious politeness rather than courtship. God forbid the Earl of Lilford should be suspected of wooing a woman of her reputation.

"I didn't mean to imply that you would deliberately spread gossip," Giles said, proving her point about his civility.

"You didn't imply. You stated just that." There was no reason to spend any more time with the man. But the absurd fascination she felt toward him prevailed, and she found herself saying, "Very well. I'll walk into the garden with you."

By now, Lydia would be heading back inside. In the past few weeks, Yasmin had noticed two important points: the girl invariably left the ballroom while Yasmin waltzed with her brother—

and Lydia was always careful to be back in the room when the next dance began.

The Honorable Algernon Dunlap trotted up to them, and Yasmin shook her head. "We'll have to dance later, *mon chèr*. The earl has kindly agreed to accompany me into the garden for a brief respite from the heat."

"I'll accompany you, Lady Yasmin," Algernon said eagerly. He stuck out his bony elbow.

Giles cast him a look, and he clapped his arm to his side.

"Alas, I could not accompany you into the gardens, Mr. Dunlap," Yasmin said, lowering her voice. "What would your mama think if I compromised you, albeit accidentally?"

"But—"

"As everyone knows, Lord Lilford and I have no affection for each other, so I regularly allow him to accompany me for a breath of fresh air."

Yasmin paused to see whether Giles would counter her description of their relationship, but his face didn't move. She could hardly say that was a surprise.

She smiled at Algernon. "You might tempt me to an indiscretion." He tipped toward her, like a statue poised to crash to the ground.

"Lady Yasmin," Giles said, unmistakable impatience in his voice. His eyes had darkened to sea green. In another proof of her idiocy, Yasmin had wasted an absurd amount of time thinking about the color of Giles's eyes.

Last Season, when he was wooing her friend Cleo, they had been a silvery gray. After Cleo married Jake, sunny had turned wintery. This Season the earl stalked around the ballroom on the hunt for the perfect countess, his eyes darkened to an icy green. She'd never met anyone whose eyes shifted like that, from one color to another.

As Giles led her through the ballroom into the large drawing room, she caught sight of Cleo and waggled her eyebrows. "Supper," Yasmin mouthed. Cleo smiled and nodded.

On the far end of the drawing room, large doors stood ajar, leading to the gardens. A few couples were standing just outside, within sight of sharp-eyed chaperones. Lydia was not among them.

"Neither Lydia nor Pepper are here," Giles said as they reached the door, evident relief in his voice. He wasn't as certain of his sister as he claimed.

"I expect she tore a flounce," Yasmin said. "Lord Lilford, if you'll excuse me, I see friends seated in the far corner, so I shall join them."

"No."

She blinked at him.

He narrowed his eyes in return.

"I'm sorry I mentioned your sister's absence from the ballroom," Yasmin said. "Surely we needn't actually go outside."

For one thing, that would have everyone chattering about *them*, which she was certain the earl would loathe. And for another, it might start raining. She dampened her skirts, but a damp bodice would be a step too far. She was wearing a short corset, and her breasts were generously sized.

"If there is any chance that Lydia is in that garden with Lord Pepper, I must know." Giles's voice was so grim that Yasmin sent up a special prayer to the patroness of naughty young ladies. There was no need for the earl to catch his sister canoodling with a man; after this evening, he would surely keep a closer eye on her.

Moreover, Lydia had been using her brother's waltzes with Yasmin to cover up her indiscretions. But Yasmin didn't intend to ever dance with Giles again.

Problem solved.

CHAPTER THREE

Giles Renwick was accustomed to getting his own way, which invariably had a terrible effect on a man's character. Luckily, Yasmin had no interest in taming the Earl of Lilford. His mother should have taught him manners long ago, and since the lady had failed in the task . . . it was too late.

If she kept telling herself that, one of these days she would believe it.

He would be a dictatorial, obstreperous husband, not even taking into account that if she, Yasmin, were waiting at the altar, he likely wouldn't show up.

The two of them in proximity at an altar was as likely as shrimps learning to whistle.

Taking a deep breath, she allowed the earl to escort her onto the terrace, ignoring the curious glances that made her back prickle.

"I don't see Lydia," Giles stated.

Yasmin kept her gaze steady. "I expect that I was wrong."

His brows drew together.

"Very wrong," she added. "I'm often wrong."

His frown deepened, but he didn't respond.

"Shall we return inside? I think it might rain any moment." Yasmin glanced to the right, where the mother of her dance partner Algernon was standing with a friend, both of them openly staring. She smiled and raised her hand, and Lady Dunlap turned away.

The cut direct, and not for the first time. No one in England seemed to know the details of her scandalous past with Hippolyte, but that didn't stop the rumors from circulating.

It wasn't her fault that Algernon Dunlap chose to write sonnets to her eyes. If he were a turkey, Algernon would be the first to drown in a rainstorm after looking up at the sky. Yasmin had never encouraged his attentions, but he persisted in his poetic efforts, anyway.

Actually, that was one of the reasons why Yasmin preferred English men to French. Algernon wrote poetry without the faintest hope he would successfully gain her attention, whereas Frenchmen used their lyrics to seduce the innocent and unwary.

Giles glanced at the women, both of them now gazing out at the gardens as if they never had an unkind thought. Then he said, "Fresh air will help your headache, Lady Yasmin," and drew her down three steps to the garden walk.

"I never have headaches," she informed him. "Besides, I thought I was feeling faint? You're making me out to be a weakling."

"You are no weakling," Giles stated.

She glanced at him in some surprise, but he was

looking about the garden, presumably searching for Lydia's yellow topknot.

Lord Boodle's gardens were laid out in the French manner, with shoulder-high walls enclosing small grassy quadrangles. In front of them one couple—married, of course—idly strolled down the straight walkway, and to the right, another path curved away and disappeared between stone walls. Lord Pepper would have guided Lydia to the right, out of the sight of those on the terrace.

Yasmin began to walk forward, trying to think of a subject for conversation. If Lydia heard her brother's voice, she would surely head back to the house. "I am a great admirer of British cottage gardens," she announced.

Giles threw her a glance that said, "So?"

"I should have known that Lord Boodle was an admirer of the French," Yasmin improvised.

"Why?"

"He named his daughter Blanche."

"And?"

Yasmin lowered her voice. "Blanche Boodle! The girl must be desperate to marry and change her name."

Rather surprisingly, one side of Giles's mouth twitched, as if he contemplated a smile. "I think that is a fair observation. She is my sister's closest friend and spent time with us last summer. Miss Boodle was disappointed not to marry in her first Season." He cleared his throat. "I saw her dancing with Gerald Boyle earlier this evening."

"Why don't you smile on occasion?" Yasmin

asked. "Are earls constitutionally stern or are you the exception? Blanche Boyle would be unfortunate, but Blanche Booble would be worse!"

"Not a real name," Giles said.

"I assure you that I met a Mr. *Booble* just the other day. Granted, he was a member of the Worshipful Company of Grocers, and Lord *Boodle* has higher aspiration for his daughter."

"You 'met' a grocer?"

"I did," Yasmin said. "I wanted to buy fresh strawberries, so I went to Covent Garden. It's one of my favorite places in London."

Giles's brows drew together.

"You have visited the market, haven't you?" Yasmin asked.

"Never. I hope you did not make this excursion unaccompanied?"

"For goodness' sake, it's a daily market, not a rookery! The worst that could happen is that I'd be pickpocketed. Since I am accompanied by a footman, I needn't worry about someone cutting my reticule strings. I find it one of the most fascinating places in London. Truly, you must pay it a visit."

She almost offered to accompany him to the market . . . and rethought it. Giles wouldn't even dance with her twice; he certainly wouldn't wish to be seen at an open-air market so far beneath him that he'd apparently never descended from his carriage to explore it.

More importantly, she was determined to stifle the irrational impulses she had to make his expressionless eyes light up with interest or humor.

The earl had turned away and was peering over the stone walls, as if Lydia might be hiding in a quadrangle. Each grass oblong held two rows of stone posts topped with marble pineapples. Singularly unattractive to Yasmin's mind—if rather funny.

He turned. "Why are you laughing?"

"Those dreadful pedestals," she said, chortling.

A row of stone pillars set on square pediments rose into the air just high enough so their bulbous pineapple finials showed above the garden walls. But if someone glanced over the wall and viewed pillars from the ground up . . .

Giles made a humming sound, and the edge of his mouth twitched again. A belly laugh in another man, one had to presume.

"Once seen, you'll never unsee," Yasmin said. "No matter how much you might wish to. It casts a dubious light on our host's notion of elegance, don't you think?"

"His grandfather's notion, I would think. It took time to scour stone pineapples to that smoothness."

"But just imagine when they were new," Yasmin said. "Most of them have lost the flourish of leaves on top, but if you consider that one, closest to the wall . . ."

"*In medias res*, as it were."

"My education is inadequate as regards Latin," Yasmin told him. "What does that mean?"

"In the midst," Giles said. He hesitated, then elaborated. "In mideruption, in this case."

Yasmin laughed. "I like you so much better

when you aren't imitating a Quaker. Look, your lips are actually curling upward."

Unfortunately, that comment turned him back to a block of wood.

"Shall we continue, Lady Yasmin?"

"There it went," she said with exaggerated mournfulness. "No more of this phallic foolishness. All hail the moment of joy, for it hath met its demise."

"'Hath met its demise'?" he repeated.

"I was caught in an extraordinarily long church service last week so I amused myself by memorizing bits from *The Book of Common Prayer*. Very good for my English, if a trifle antiquated." Yasmin reluctantly began walking again. "We ought to return. I don't want to turn the corner and be out of sight of the terrace."

"You were certain that my sister had entered the garden with Lord Pepper. We should follow the path to its end."

"Not unless you want everyone in that ballroom to be gossiping about us." She caught sight of Giles's instinctive flinch. *Instinctive.* He must positively loathe her to have that reaction without thinking.

Enough was enough. Later, she ought to give serious thought to why she always waltzed with a man who disliked her. Despised her, even.

After all, she had plans for this Season: she meant to find a husband.

A kind and charming Englishman, preferably one who had reached forty years of age, when the blood didn't run so quickly. A man who would show her respect and give her children, without making false promises. A man generous in spirit to whom she could confide her scandalous past. He would understand rather than condemn.

Even contemplating how Giles would respond to her story made her instinctively flinch, just the way he had after the suggestion that people might gossip about the two of them.

"It's growing cold," Yasmin said, turning around. "I'm wearing fewer layers than you are, and my next dance partner will be looking for me."

He began to remove his coat.

Yasmin raised a hand. "Don't—"

She changed her mind as the earl's broad shoulders emerged, clad in linen so fine that she could see the contours of his chest. His muscled chest. "On second thought, I *am* chilled."

Even his shoulders had pads of muscles on them. It was something of a revelation. Most of her suitors had slim silhouettes. Even Hippolyte— with the ease of long practice, she dismissed that thought.

Giles shook out his coat and wrapped it around her. Unlike ladies—such as his sister—who piled all their hair on top of their head in a big puff, Yasmin let a few strands fall over one shoulder. Her curls bunched against the collar of his coat, and he carefully drew them free.

In another man, it would have been a tender gesture, but Giles's expression was verging on a glare. There was no rational reason to be so attracted to him, and yet his chilly gaze felt like a caress, and the touch of his fingers on her neck made her shiver.

What she needed was an older, cuddly version of Giles. "Cuddly" was a new-to-her English word, one that summed up so much, to Yasmin's mind: it meant to hug or embrace, but also to be comfortable with.

Their silence was growing embarrassing. "You show to advantage without a coat," Yasmin said. "Do you box?"

"Yes," Giles stated.

A raindrop splashed on her cheek, and he reached out and brushed it away. Their eyes caught.

"You're right. We should return," he said, looking back at the mansion. The ladies had retreated inside. "Even if my sister had been imprudent enough to venture into the garden, she hates discomfort. Lydia would never play the coquette in this weather."

"All right," Yasmin said. She felt a bit shaken, unable to come up with another playful comment, her stock-in-trade. There was something about Giles's uncompromising gaze that made it difficult to flirt with him.

Before she could move, his hands closed on her shoulders. Yasmin's eyes widened at the sensual intent in his eyes, but she didn't stop him when he slowly drew her closer, or when he leaned down, and his mouth touched hers. Their lips met and clung. He didn't press her, and she didn't open her mouth.

The man had no warmth in him and yet a brush of his lips sent heat racing down her limbs. One kiss ended and another began. Yasmin swayed toward him as his lips met hers in yet another chaste kiss that sent pure lust quivering through her body.

"You are so—" His voice broke off, but that raw, abandoned tone spoke for itself.

Yasmin felt dazed, her heart beating too fast, her mind unable to keep up, but one thing was clear: she didn't want to feel like this. She wanted nothing to do with kisses that made a woman dizzy. She'd experienced those before and still had the scars. Lust led to horrendous decisions.

The earl pulled back and dropped his arms from around her. "That shouldn't have happened."

He was back to the clipped, aristocratic tones of an earl. His gaze was remote, with all the warmth that he might show a parlor maid. A misbehaving parlor maid, given his hardened jaw.

Even though Yasmin agreed, she felt a flash of anger. "Because you don't like me?" she asked, the question slipping from her lips before she thought better of it.

His lips tightened. Silence answered her.

The blow felt almost physical, which was so stupid. She'd known that truth for months, after all. "True, you don't have to like someone to desire them," Yasmin supplied for him, slipping off his coat and pushing it into his hands.

She walked quickly back, ignoring the silent man pacing at her side. She was battling with shame. How stupid could she be?

So many men had tried to seduce her, yet after her experience with Hippolyte, she had easily refused them. That was her secret defense when English ladies sneered at her: she had nothing to be ashamed of. Their husbands, brothers, and sons may desire her, but she never returned the compliment.

Yet Giles Renwick, Earl of Lilford, hadn't even bothered to flatter her. Presumably, he couldn't think of anything complimentary to say. She tried to imagine him praising her: "You are so . . ." what?

So frivolous. So loose. So beneath him.

The words beat through her head in a pitiful melody that made her irritated with herself. And with him, that stupid man who thought she wasn't good enough for a second waltz but kissed her when no one was watching.

They walked silently through the drawing room. When they reached the ballroom doors, Lydia's yellow topknot was instantly visible.

"My sister is waltzing with Pepper a second time," Giles observed blandly as if nothing had happened between them.

Lydia's cheeks were pink and her eyes shining, though it was a question how her brother would interpret her expression. Presumably, he was aware that it was improper for a young lady to waltz twice with the same gentleman. One might accept two invitations to dance, but two waltzes?

To Yasmin's mind, Lydia was positively begging to be labeled "brazen," if not worse. Yet, the last thing either sibling wanted was her opinion. Clearly.

"Good evening, Your Grace."

She turned away and curtsied in front of her waiting dance partner, London's most eligible bachelor, Silvester Parnell, Duke of Huntington. He wasn't precisely cuddly, but at least he didn't look at her with icy dislike.

The duke bowed. "Good evening, Lady Yasmin. Chilled to the bone?" he asked as they slipped onto the dance floor, joining the waltzing couples.

"Are my gloves very cold?" Yasmin asked. "I've been outdoors and it's beginning to rain."

"Not the weather," Parnell said. "The earl. Lilford." He waggled his eyebrows. "Chilly bugger, isn't he? Oh, dear, I shouldn't have used that word in front of a lady." His eyes laughed at her.

Yasmin let his cheerfulness replace the sick feeling in her chest. This duke liked her as she was. "Bollocks!" she said, grinning back at him. "You don't care for the earl?"

"We were at school together, but he decided early on that I was a frivolous excuse for a man and not worth his time."

A shared confession felt soothing. "Alas, the earl has a similarly low opinion of me."

"More the fool he," the duke said, twirling her in a circle.

"No flirtatious comments," she ordered, letting her smile fall. "I like you too much for that."

"*I* am not fool enough to join the parade of besotted men at your heels. Of whom, I might add, the Earl of Lilford is definitely one. I've caught him more than once standing at the edge of the ballroom, staring at you like a mooncalf."

"Nonsense. Lord Lilford was preparing his next insult." Yasmin had no intention of discussing Giles with anyone, let alone one of her suitors.

"It's irresistible, given how you look in that gown."

"Enough," Yasmin ordered. "I'm sick to death of flattery." Silvester Parnell was fast becoming one of her closest friends—but only as long as the duke avoided the kind of flummery that made her uncomfortable.

"It's irresistible to tease you."

She frowned.

"Anyone who watches you closely will notice that you are a flirtatious minx in public and prudish in private. Most of my fellows haven't noticed because they're imbeciles in public *and* private."

"Do not watch me closely," Yasmin ordered.

"Do not watch me closely, *Silvester*?" he amended.

She wrinkled her nose at him. "Very well."

Silvester's grin was charming; he was intelligent, fairly handsome, titled. Giles didn't have his charm, so why was she still thinking about his kisses? It was absurd. Obviously, she should marry the friendly duke, who liked her, and laughed at her jokes.

If her grandfather had attended this ball, His Grace would be nodding with approval from the sidelines.

Her grandfather was under the fixed conviction that the only way to heal the shame Yasmin's mother had brought upon the family was for her daughter to marry a highly respected peer. "If only Mabel had chosen to engage in garden-variety adultery," he had told Yasmin a few days ago, "no one would give a damn. But no. She had to sleep with an emperor!"

Yasmin reserved judgment about adultery; it seemed to her that malicious gossip circulated widely, no matter the indiscretion.

Still, according to her grandfather, marriage to a duke would remedy the family disgrace.

Yasmin had the distinct sense that Silvester—for all his claim not to be one of her suitors—was a purposeful man. In the past three weeks, he had danced with her, plied her with champagne, and told her stories of his family.

One of these days he would pull out an heirloom ring, likely a rock as big as one of his knuckles.

And then what would she do?

CHAPTER FOUR

Breakfast the following day
82, STRATTON STREET, LONDON
THE DUKE OF PORTBELLOW'S TOWNHOUSE

As a little girl, Yasmin and her nanny used to visit her mother every morning promptly at eleven a.m. Her mother would be half-buried in rosy satin pillows, a matching eye shield pushed to her forehead and a band of satin snugly wound around her chin in an effort to combat much-dreaded jowls.

It wasn't until Yasmin was older that she understood that her mother's grogginess was due to the soothing drops she took in her morning chocolate. She would languidly touch Yasmin's cheek. "You are pure sunshine, *chérie*," she would murmur. "You have a beautiful smile. Your teeth shine so. Always smile, even when the world frowns at you."

Yasmin learned to brush her teeth without complaint, and to smile even when French ladies sniggered. People didn't know what to make of

Yasmin's smile. It made them uncomfortable that she wielded happiness like armor.

But this morning she was having trouble summoning even a grimace. She had woken with the conviction that it was time she found a husband whose respectful manners would dispel her grim memories of Hippolyte Charles and his stupid long whiskers.

Someone in whom she could confide her past, without fear of contempt.

Someone who would make her forget all about Giles.

Her grandfather, the Duke of Portbellow, was seated opposite her at the breakfast table, attired in the grand style of his youth. He had once told her that a gentleman without a wig was no better than a crusader without a helmet. And a gentleman without lace at the wrists?

No better than a chimney sweep, in His Grace's opinion.

His wig was white, his morning coat was black, and the white flounces covering his hands were fashioned from lace as delicate as cobwebs. A footman stood behind him, painstakingly applying butter to toasted bread.

"You seem tired, Granddaughter," the duke observed.

When she first arrived in England in February of last year, Yasmin had been certain he disliked her: certainly, His Grace despised the sensuality of her dress and the pleasure she took in frivolous subjects. Unlike her mother, the duke didn't care for her smile and told her that if he wanted to see so many teeth, he would tame a lion. "I have it on the best authority that they smile just before they eat you," he had told her.

But when one Season, followed by a tranquil summer, turned into a second Season, she decided that the duke rather liked her. In fact, her grandfather might be lonely if she returned to France, not that she had any such intention. Her mother had retired to Provence a few years ago, before Napoleon's first exile, and neither the *duc* nor *duchesse* had evidenced a wish for their daughter's return.

"You're not smiling," her grandfather said now, revealing a rarely attempted ability to assess another person's emotional state.

"'Twas a long night," Yasmin said, accepting a plate containing a preparation of eggs done four ways.

"You could eschew the Duke of Trent's ball tonight. Inspired by *A Midsummer Night's Dream* indeed! Only an American would think that amusing," His Grace said. He raised a finger, and a footman sprang from the wall. "Bring my granddaughter a portion of haddock. Your grandmother believed that young women," he said to Yasmin, "require fish on a regular basis." He raised the finger again. "And a small mug of beer. Good for a nursing woman."

"I'm not nursing!" Yasmin was startled into saying.

The duke would never be so inelegant as to

shrug, but he ignored her. "Beer," he commanded. A footman scurried out the door.

"I am looking forward to the Trent ball tonight. I have a new gown, and moreover, I am very fond of Merry. She and Cleo are my closest friends," Yasmin said, poking at the haddock that appeared before her.

"'The American Duchess,'" her grandfather said with an air of disapproval.

She frowned at him.

"Although one must admit that Her Grace is an admirable mother who seems to have largely overcome her unfortunate ancestry," he amended. "I would also note that she is an excellent influence on you, being older and mature."

The last time Yasmin saw Merry, they had drunk a lot of brandy and reeled around the room practicing the *Danse Écossoise*, one of Yasmin's favorite quadrilles, often danced in France, but not yet accepted in England.

If the august leaders of British society had seen Merry, Cleo, and Yasmin laughing and stumbling over each other, they might have retracted their conditional approval of the American Duchess. Merry's claims to being "mature" were dubious; if Yasmin remembered correctly, Merry was still prancing around the room in fits of laughter after she and Cleo had collapsed under the influence of four glasses of brandy.

"My morning correspondence indicates that last night you waltzed with the Duke of Huntington, as well as the Earl of Lilford," her grandfather said. "A duke and an earl. I must offer my congratulations. Lord Ferble described you as shining like a diamond of the first water."

Yasmin sighed. Every morning, His Grace received a bevy of letters from his cronies, assessing her activities. During her first Season, his elderly friends had watched for signs of scandalous behavior—to no avail because she loved flirting but had no interest in further intimacies.

"What does that mean?" she inquired.

"Diamonds are judged by their brilliance, or 'water,'" her grandfather replied. "Which reminds me that I must give you your grandmother's diamonds. They were her personal possession and not entailed with the estate." He turned to his butler, waiting by the sideboard. "Take the diamonds from the safe, Carson, and give them to Lady Yasmin's maid."

"Certainly, Your Grace," Carson said, bowing.

"I have no need for diamonds!" Yasmin said, startled.

"I was waiting until you agreed to be presented to the Queen," the duke said with a waggle of his eyebrows.

Yasmin didn't say anything. She had no intention of putting herself through such an uncomfortable experience. "I've had enough of royal courts, Grandfather."

"Your grandmother would wish you to have her diamonds. There's a necklace, earrings, bracelets, and an aigrette for your hair. It will encourage the fortune hunters, of course, but they already have you in their sights." The late duchess had left her personal fortune to Yasmin, bypassing her scandalous daughter, Mabel. In retaliation for the insult, Mabel had bequeathed her daughter a generous dowry that originated in Napoleon's coffers.

"Neither the Duke of Huntington nor the Earl of Lilford are in need of a fortune," her grandfather said. "Their attentions can be assumed to be genuine."

It was horridly unfortunate that Yasmin felt nothing other than friendship for Silvester, and even more unfortunate that she couldn't get Giles's muscular silhouette out of her mind. Of course, now that she was resolved to stop waltzing with him, she would quickly lose the absurd infatuation she had for the grumpy earl.

"I did indeed dance with both gentlemen." Yasmin put a forkful of haddock into her mouth and forced herself to swallow.

Her grandfather raised his lorgnette and stared through it, his right eye hideously enlarged. "My good friend Mr. Happle seems to believe that you permitted the Earl of Lilford to escort you into the gardens. For an unremarkable perambulation, it need hardly be said."

"That is also true." Yasmin gave up on the fish and nodded to James, the footman assigned to stand behind her chair. He waited until the duke turned his attention to his breakfast, then whisked the plate away.

She smiled, and James winked at her.

"I found that surprising," His Grace announced. "I myself have witnessed you and Lilford glowering at each other. In short, I thought you didn't like the man."

"I rashly informed him that his young sister, Lady Lydia, had left the ballroom in the company of Lord Pepper. He wasn't pleased."

Her grandfather's eyes sharpened. "I agree with him. Not a good prospect, not good at all. I hear that Pepper is under the hatches, having wasted his money in rash bets."

"The earl did not disapprove of Lord Pepper. He simply did not believe me. He was convinced that I would share untrue gossip about his sister, so he insisted that I accompany him into the gardens to prove that she had not done anything imprudent."

At seventy-one years old, the Duke of Portbellow was still a formidable man. His brows drew together over a hooked nose that Yasmin was grateful not to have inherited. "Did he indeed?" His voice dropped an octave. "He thought you would destroy his sister's reputation? Why? For the pleasure of it? That would not be the action of a lady, and while you may dress with a certain *joie de vivre*, you are nothing if not ladylike."

Yasmin found herself smiling. Her heart had felt tight and pinched on waking, and it helped that her grandfather looked as if he was about to throw away his cane and slap Giles on the face with a glove. "He doesn't like me, Grandfather. That is acceptable."

"No, it isn't. You are my granddaughter, and as such—"

"As such, every eligible peer must like me? You know that's not the case. The Earl of Lilford is a good man, if somewhat rigid. He doesn't care for my gossiping, my scanty gowns, and my mother's influence on my conduct."

"Your mother has *no* influence," His Grace thundered.

Yasmin nibbled on her toast, raising an eyebrow at her grandfather. A good part of their détente was based on a mutual understanding that they both loved her mother. Mabel was infuriating and distinctly immoral, by civilized standards.

But they both loved her.

Sure enough, the duke subsided. "A small influence," he grumbled. "I count Mabel responsible for those Frenchified gowns you wear. More to the point, Lilford should not have been so impolite to you, and so I shall tell him. Tonight!"

"I thought you didn't plan to attend the Trent ball," Yasmin said. She didn't spare any sympathy for Giles. He deserved the scolding coming his way. Given that she would never waltz with him again—which meant they would no longer converse—she might as well leave his life in a burst of glory.

So to speak.

"I have changed my mind."

"You will have to wear pink, red, or purple.

Merry told me that her butler is going to turn away those who do not comply."

His Grace snorted again. "My wardrobe will suffice." He glanced to the side. "Toast!"

The footman snatched up another piece of toast and began hastily buttering.

"Don't terrorize poor Edward," Yasmin said. "Save your vehemence for this evening."

"Oh, I shall," His Grace said, a ferocious smile curling his lips. "It's a pity that the earl's parents aren't alive, because I would—Well, no. That would be useless."

"What were they like?" Yasmin asked, contemplating the surfeit of eggs on her plate.

"The late Earl of Lilford was a rotter," her grandfather said bluntly. "And a coward. Shot himself when everyone found out his true colors."

Yasmin put down her fork. "Shot himself?"

"Ugly affair," her grandfather said, nodding. "The countess was never seen in society again. When she came to the city, it was only to visit the Inns of Court."

"To visit her solicitor? Whom did she sue?" Yasmin asked, picking up a piece of toast. She felt a reluctant pang of sympathy for Giles.

"She sued the makers of the gun that her husband used to kill himself. She lost, but it put wind in her sails, and after that, no one was safe. She sued anyone who gossiped about her husband. She became obsessed."

Yasmin thought about the scowl on Giles's face

when he reprimanded her for mentioning Pepper's reputation. His stance apparently had deep roots.

"She couldn't deny her husband's scandalous past—he was a thief, earl or no—but she vowed revenge on everyone who shared the story." The duke cast down his half-eaten toast and barked, "Fresh tea."

Noah, the footman charged with tending a small burner on the sideboard, carefully poured boiling water into a waiting teapot and placed it on the table, whisking away the lukewarm pot and both of their teacups.

"I used to feel pity for their son," her grandfather said while they waited for the tea to steep. "The present earl, that is. You wouldn't know it to look at him now, but he was a puny boy, with legs like sticks. He looked unhealthy."

Yasmin definitely did not want to think about Giles being thin or unhappy.

"I have made up my mind to accept a marriage proposal," she said, changing the subject. "It only remains to choose the groom, and though I am sad to disappoint you as regards my dance partners from last night, I actually believe I would like to marry an older man. One who is steady and unemotional."

Her grandfather's eyebrows flew up. "Indeed? In truth, I'd like to see you happily married before I shake off this mortal coil, and my nephew inherits the title. An older man, eh? How many proposals have I rejected so far? A couple of them were in their forties."

"I haven't yet met the man whom I can imagine marrying," Yasmin said. It wasn't entirely true, but some secrets are so humiliating that they had to be kept to oneself.

"Marriage is not about desire," the duke said flatly. "Marriage is a matter of compatibility and prudence. *Wanting* to marry someone leads to disasters like that which has overtaken your mother. Having indulged herself in matters of the heart by eloping with a Frenchman, Mabel could not restrain herself when *Le Chapeau* knocked on her door."

"Actually, Napoleon offered her an emerald in full sight of Joséphine and her ladies," Yasmin said, fiddling with her fork. "I was thirteen and not yet introduced to the court, but the household talked of nothing else."

Her grandfather shuddered. "Do not repeat that detail to anyone, child. Ever."

"Mother is still in love with the emperor," Yasmin said. "Her latest letter informed me that she is making a tapestry to celebrate his triumphs as Emperor of France. She plans to send it to Saint Helena to cheer his exile."

"An unsavory subject," the duke said.

Noah stepped forward to pour fresh cups of steaming hot tea.

Yasmin cleared her throat. "More to the point, Grandfather, I have a disgrace in my past as well."

He smiled faintly. "Child, don't you think I know?"

"You do?"

"Within a week or two, I received detailed letters recounting the scandal. Two years later, I learned you had returned to the court. I rejoiced at a detailed description of your exquisite snub of Hippolyte Charles. I have never been prouder of any family member." Apparently considering the subject closed, he picked up his teacup.

Yasmin had to fight not to cry. Her parents had never expressed anything other than disgust for her stupidity.

The duke put his cup down before taking a sip. "Let me assure you that if that blackguard Charles ever broaches these shores, I'll have a sword in his gut before he walks more than a step or two." He leaned in. "I may be old, but I will avenge you, my dear, if I have the chance."

She managed a wobbly smile. "He would never fight a duel over me."

"Luckily, poverty is a revenge in itself," the duke said, a twinkle in his eyes. "I made sure of that."

"You didn't—"

"Oh, but I did. I have many connections in France, even given all the unpleasantness, and it wasn't hard to shear that particular ram. These days, with Joséphine gone and Napoleon in exile, the man can scarcely afford the pomade for those overgrowths he terms mustaches."

Yasmin shook her head. "You are wicked, Your Grace."

Her grandfather smirked and raised a finger. "Carson, where is that beer?"

The butler bowed so deeply they heard his stays creaking. "I shall visit the buttery myself, Your Grace."

The duke turned back to Yasmin. "The lesson to be learned from dubious Frenchmen such as Napoleon and Hippolyte Charles is clear: one must never indulge one's baser instincts."

Or, to put it another way, *no more waltzing with Giles Renwick, Earl of Lilford.*

And definitely, without question, no more kissing him.

CHAPTER FIVE

Later that evening
EN ROUTE TO THE DUKE OF TRENT'S
BALL

Giles and his sister, Lydia, rarely talked about things of consequence. Their sibling bond had been forged in an unhappy childhood that they never discussed. Being so much younger, there was a great deal Lydia didn't know about their parents, and Giles had no intention of revealing any of it.

From the minute she was born, he'd devoted himself to protecting her from the secrets that poisoned their household. But he couldn't keep everything from her. When she was seven years old, she'd asked how their father died, and Giles told her the truth: he took his own life.

"Why?" she had asked.

He had given her the truest and yet most evasive answer: "He was unhappy because people said cruel things behind his back."

They never discussed it again. When their mother expired due to an apoplectic fit after a judge had the temerity to rule against one of her lawsuits, they never discussed that, either.

During Lydia's disastrous first Season, she gained a reputation for clumsiness before the dreadful mistake of fizzling, as Lady Yasmin had termed it, in the presence of the queen. She didn't receive a single proposal and had cried all the way home to their country estate.

This Season seemed to be going better than her first, from what he could tell. But Giles couldn't stop wondering why Lydia had left the ballroom in the middle of a waltz. When his sister had told him that she didn't want a chaperone, he hadn't hesitated to agree. But now he was prickling with misgivings. He felt another stab of annoyance. Yasmin had gossiped to him about his sister. She had listened to unkind chatter, and what's more, she had believed it.

This evening, he would not ask Yasmin for a waltz. Nor on any future occasion.

It was one thing to indulge his fascination with an occasional dance. But given his certain knowledge that she had listened to blather about his family, if not shared it herself?

He and Lady Yasmin weren't exactly friends. But he would have thought—

Anyway, he didn't believe that Lydia would walk into the garden with a gentleman. Rumormongers always believed the worst. They jumped on the ugliest interpretation of an innocent action.

He cleared his throat. "Are you looking forward to this evening, Lydia?"

"Of course I am! The duchess has such novel ideas." She removed the reticule tied to her wrist, pulled off her gloves, took out a talcum bottle, and began to powder her nose.

"Ought you to be wearing face powder?" Giles asked. Now that he looked closely at his sister's face, he realized she was wearing lip color too. "Have you blackened your eyelashes?" They fringed her eyes in a startlingly sooty fashion.

Lydia flicked her brush in the air and then hooked it back on the talcum bottle and stowed it away in her reticule. "Of course."

"Is that . . . Do debutantes paint their faces, then?"

Lydia cast him a pitying look. "I am not a debutante, Giles. I am in my second Season." She pulled out a tiny pot and dipped her finger into the geranium-pink paint, rubbing it across her bottom lip.

Giles came to the blinding conclusion that he'd made a huge mistake. How could he have considered himself able to guide a young lady into society, sister or no? "Where did you buy those cosmetics?"

"They are sold everywhere." She pulled her gloves back on, shaking her head at him. "I suppose you think that women such as Lady Yasmin don't paint their faces?"

Giles studied Yasmin's face every time they danced. Her skin was creamy and translucent, and her cheeks turned pink when she was embarrassed. Sometimes, if she was making a particularly dramatic point, she would close her eyes in exasperation. Her lashes were thick and dark brown, with golden tips. Not pitch-black, the way Lydia's were.

"I don't think she wears cosmetics other than on her lips."

Lydia snorted. "Not that I'd *ever* want to model myself on Lady Yasmin, but of course she paints, not to mention wearing that scarlet lip color which, by the way, is a huge mistake. Given how puffy her lips are, it makes her look debauched."

The disdain in Lydia's voice made Giles's jaw tighten. He may have private misgivings about Yasmin but— "Why do you speak so disparagingly of the lady?"

"I don't say anything that isn't repeated everywhere," Lydia told him, wrinkling her nose. "She wouldn't be welcome in society, except that her grandfather is foisting her on to us. I've heard any number of people say the same. Plus, she's old."

Giles caught back a snarl.

"Will you please tie my reticule back on my wrist?"

As he bent forward to comply, she said, "On that subject, I've been meaning to mention to you, Giles, that you shouldn't dance with that woman anymore. I assure everyone that you dance with Lady Yasmin out of respect for her grandfather, the Duke of Portbellow. However, it would be more prudent to ignore her altogether, the way most people do."

Most people? Every night, he had to fight his

way through a thicket of suitors to reach Yasmin's side. She was best of friends with their hostess this evening, the Duchess of Trent, not to mention Mrs. Addison, her friend Cleo. Mr. and Mrs. Addison had become remarkably influential in society in just over a year, perhaps because they made it so abundantly clear that they didn't give a fig what anyone thought of them.

Giles straightened and moved back in his seat. He could feel anger stirring inside him at Lydia's unfair statement.

"Don't waltz with Lady Yasmin tonight, if you please," Lydia ordered.

He had come to that decision himself. But he wasn't a man who took commands from anyone, especially his younger sister.

"It's only because I want to protect you," she continued, when he didn't reply. "It has even crossed my mind on occasion that you might consider her as the future Countess of Lilford, and Giles, that would be a frightful mistake. Our father tarnished the family name but *that* would make you—us—a laughingstock."

How were Lydia's conclusions different from his own? He had decided months ago that this particular lady wasn't eligible. "I have no intention of marrying Lady Yasmin, nor am I courting her. I merely enjoy her company."

There was a moment's silence in the carriage. "I know you," Lydia said. "We both know that you aren't dancing with Lady Yasmin out of politeness. But marriage to her would be disastrous,

Giles." Her voice wasn't commanding now, but earnest, even pleading.

His jaw tightened.

"You're my brother, my only brother. I've seen the way you look at her. And she—she's so beautiful. Delectable, really. I do see that. But she would create scandal after scandal. You would never know if your children are your own. Some say that she is Napoleon's bastard. Did you hear that? Or that she was his *inamorata*, rather than her mother."

"Absurd," Giles said. "Logically, Lady Yasmin cannot be his daughter, because she was born long before Napoleon became First Consul, let alone Emperor of France. She told me that her mother gave her one of Napoleon's hats. She brought it here as a gift for her grandfather, who adorned a skeleton with it."

"I suppose she couldn't be Napoleon's daughter. For one thing, she is disagreeably tall."

"As I already told you, I have no intention of marrying Lady Yasmin," Giles stated.

"You can't make such an important decision yourself. We're talking about my future sister."

He looked at her incredulously.

"You look so stern all the time that probably no one will wish to marry you anyway," Lydia muttered. "No, that's not true. You're an earl. The only time those dreadful girls at the seminary would talk to me was when they were trying to figure out how they could catch your attention."

He should have listened years ago when his

sister first told him how much she disliked the school. Their carriage slowed, joining a block-long line of vehicles waiting to drop guests at the Duke of Trent's townhouse.

The unpleasant gossip that Lady Yasmin had told him was surely untrue, likely started by disagreeable schoolgirls. That would make sense. The last thing he wanted to do was tell Lydia that people were speaking unkindly about her.

Still, Giles had to say something, something a chaperone would say.

"Lydia," he said, clearing his throat.

"Yes?"

"You do know that you mustn't visit darkened corners in the duke's gardens without a chaperone?"

Lydia's eyes narrowed, and he instantly knew that Lady Yasmin had been right.

"Who told you that rubbish?" she demanded.

"Did you leave the ballroom yesterday and go into the garden, accompanied by a gentleman, without a chaperone?" he countered.

Lydia straightened, thrusting her chin forward. "I know who told you," his sister hissed. "*She* did, didn't she? The *strumpet* told you."

"I don't know who you mean."

"You know exactly who I am talking about!" Lydia cried. "The woman you are making a fool of yourself over. Do I really have to name her? The French coquette. The flirt. People use other names too." Whatever she saw in Giles's eyes made Lydia's jaw set even more firmly, and her eyes flare with anger.

"Lady Yasmin is a *lady*," he said. "You do yourself a disservice by speaking about another woman in such a fashion."

His sister barked with laughter, and he saw a flash of his mother in her face: the implacable rage, the dislike of being questioned.

"She's after you," Lydia said with unforgivable informality. "She wants you and your title. You're too naïve to see it, Giles. Although they also say that she dare not accept a marriage proposal because she's no innocent."

Giles fought to control a stab of pure fury. "You and I know better than most that cruel gossip should never be shared or even listened to."

She tossed her head. "If you are referring to our father, I consider that a lamentable episode that should be forgotten."

Episode? Of course, she had been very young when the late earl took his life.

"Our father was weak." She said it fiercely. "I'm old enough to acknowledge the truth about him. He wasn't just unhappy. He was a criminal, a thief."

Giles flinched. "Who told you?"

"Those girls at the seminary," Lydia stated. "They were never my friends and they never will be. Not given who my father was. Blanche was the only one who didn't care."

The carriage was silent for a moment, the only

sound the rattle of carriage wheels over cobble-stones.

"Our father was hounded to death by gossip, which is why I am not happy to find you engaging in it. He left a letter saying as much."

"Why shouldn't they gossip about him? He stole money from a church. That's what they all said. From a *church*."

"He was a very young man, not old enough to think clearly. Sometimes young people do foolish things," Giles said, watching Lydia closely. "Things that society doesn't approve of."

The carriage jolted to a halt.

Lydia laughed, quick and fierce as a fox's bark. "You can't possibly be comparing the fact I've kissed a few men to stealing money from a church. Hundreds of pounds, as I heard."

"Both things can wound a person's reputation."

"Those girls that I mentioned, Giles?"

"Yes?"

"Their brothers, Lord Pepper among them, follow me like lambs to the slaughter." Her mouth curled in a smug smile. "I could have any of those men with no more than a snap of my fingers. Any of them. I am an earl's daughter, after all, and my dowry is one of the largest on the marriage mart."

"That is a remarkably vulgar statement," Giles said, keeping his voice even. "Ladies risk more than their reputation by accompanying gentlemen into secluded pathways. You could be injured, Lydia. No more improprieties with Lord Pepper."

He was fairly sure his sister was grinding her teeth.

"I will agree only if you never again waltz with Lady Yasmin!" she retorted.

A groom opened the door, and Giles nodded to him. When Lydia stepped off the mounting block, he tucked her hand into his arm and began to escort her to the Duke of Trent's imposing mansion.

Two matrons dressed in purple gowns charged the front door ahead of them.

"Everyone knows you accompanied Lady Yasmin into the garden last night," Lydia said in a low, vehement voice. "*You* engaged in improprieties. If you're not careful, Giles, she will contrive to compromise you."

He held his tongue.

"Fine," Lydia said, once a footman had taken her pelisse. "I will avoid Lord Pepper. But only on the condition that you have nothing to do with Lady Yasmin."

Giles blinked at her. "I have almost nothing to do with her now, Lydia."

"Lord Pepper for Lady Yasmin. No dancing. Absolutely no walks in the garden. You should have heard Lady Dunlap gossiping about the two of you last night!"

"Very well."

"Of course, if Lady Yasmin becomes the Duchess of Huntington, you may dance with her as much as you wish," Lydia said in a conciliatory way, just as they reached the end of the receiving line. Her lips tipped up into a smile, though her eyes were cold. "Make her your mistress, if you wish. I merely want to ensure that she doesn't weasel her way into marriage with you, ruining our family name."

Giles bit back a retort and said, instead, "I'd rather you didn't dance with Pepper even if you become a duchess. He's not a gentleman."

Her face eased. "You are a stick in the mud, Giles, you do know that? My friend Blanche thinks it's quite adorable."

Giles hid a shudder.

"Come along," Lydia said. "Blanche saved a waltz for you. I told her you would be wearing a pink cravat, and she chose her gown as a pleasing counterpoint."

She was his baby sister. He loved her.

He followed her.

CHAPTER SIX

The Duchess of Trent's ball was the high point of the social Season. Merry scorned the idea of renting a few lemon trees, scattering them around the ballroom, and calling it a day. Instead, the American Duchess used her remarkable gardening skills to create extravagant events. Months ago, she had announced that this year's inspiration was Titania's bower from *A Midsummer Night's Dream*.

Yasmin and her grandfather strolled into the Trent mansion and were promptly greeted by their hostess, who deserted the receiving line and sped toward her, hands outstretched.

"You look delicious!" Merry cried.

Yasmin smiled and spun in a circle. She wore shell-pink satin with a tiny, high bodice, cut low back and front. Her skirts were gored and floated around her ankles, trimmed with small net roses gleaming with spangles.

"And your diamonds are pink!" Merry exclaimed, clapping her hands. "I may be Queen Titania, Yasmin, but you are surely my lady-in-waiting! Or perhaps a visiting queen from another land. Wait until you see Cleo; she too is practically festooned in diamonds."

"My granddaughter wears the Portbellow diamonds," the duke announced.

"They are exquisite, Your Grace." Merry caught Yasmin's hand. "I must show you the ballroom!"

The large chamber was hung with strings of flowers graduating from pink blossoms to raspberry-colored roses, with exquisite white ferns providing a lacy border. The chandeliers were hung with blowsy silk, and in all four corners of the room, women costumed like fairies, with bodices made of roses and skirts of fern, strummed golden harps.

"It's astonishing!" Yasmin exclaimed, awed. "Better than anything I saw at Versailles, Merry. I promise you that."

"I love hearing that! I am already planning next year," Merry said, laughing.

Dancing wouldn't begin until later; at the moment ladies and gentlemen dressed in shades of rose and purple strolled through the grand ballroom, the ladies' skirts brushing aside shoals of rose petals.

Having caught sight of Yasmin, gentlemen began arrowing toward the entry to ask her to dance. Merry squeezed her hand and returned to the receiving line.

"Granddaughter," the duke said, appearing at her side. "May I present Viscount Templeton?"

The gentleman was tall, his dark hair just touched with frost. His eyes smiled down into hers. "It is my great pleasure, Lady Yasmin," he said, bowing as he kissed her gloved hand.

Her grandfather's introduction was a delightful start to the ball.

Since their hostess, Merry, was admired, powerful, *and* Yasmin's friend, no one dared be openly rude. It didn't bother Yasmin much to be mocked from behind the shelter of a fan. Even when ladies summoned up their courage and hissed a nasty word or two in the privacy of the ladies' withdrawing room, she merely smiled at them and sailed out of the room.

Ladies at the French court—not to mention a furious empress—had provided an excellent training ground. Insults offered by a British noblewoman paled in comparison. All the same, it was a joy to be surrounded by genuine friends who cared for her, and a grandfather who seemed to like her more than her mother and father combined.

Moreover, after a second dance with Viscount Templeton, they sat at the side of the ballroom and discovered that they both disliked hunting, long sermons, and Gunter's lavender ice cream.

"Yours, if you want him," Merry whispered after the viscount reluctantly left to dance with another lady. "I like being a noblewoman, by the way. I oughtn't to say that, as an American, but I do." As Silvester emerged from the crowd, she added mischievously, "We could be the most fashionable duchesses in London."

Yasmin rolled her eyes and allowed Silvester to

draw her into a waltz. After their second dance, a somewhat boisterous quadrille, he tucked her beside him on a snug sofa.

"Where's your most devoted swain, the Earl of Lilford?" Silvester asked now.

"Swain?" Yasmin asked, frowning.

"Suitor. Lover. Wooer."

She tucked the new word away in her memory. "Lord Lilford dances with me out of courtesy."

"The man has been asking you for the first waltz all Season. Don't tell me you haven't noticed, because you always save it for him." Silvester picked up her dance card. "Dear me. Perhaps there's a chance for me, after all. It seems Viscount Templeton had the pleasure of your first waltz tonight."

"You didn't request that waltz."

"I assumed you were saving it for Lilford. I would have preferred the supper dance, but you had already given it to your grandfather. In case you'd like to start saving a dance for me every night, I choose supper."

Yasmin smiled. "I like my grandfather, and I enjoy dining with him."

"Then you'll be glad to know that *your* grandfather was one of *my* grandfather's close friends. Gramps was not what you'd call an ordinary peer, but your grandfather liked him anyway."

Silvester waved her dance card in the air. "Even if you don't marry me, you shouldn't dance with Edwin Turing, darling—" He bit off the endearment when she frowned at him. "Why do you hate that word so much?"

"I dislike empty endearments in general," Yasmin said, accepting a glass of champagne from a passing footman. Generally, she didn't drink much wine—though she loved a sip of brandy—but she was feeling oddly melancholy not to have a waltz and a squabble with Giles to look forward to. It made the evening ahead feel long and dull.

After what Giles said about her—what he *thought* about her—they should never dance together again. Nor kiss, obviously. She had stayed up half the night rehearsing the moment when she would carelessly inform him that she hadn't saved the first waltz.

It had been ferociously disappointing when he didn't ask for it.

"Edwin Turing is a loose fish," Silvester stated.

"I'm surprised to hear that," Yasmin said. Her grandfather had unceremoniously refused Turing's proposal of marriage, telling her that the man had neither the requisite money nor status. But he hadn't mentioned moral failings.

"I know Turing has written a sonnet or two to your eyes, but setting aside his public adoration for you, he's a voluptuary. He practiced his seductive wiles on one of my sisters, but she unceremoniously gave him a clout on the cheek."

"He hasn't offered me an affront."

"He knows he wouldn't get anywhere with you. You're too—"

"Old?" Yasmin supplied. "I do feel like a spinster at times. One of these days I'll dwindle into a wallflower."

Silvester blinked at her, startled. "Spinster? You're the most beautiful woman on the marriage mart this year. All eligible gentlemen are at your feet. The grumpy earl as well, for all he hasn't asked you to dance this evening."

Yasmin felt a rush of affection for Silvester, along with a strong suspicion that he was a good deal more perceptive than he allowed others to know. She leaned over and tapped him on the cheek. "Your Grace, you are a great flatterer."

"You should do that again after Lilford has made his appearance," Silvester said, laughter running through his deep voice.

"Why?"

"To convince him that he has no chance. Because he has no chance, has he?"

Yasmin shook her head.

"In fact, perhaps you should kiss me." He caught her hand in his. "On the very cheek where you just caressed me."

"I didn't caress you!"

"The earl would think you did," Silvester said smugly. "If he had the ability, he'd probably throw a spare lightning bolt at me. I've seen him glowering at your suitors."

Yasmin broke out laughing. "A lightning bolt? As in Jove's favorite weapon? You have completely misjudged that man's power, not to mention his interest."

"For months now he's claimed the first waltz with the most beautiful woman in London without even bothering to smile at you. Godlike powers or magic? To us poor mortals, it felt like Jove had come down from Mount Olympus."

Yasmin shook her head, giggling. "I do hope you are not implying I could end up in love with a swan?"

One side of Silvester's mouth crooked into a smile and he said, "That would never be you, Yasmin, would it?"

"No gods have paid me visits clad in feathers. Didn't Jove show up as a cuckoo bird as well? If I encounter a bird with amorous intentions, I will kick it solidly, god or no. So no, that is not me."

Silvester's smile deepened. "I mean, darling, that you are an incredibly good girl, aren't you?"

Yasmin felt herself going pink.

"Lilford is not the right man for you."

"I agree," Yasmin said instantly. "I dislike him."

"Hmmm," Silvester said. "I wish that was so. Perhaps in time it will be true. I've watched you dancing with him. You flare into life. Instead of smiling all the time, you scowl and fuss and generally resemble a woman rather than an extremely pretty china figurine."

"I scowl at you regularly," Yasmin said, finishing her champagne, because the conversation was making her uneasy.

"A point in my favor, I admit."

"The earl irritates me," she confessed. "I am tempted to drive him to rage, which is childish in the extreme. I have decided to stop the practice."

"Thereby giving me hope," Silvester said lightly. He glanced down at the dance card he still held. "I do believe that you're supposed to be waltzing with Algie Dunlap at this very moment. Let's stay here, shall we? He's a tiresome young fool and likely won't glimpse you in this corner."

"Another bad poet," Yasmin sighed.

"Yes, but at least Dunlap's poetry is original. No one would crib a line that described his love as being 'faultless as a blown rose in June.'"

Yasmin started giggling. "The 'blown' was unfortunate, wasn't it? He explained that he needed another syllable."

"I'm not a poet." His eyes were lit with wicked mischief. "Faultless as a flea?"

"I don't have fleas!"

"I'm glad to hear it," Silvester said, a silky tone entering his voice. "A duchess shouldn't be infested."

Yasmin rolled her eyes.

"It would make the marital bed so uncomfortable, don't you think?"

Yasmin snapped her fan shut and stood. "I should find my dance partner."

Silvester stood as well. "I went too far. Forgive me?"

"No need," she said, glancing around for Algernon.

He took her hand. "I made a coarse jest, and I apologize."

Yasmin could feel herself turning pink again. "I am not . . ." She tried again. "I am somewhat prudish." Then she remembered saying "bollocks" to him. She was a hypocrite who loved bawdy words, but not when deployed in flirtation.

"*You* are a constant surprise and a delight. Please, won't you sit down, Yasmin? I promise to be good."

She somewhat reluctantly allowed him to draw her down onto the sofa again. "I really mean it, Your Grace. No more flummery, and *no* improper jokes. I don't like them. That is, I do like them, but not when they are like that."

"Like what?" he asked, a smile playing around his lips.

To her discomfort, it was an affectionate smile.

"Lewd. I may never marry," she added, succumbing to a sudden impulse to tell him the truth.

"You might change your mind about that. Even if your heart is bruised."

He was entirely too perceptive.

Yasmin managed a careless smile, though it was not easy. A mere hint of weakness would give the gossips reasons to rejoice, and the last thing she wanted to do was admit that her heart did feel bruised, as if she were a girl in the French court once again.

Giles wouldn't care that he had wounded her feelings.

"My heart is whole," she said airily, her facade firmly in place.

CHAPTER SEVEN

Yasmin and Silvester were still nestled on the sofa when he said, "Jove himself just entered the drawing room with his sister, darling."

"Don't call me that," Yasmin said automatically.

"Wearing black, of course, although he complied with the duchess's request by wearing a pink neck cloth," Silvester continued, ignoring her. "His valet must have washed it in beet juice. Lilford is broodingly handsome, don't you think?"

Yasmin did think, but she wasn't going to admit it. She deliberately did not look about the room for Giles. "*You* are just as handsome."

"Not a bit of it," Silvester said cheerfully. "I have the family nose, and I'm no good at looking stern and moody, which my sisters tell me is what makes the earl so desirable. Personally, I think it signals nothing more than irritability and likely indigestion. Just look at him now. He's in a fury. Perhaps he ate too many beets in preparation for the ball."

Yasmin gave up her principles and looked around for Giles. "Where is he?"

"Over there with his sister, talking to our host."

Yasmin could only see Giles's profile. She couldn't crane her neck, as that would lead to gossip that she had ogled the earl. Yet even from here, she could see that the tendons in his neck were strained. Likely he was clenching his jaw, which in her experience, he did when he was furious.

"I don't care for his sister," Silvester observed. "Lady Lydia always looks at me as if she were measuring me for a wedding coat and finding that I come up short."

At that moment Lydia turned away from the group and began strolling toward the ballroom, her hand on Lord Turing's arm. Her eyes paused for a moment on Yasmin's face before she looked away.

The duke let out a low whistle. "My grandmother used to have a little dog who would bare her teeth the way that woman just did. Is Lydia the reason why he hasn't strode over here like a disapproving god and demanded your hand for the next waltz, since he missed the first?"

"Quite possibly," Yasmin admitted.

"That woman will do you an injury if given a chance. What on earth did you do to her?"

"Nothing," she said, untruthfully.

Obviously, Giles had told his sister that Yasmin was the source of gossip about Lydia's escapades in gardens. In fact, she never shared unkind gossip about a woman. In France, gossip was a blood sport. People who hadn't known the details of the week she spent with Hippolyte had made them up.

The last straw before Yasmin accepted her grandfather's invitation to visit England had been when a lascivious gentleman made a jest about clipping one of the emerald buttons on his coat and offering it to her, as emeralds were her family's favorite gem.

Everyone around the dinner table laughed, which was when she realized that she would never escape the French court's fixed conviction that she could be bought for an emerald, as Napoleon had bought her mother. She had informed her parents she was leaving for England the very next day.

Mabel had nodded and said, "I *do* find it dismaying to have a young girl living with me."

None of the sentences that had come to mind— *But I'm your daughter!*—were worth saying aloud, so Yasmin offered the airy kisses that Mabel preferred, ordered her trunks packed, and left.

"Lady Lydia doesn't care for me," she told Silvester.

"Why not?"

"I believe she considers me shamefully dissolute."

Silvester raised an eyebrow. "*You* don't kiss men in alcoves. I accidentally walked into her canoodling with young Harriford a few weeks ago. Not that I had ever considered marrying her, but the way she smirked when she saw me was enough to put me off."

"You mustn't tell anyone that," Yasmin said.

"I never do," Silvester said. "Gossip of that nature is so dreary. Her brother's behavior is far more interesting."

"Why?"

"He's handed off his sister, but he is not coming straight to your side like a homing pigeon. In fact, he's not looking in this direction, which suggests that he knows exactly where you are."

Yasmin flipped open her fan and waved it lazily before her face, just in case Giles did look in their direction. But he didn't. As she watched, Merry introduced him to a soberly dressed young woman with her hair in a no-nonsense chignon and spectacles perched on her nose.

"The Marquess of Tatton's granddaughter, Lady Stella," Silvester said.

"She looks very serious."

"Indeed, she is not a fribble like ourselves. Doesn't give a damn about appearances since, as you'll notice, she's wearing spectacles, rather than carrying a lorgnette. The earl could always instruct the family portraitist to pretend the spectacles don't exist. I'm sure he expects perfection in his wife—or at least will want to pretend he's found it."

"You're being rather unkind," Yasmin said, unable to stop herself. "I don't think Lord Lilford is so shallow that he'd pretend his wife doesn't wear spectacles."

Silvester's gray eyes were sharply ironic. "The earl is so shallow that he won't allow himself to court you because he doesn't approve of your gowns."

Yasmin waved her fan while she thought about that. "You underestimate his dislike of my frivolity." By which she meant her reputation.

"Lady Stella should suit him. She wields her intelligence like a hammer. It's her most obvious characteristic, the attribute she presents to the world." He glanced at Yasmin's bosom and waggled an eyebrow.

"You're suggesting that I do the same with my bodices?"

"I cannot answer because I promised never to make an improper remark to you again," Silvester murmured. But his eyes laughed at her.

"What do you present to the world?" Yasmin asked. "What is your most evident characteristic?"

He shrugged, humor disappearing. "Oh, Lilford and I don't need a character or any characteristics. We carry our titles with us, as if they were emblazoned on our foreheads. They prove irresistible, in my experience."

Yasmin gave him a frank look. "I wouldn't count on that."

"You are the exception," he said, catching up her hand and kissing it. Yasmin looked up to find Giles's eyes on them, but he turned away and walked into the ballroom, the bespeckled lady on his arm.

Somehow, after that, the evening lost its sparkle. Yasmin and her grandfather had the honor of dining with Queen Titania and King Oberon—Merry and her duke—but even the fact that Silvester had been invited to join them didn't raise her spirits.

Her grandfather, on the other hand, enjoyed himself thoroughly, arguing with Merry about the cultural differences between America and Britain.

"You British have honed the art of rudeness," Merry informed him.

"Rudeness is like cockfighting," the duke retorted. "I'll grant you it's an unpleasant sport, but hardly confined to my nation."

Silvester had been talking to the young lady whom he escorted to supper, but he turned to Yasmin. "What particular rudeness is in question?"

"Nothing important," she answered, leveling a frown at her grandfather.

"I was describing my conversation with the Earl of Lilford," her grandfather chortled. "The man had the temerity to imply that my granddaughter would spread squalid gossip about one of his relatives! I set him straight."

"He doesn't know Lady Yasmin," Silvester said.

Yasmin couldn't help thinking of all the waltzes she'd shared with Giles, far more than she'd shared with Silvester, whom she'd only met this Season.

"Aye, there's something to that," her grandfather muttered.

Yasmin summoned up a smile, a bit tremulous. What Giles did know of her, he didn't like.

So why should he care to know more of her? The truth hurt, a dull pain in the area of her heart, but that was absurd.

The only relationship they had stemmed from waltzing and bickering.

Yasmin felt a touch on her shoulder and looked up to find Giles nodding in a tight-lipped way at the table. "Good evening, Lord Lilford," she said, her heart suddenly thudding in her throat.

"I wonder if you could spare me a few minutes, Lady Yasmin," he said.

"The first waltz has come and gone, and her dance card is full," Silvester said, his voice a nice blend of courtesy and something else. Something a bit possessive.

No, *very* possessive, since he followed that up by putting an arm on the back of Yasmin's chair.

"I am Lady Yasmin's escort this evening," her grandfather said, eyeing Silvester with a distinctly mischievous expression. "I suppose I will allow the Earl of Lilford a brief conversation." He waved his thin hand, making the lace ruffles at his wrists flutter. "Off with you."

Yasmin sighed and rose. "If you will excuse me," she said to the table, curtsying.

They walked a few steps in complete silence before she said, "Is there some way by which I might help you, Lord Lilford? Or did you simply wish to stroll?" She allowed disbelief to leak into her voice.

"She's gone," Giles said, staring straight ahead

and speaking so quietly that no one could catch his words.

Yasmin drew in a sharp breath. "Your sister? Where did she go?"

"I'm not sure. I didn't accompany her to supper."

"You were seated with Miss Boodle," she said, revealing that she knew where he sat before she could stop herself.

"My sister's closest friend," Giles said. "When I realized that my sister was nowhere to be seen, I excused myself. But I have been unable to find Lydia. She's not in the drawing room or the ballroom. I have to ask you to go into the ladies' retiring room. I didn't . . . I didn't want anyone else to know my concern."

"I am certain that Lydia did not elope, if that's what you're worrying about," Yasmin promised him. "She is still in the house."

The Duke of Trent's dining room opened into a grand foyer draped with strings of roses and ferns. They strolled out as if they were merely admiring the Shakespearean embellishments.

"We had an argument in the carriage so it occurred to me that Lydia may have run away."

"It would have to have been a ferocious argument for your sister to flee the house. She is not a foolish young girl."

"Did you run away when you were a girl?" Giles asked, frowning at her.

"Yes," Yasmin said baldly. "But that doesn't

explain why you think that such a well-brought-up lady as your sister would do the same."

"I fear she didn't run away alone," he said, a harsh note in his voice. "I believe I owe you an apology, Lady Yasmin. You were right when you suspected my sister of unladylike behavior."

Yasmin's heartbeat thudded in her chest at the expression in Giles's eyes. It wasn't disapproving. She wasn't sure what it was, but he didn't look as if he despised her. She reminded herself that she wanted nothing further to do with him, but she could feel herself growing hot in the cheeks anyway.

All because he was looking at her.

As if he actually saw her.

She hurried into speech. "I'm sorry that I shared such distressing information about your sister. I promise that I hadn't heard it from gossips. I'd merely noticed that Lady Lydia occasionally absented herself from the dance floor."

"Once I knew you were right about her behavior, I realized that I had been unfair. I apologize."

"I do love a good story," Yasmin admitted. "But not about improprieties of that nature," she added, allowing him a tiny glimpse of herself in hopes that he would see beyond her reputation.

He didn't look remotely interested.

"I don't believe for a moment that your sister eloped," Yasmin said, to bridge the silence between them. In her opinion, Lydia was far too hardheaded to elope, an action that would put her standing in society in serious jeopardy. Kissing was one thing; eloping was another.

"She might have done so out of anger. I told her she was not allowed to have anything more to do with Lord Pepper."

"A wise decision."

He grimaced. "I hadn't thought about how akin Lydia is to my mother. Once thwarted, the late countess became quickly enraged, illogical, and revengeful."

"Did you forbid your sister to see the man without explaining why?" Yasmin couldn't help looking at him pityingly.

Giles's jaw tightened. "Everyone, including Lydia, is aware that Pepper's estate is impoverished."

"At least she is not making mercenary decisions."

"She deliberately made Pepper think that he had a chance of marrying her in order to gain revenge on his sister, who was rude to her when they were schoolgirls," Giles said bluntly.

Yasmin bit her lip.

"Lydia's anger stems from unkind talk at school," he continued. "About my father's death."

"How horrible for her," Yasmin said.

Giles cleared his throat. "She boasted of making the brothers of those girls come at the lift of her finger. She is toying with them, like a cat with mice."

Yasmin could understand Lydia's wish for revenge, but the girl would only harm herself if she continued in this mad fashion. "I'm sure that she is still in the house. I'll check the ladies' retiring room first. After that, we'll have to ask the butler."

She ran up the marble steps to the first floor. Merry had designated a pleasant room for the use of ladies who needed to rest their feet or to ask a maid to mend a ripped hem. The maid had likely been reassigned to help with supper, because the room was empty. Yasmin even peeped into the adjoining water closet, outfitted with a Lewis commode, but Lydia was nowhere to be seen.

Leaving the room, she saw Giles waiting for her at the bottom of the stairs. Did he have to be so broad shouldered? She had never imagined a man with such a deep lower lip. And he was so protective about his wretched sister, making him fifty times more desirable to her, which was stupid, stupid, stupid.

She ran back down the stairs. "There is no sign of her. Perhaps she is in one of the parlors."

"Lydia wouldn't—"

"Yet, you think she might have eloped?" Yasmin asked, cutting him off. Just then the butler emerged from the dining room, so she walked to meet him. "Peters, Lord Lilford is concerned about his sister, Lady Lydia. I wonder if you have seen her."

The butler's expression didn't change, but his eyes did.

"To make certain that she is safe," Yasmin added.

Peters cleared his throat. "If the young lady felt faint, she may have taken refuge in the library or a smaller drawing room."

"He knows," Giles said as they walked down the marble passage. "He knows where she is and with whom." Then he muttered, "Damn it."

"Butlers know everything," Yasmin said. "Here's the library."

She turned the doorknob and walked in. The library was lined with books, of course, with an imposing desk positioned straight ahead. But what caught Yasmin's eyes was a hairy male bottom, breeches down around his knees.

A flood of embarrassment went over her. The man in question was vigorously tupping a woman in a garish crimson gown, unquestionably the one worn by Mrs. Dyne. The lady's spouse was considerably older than this energetic fellow.

She whipped around. "It's not Lydia!" she whispered frantically, pushing Giles backward.

CHAPTER EIGHT

Giles only caught a brief glance of the room before Lady Yasmin turned and pushed him back into the corridor.

"It wasn't your sister!" she whispered, pulling the door shut behind them. Her cheeks had stained rosy pink, and she didn't meet his eyes.

Giles felt a pang of guilt for having placed her in such an invidious position. He hadn't glimpsed more than a man's hairy arse, but no lady wanted to see that. "I apologize for placing you in a situation in which you witnessed something abhorrent. Shall we return to the dining room?"

He knew perfectly well he could investigate these rooms by himself. But if he let her go, she'd return to sitting next to Silvester.

"Nonsense," Lady Yasmin said, raising her chin in a decisive fashion. "Once you've come across your mother kissing an emperor, nothing else can disturb you."

Giles didn't think that was true, given the hectic color in her cheeks. It made him wonder how much of the lady's sophisticated manner was genuine, and how much was pretense. It also made him want to kiss Lady Yasmin until she lost the vaguely horrified look in her eyes.

"You're certain that my sister was not in the room?"

"Indeed." She cast him a narrow-eyed look. "Do not ask me for the names of that couple, Lord Lilford. You may believe what you wish about me, but I do not gossip about extramarital dalliances."

She rapped on the next door, but before she could open it, Giles nudged her. "I'll enter first this time."

He walked into the room. Since it was empty, he moved to the side so that Lady Yasmin could join him. The chamber was lit only by a large candelabra on the mantelpiece, its light amplified by a gilded mirror. The room was apparently used by their hostess for informal moments with her family, given the books stacked on the floor, the toy elephant lying on its side, and the unfinished sampler on a side table next to a huge bowl of plump roses. Comfortable chairs covered in purple velvet clustered before a matching sofa with its back to them.

"*Une belle chambre*," Lady Yasmin murmured.

Giles felt a bolt of lust at her husky voice that went straight down his limbs. "I've never heard you speak French."

"I try to speak English as much as I can. Last Season I kept slipping into French, but I am better at English now."

He'd noticed her voracious love of language, extending from American slang to the *Book of Com-*

mon Prayer. Before he could respond, he heard a rustle.

Like a jack-in-the-box, his sister popped up on the other side of the sofa.

"Lydia!" he exclaimed.

She pointed imperiously at Giles, for all the world like a furious Lady Macbeth.

"You *lied* to me!" she screeched.

During the stunned silence that followed, a young man got to his feet, hastily adjusting his coat. Somewhat to Giles's surprise, it was Edwin Turing. He had been under the impression that Turing was one of Lady Yasmin's most devoted suitors. Certainly, he played that role in public with a good deal of poetic vigor.

"Good evening, Mr. Turing," Lady Yasmin said evenly.

He winced. "Good evening, Lady Yasmin. Lord Lilford."

"What are you doing here, Giles?" Lydia demanded, ignoring this exchange. She scowled, apparently not realizing or caring that her topknot was falling halfway down her back, and she was thoroughly disheveled. "You *promised* that you would have nothing to do with Lady Yasmin!"

"You promised to avoid improprieties." Giles folded his arms over his chest.

"With Lord Pepper," Lydia retorted.

She rounded the sofa. More curls sprang free of her topknot, making her resemble a furious turkey-cock.

Lady Yasmin backed out of her way as Lydia

walked straight to Giles and gave him a shove with both hands. "You're a liar!"

"We will return home now, Lydia," he said with icy precision. "Please compose yourself and make yourself presentable. Your hair is untidy."

He turned to face Edwin Turing. The light was dim, but Giles thought the young man had turned rather pale. As well he might.

"Given the sonnets addressed to Lady Yasmin that you have been publicly reciting, I assume that you had no intention of offering marriage to my sister. Unfortunately, that decision is now out of your hands."

"I understand," Turing said, bowing.

"As if I would accept such a nincompoop!" Lydia snapped, curling her lip.

Turing dropped his air of civility and glared at her. "I don't care to marry someone with hair that looks like a hedgehog."

"That's enough!" Giles barked.

"At least I'm not as stupid as a post!" Lydia cried.

"You're meaner than one," Turing said.

Lydia raised her hand into the air, but Giles caught her wrist before she could strike her erstwhile suitor. The reticule she wore tied around her arm ripped down one side, its contents scattering on the carpet.

Giles kept his eyes on his sister's face. "Lydia, I must ask you to remain silent before you further disgrace yourself."

"I am not disgraced!" She twisted her hand free

and glared at Lady Yasmin, who had bent over to gather up her cosmetics. "I'm not compromised unless *she* tells the world."

"I shall tell no one."

"Then you needn't bother with a proposal, Turing," Lydia said.

"You have been compromised, Lydia," Giles said, feeling an errant thread of sympathy for his little sister, even in the midst of his anger. "The butler knew where we could find you and presumably who you were with. Mr. Turing must marry you."

"Oh, a butler! Who cares for that!" Lydia cried.

As Lady Yasmin placed a comb and several hairpins on the chair, Lydia kicked a tiny bottle of scent so that it rolled under the sofa. "Don't touch my things!"

Lady Yasmin put the pot of lip color on the chair and regarded Giles's sister with a steady expression. Lydia shut her mouth and shifted her gaze away.

"Mr. Turing, perhaps you would be so kind as to escort me back to the dining room," Lady Yasmin said, her voice as low and pleasant as ever.

He bowed hastily, sweeping a hand through his hair in an attempt to return it to the popular "frightened owl" style that he had affected earlier that evening.

"I shall expect you to pay me a morning call, Mr. Turing," Giles said.

"No, no!" Lydia cried, her eyes widening. Apparently, she was only now starting to understand that her future had been decided. "I don't want to marry him!"

"The feeling is mutual," Turing said, adding with impatience, "We're not the first or the last couple compromised, Lydia. You might as well put up with it."

"You probably arranged for this to happen!" she retorted shrilly.

The young man stared at her. "I'd arrange to be struck down by a carriage first. I'm a gentleman, though you've little claim to—"

"Mr. Turing," Lady Yasmin said.

He shut his mouth.

Lydia wheeled, turning back to Giles. "I won't marry him!"

Turing bowed before Giles. "I will pay you a visit in the morning, my lord." He turned to Lydia and bowed again. "Lady Lydia." Before Giles could say a word, Lady Yasmin whisked him out the door and shut it behind them.

"I hate him, and I hate her!" Lydia burst out. "You *promised* me that you would have nothing to do with her. You promised! Yet, here you are, entering a room with her. I supposed you were planning to have relations with her!"

Giles took a deep breath. He apparently didn't know his sister, but he thought . . . Whatever he thought was obviously wrong. It occurred to him that Lydia might have toyed with Turing simply because he was known to be one of Yasmin's suitors.

"When I couldn't find you, I had to ask a lady

to enter the ladies' retiring room. I didn't want to admit to anyone else that you were missing." He paused and added, "In case someone in that ballroom didn't already know about your behavior, Lydia."

"I was only kissing him out of boredom, really. I don't believe that explanation. You meant to toss up Lady Yasmin's skirts, didn't you? You've probably been doing that every night. Or she was the one who followed us!"

"Nonsense," Giles said. "I asked Lady Yasmin for assistance—"

"Why? Why did you do that?"

"As I said, I didn't want anyone else to know what you were doing. I trust her discretion."

"You could have asked Blanche!"

"So Miss Boodle knew where you were?"

"No, but she's not as hidebound and stuffy as the others." Lydia crossed her arms over her chest and fixed him with a glare that was the precise image of their mother's. "You've ruined the whole night, so we might as well go home. Lady Yasmin will be scuttling back to our hostess and telling her everything, I suppose. You didn't order her to hold her tongue."

"She promised not to say a word to anyone."

"You're so naïve." Lydia glanced at the mirror, pulled up her hair, and stuck a number of hairpins into it. Then she turned to the chair where her cosmetics were piled and stuck them into her pocket. She bent down and looked around the chair, though she didn't bother to reach under the sofa and retrieve her scent bottle.

"Is something missing?" Giles asked.

"Either that, or it was taken," Lydia said unpleasantly.

A wave of rage swept over Giles, so deep that he felt fire in his lungs. "I gather you are accusing Lady Yasmin of stealing a jewel of yours? You are embarrassing me, Lydia. More than that, you are saddening me. Why were you with Turing?"

Lydia scowled at him. "His sister Cordelia is a despicable human being, if you must know. They both act so proper. Just look at him, reeling off those absurd little poems about Lady Yasmin, though he followed me here eagerly enough." She smirked. "His sister looked positively sick when we left the room together. All the same, you can't make me marry him, Giles! You just can't!"

"You're compromised," he said, watching as she turned to the mirror and miraculously managed to trap her yellow hair on top of her head again.

She whipped around from the mirror. "No one who matters knows. If Lady Yasmin tells, we could just say that she was lying."

"But she wouldn't be lying."

"She's *French*," Lydia said contemptuously. "No one will believe her. We can bribe the butler. Turing doesn't want to marry me."

Giles was so enraged that he was having trouble shaping words. One part of him thought that

Lydia should suffer the consequences and marry Turing. But he didn't like the man. He hadn't liked him when he was babbling poems about Lady Yasmin's eyes, and he liked him even less now.

Another part of him was struggling with guilt. Lydia had no chaperone, and that was *his* mistake. How had he not realized that she was exactly like their mother, consumed by anger and thoughts of revenge? Their mother had flouted every civilized rule in pursuit of what she called justice.

"Please, Giles?" Lydia clasped her hands together, tears suddenly glinting in her eyes. "I can't marry Edwin Turing. Better men will propose to me."

"Not if you lead them into a room and grapple with them on a sofa," Giles stated. "No gentleman will marry you under these circumstances unless he is forced."

"I know that!" Lydia cried. "It was just . . . boredom."

"And revenge," Giles added.

She nodded. "Please, please, Giles? If I promise never, ever to be alone with a man again until I'm married?"

Giles caught a glimpse of the young girl she had been in her first Season, making mistakes and suffering for them. Kisses were mistakes with more serious consequences, but they were still mistakes, not felonious sins.

"I will hire a chaperone immediately. And speak to Turing."

"Don't forget the butler," Lydia said. "Oh,

and that—and to Lady Yasmin. You'll make her promise to be silent, won't you? She's desperate to marry you, so she'll do whatever you say."

Giles snorted. "No, she is not."

"She wouldn't help you if she wasn't."

"She helped me because she is kind, Lydia." He watched his sister carefully.

Lydia's jaw jutted out. "She helped you because she wants to be your countess, Giles. I've seen the way she looks at you."

Giles poked a last curl behind Lydia's ear. "I shall escort you to the carriage, and then return to speak to Turing."

"All right." She slipped her hand into his arm. "You worry too much. I can bring Lord Pettigrew up to scratch. We've known each other since we were children, and I heard yesterday that he is determined to find a wife."

"He's a good man," Giles said. He hesitated and added, "A decent man."

"More to the point, he'll be a marquess some-day, and the Chichesters aren't impoverished. He doesn't gamble or take laudanum. If he'd just get rid of his facial hair, he'll do. Most of all, he likes me, and he's never said a word about Father."

Giles nodded. The fellow had a short, pointed beard, but it wasn't the sort of detail he cared about. Obviously, his sister did.

"I have never allowed Lord Pettigrew to even touch my hand, though we danced together any number of times last Season," Lydia said ear-nestly, looking up at him. "I will behave, Giles. I promise. I just haven't concentrated because I was enjoying the game."

"Revenge is not a game," he said evenly.

Lydia nodded. "The wrong game," she amended. "Courtship is another, and I promise you, Giles, that I know how to play it."

"Excellent."

Giles couldn't help wondering if *he* knew how to play it.

He had a sinking feeling that he did not.

CHAPTER NINE

The following day
12, MAYFAIR PLACE, LONDON
THE DUKE OF HUNTINGTON'S TOWNHOUSE
THE DOWAGER DUCHESS'S SCAVENGER HUNT

Yasmin strolled into Silvester's townhouse the day after the Trent ball with her feelings in a jumble. Her grandfather was prancing beside her, beaming with satisfaction. He had decided that the Dowager Duchess of Huntington's invitation to a scavenger hunt was a thinly disguised attempt to get to know Yasmin better before her son proposed marriage.

The house was brimming with members of the ton, all chattering in high voices. At first glance, Yasmin caught sight of two ladies who disliked her and—

Lydia.

Make that three ladies who disliked her.

"Dear me," her grandfather said after the butler announced them. Scarcely a head turned in their direction; people were too busy peering at scrolls being handed out by footmen.

The dowager duchess, a stout lady with a monocle fixed in her eye, clambered up on top of a low table with the help of a footman. "Hear ye, hear ye!" she bellowed. She looked around, people quieting as soon as her eyes fell on them. "Oh, there you are," she called to Yasmin's grandfather. "Better late than never, I suppose. You and I are the judges. I'm not haring about London."

"I can partner my granddaughter," the duke replied. "Unless you intend to match her with your son."

Her Grace scanned the list she held. "My son is with Lady Stella."

Either Silvester hadn't told his mother that he was courting Yasmin, or the dowager hadn't welcomed the news.

"Lady Fester and Mr. Coke," the dowager bawled. "Lady Caroline Gage and Lord Elton." Mr. and Mrs. Addison were listed, but when Yasmin looked about, Cleo and Jake were nowhere to be seen.

Across the room, Silvester was bowing before Lady Stella, a cheerful smile on his face. Perhaps his mother had informed him that she had no intention of welcoming a French trollop into the family.

"*She* won't offer you any competition," her grandfather commented. "Bespectacled, poor girl, and has spots on top of it."

The dowager was still shouting out pairings, so Yasmin whispered, "Lady Stella's skin looks clear to me."

"Not that sort of spots," he said impatiently. "Freckles. The permanent kind of spots. Would have to be painted out in a portrait, along with those spectacles, of course."

"That is taking portraiture altogether too seriously," Yasmin stated.

Her grandfather snorted. "Have you taken a look at your grandmother's portrait?"

"Not closely."

"Look again. You can see where the artist painted out her double chin. We had to have that fellow back three times before he came up with a decent likeness."

Apparently, "likeness" was a malleable term.

The dowager swiveled in their direction. "Your Grace, go over there and stand next to the urn so I can find you. Or sit, if your corns are hurting you."

"I don't have corns," her grandfather said indignantly.

"Must be some other duke," she said unapologetically. "All right." She peered at her paper. "Lady Yammer, your granddaughter, is on this list somewhere."

"Lady Yasmin," her grandfather said sharply. "I introduced you myself, weeks ago."

"Lady Yasmin and the Earl of Lilford," the dowager announced, blithely ignoring that comment. "Lady Lydia and Patrick deGrey."

"Damn it, I'll have to speak to her," Yasmin's grandfather muttered. "She's trying to throw you into the arms of that sullen earl. I'll straighten her out. She'll never fix a match between her son and the spotted girl."

He patted Yasmin on the arm. "I can see Lilford headed in this direction. If he gives you a headache, send a footman for me, and we'll leave immediately."

"I'm certain that Lord Lilford and I can be pleasant to each other for the length of a game," Yasmin said. "I'll join you again in an hour or so."

Her grandfather snorted. "An hour? Is this your first scavenger hunt?"

"In France, hunting takes place on horseback."

"A scavenger hunt sends people off to find useless items."

"Why?"

"For the fun of it," her grandfather said. "There's usually a trumpery prize, but the real game is beating the competition. Takes a couple of hours at least."

Giles emerged from the crowd, bowing before Yasmin and then before the duke. "Good afternoon, Lady Yasmin. Your Grace."

"I'd better get over to the urn," Yasmin's grandfather said, eyeing Giles with dislike. "I needn't tell you to keep a civil tongue in your head, Lilford. No working off your excess bile on my granddaughter."

Giles bowed again. "I apologize again to you and to Her Ladyship for any offense."

"Humph," the duke said. "Well, I'll be off, dear." He nodded to Yasmin, gave Giles a final scowl, and headed across the room.

Yasmin felt unaccountably awkward. Not shy: she was never shy. It was just those stupid kisses in the garden that she couldn't get out of her head. "How is Lady Lydia?" she asked when Giles looked at her without speaking.

"Thriving." He cleared his throat. "She—we—would be very grateful if you could forget what you saw at the ball last night, and not mention it to anyone."

Yasmin felt a stab of hurt. For all his assurances, her reputation as a malicious gossiper was apparently alive and well.

He took a step closer. "I know you wouldn't tell anyone, but Lydia made me promise to bring it up."

"Of course," she said woodenly. "I gather Lady Lydia has resolved not to accept Mr. Turing's proposal."

"He dutifully appeared to request her hand. I never saw a man more grateful for his reprieve," Giles said. "I have spent considerable time since trying to hire a chaperone, but it isn't as easy as it sounds. There are no respectable women to be found at this point in the Season."

"It's a conundrum, isn't it?" Yasmin said. "A chaperone who is not a relative must be of the right lineage with an impeccable reputation and endless patience. I had a chaperone last Season, a dear friend of my grandfather's, and we both found it extremely challenging."

A footman paused before them. "My lord and lady, have you a scroll?" When Giles shook his head, he handed one to Yasmin.

"Hear ye, hear ye!" the dowager bellowed. "Has everyone looked at the list?"

The scroll turned out to include around fifty items. Yasmin took a quick look. Number fourteen was a footman's wig, which couldn't be terribly hard to find. A yellow chamber pot was perhaps more rare. An ostrich egg? A whisker from the beard of a bishop?

"The winning pair will receive two marvelous prizes, one for each." The dowager held up something Yasmin couldn't see over the heads of the men around her.

"What is it?" she asked Giles, breaking the silence between them.

"Looks like a lady's hair band. A tiara, perhaps," Giles remarked. He showed no inclination to read the list. Everyone around them was debating the best strategy to tackle the hunt.

She let the list roll back up. Couples were chortling with laughter as they made their plans, but clearly, her partner was not interested.

"A vulture crown!" the dowager cried, twirling it over her head. "Quite likely worn by a female pharaoh."

"Only if that pharaoh was born a couple of years ago," said a deep voice beside them. Yasmin turned with some relief to meet Silvester's smiling eyes. "My mother is taking the opportunity to get rid of some ill-advised jewelry acquired during her craze for Egyptian art."

No one in the crowd seemed particularly excited by the vulture crown, perhaps because most of the people had weathered the fashion in Egyptian culture and art and still had a pair of gold-painted china jackals poised incongruously on either side of the chintz sofa in their drawing room.

"The next prize!" The dowager held up a wooden box, about the size of a large breadbox. A hum of curious commentary rose, but she merely grinned. "I'm not saying what's inside. I'll just say that you *want it*. Every man in this room would be happy to own the contents of this box."

"Diamond cufflinks?" someone called.

"Perhaps," the dowager said, looking distinctly mischievous. But that was all she would say. Instead, she began reeling off rules for the scavenger hunt.

Silvester ignored her, embarking into a flurry of introductions. Yasmin curtsied before Lady Stella, thinking that her grandfather had been quite unkind. The spray of freckles over Stella's nose was darling, and her spectacles suited her.

"I thought perhaps we should join forces. Four heads are better than one, after all," Silvester said when greetings were over.

"Your mother just announced that all pairs must tackle the list on their own," Giles pointed out. "Two gifts for the winning couple."

His voice was positively chilly.

Lady Stella was looking embarrassed. It wasn't reassuring to have one's partner chase across the room and begin smiling at another lady.

Yasmin surreptitiously elbowed Silvester. "Of course we won't break the rules."

"The scavenger hunt begins in Covent Garden Market," the dowager bawled. "You must be checked off there by my head footman, whom you'll find at the main entrance, wearing Huntington livery. Return there at your appointed time, three hours later. A tardy couple cannot win. The couple who finds the most objects—or obtains one of the first three items—wins."

Chatter rose in the room like water in a flooded stream.

"Number two is the Bishop of Norfolk," the dowager continued. "I haven't seen my brother in ages, so if anyone manages to snag him, he has to agree to come for tea before he trots back to the cathedral. Just so you know, he *is* in London."

"How could we possibly find a bishop?" Yasmin asked the group.

Silvester glanced at his partner. "I might have an idea."

"Wouldn't that be cheating since he is your family member?" Lady Stella asked. Her tone strongly suggested that she would expect nothing more.

"It isn't based on intimate knowledge," he answered. "I read in the morning paper—"

"Don't forget to take a chaperone, if you're an unmarried chit!" the dowager barked. "I don't want any fuss and bother from outraged mothers. Every maid in the house is waiting at the front door. Take one of 'em and go. The carriages are waiting!"

"Excellent," Giles said, drawing Yasmin away

without a farewell to either Silvester or Lady Stella.

Yasmin apologetically smiled over her shoulder as he towed her to the door. "We needn't be in such a hurry!" she protested. "I haven't the faintest interest in a vulture crown. Have you?"

"I want to make sure that Lydia leaves with a chaperone," Giles said, his voice tight.

Once in the entry, she saw his shoulders relax. Yasmin came up on her tiptoes. "Wasn't she paired with Patrick deGrey?"

"Apparently, she switched partners, as her current partner is Lord Pettigrew."

"He's a nice man," Yasmin said. "I understand that he is very kind to his dogs. Oh, and you probably know this, but he studied to be a barrister for the pure fun of it. Of course, he doesn't have a regular practice, but I understand that he occasionally argues cases for those who cannot afford legal defense."

Giles looked at her. "Dogs?"

"A poodle, a dalmatian, and a pack of hounds," she told him. "Pedigreed hounds, not the regular sort."

"Do you know everything about everyone?"

Yasmin blinked. "Yes, of course. I have astonishing powers of perception. I can see into the heart and soul of a person and ascertain whether they are an adulterer or a spy."

Giles had been watching his sister leave; he looked down at Yasmin when the door closed behind Lady Lydia. "I see."

"Did you even hear what I said?"

"You are gifted with godlike powers of discernment. I expect that must prove useful in navigating polite society."

Yasmin sighed. "Do you mind if we pause for a moment before we run out the door to try to find these items? I still don't understand the game." Giles was a wooden statue without a sense of humor. She was astonished to think that she even bothered to waltz with him, let alone speak to him. Or allow him to kiss her.

"Number one," she read aloud. "Queen Elizabeth's coronation crown? That is impossible."

"Ignore the first three," Giles said. "Traditionally, the first three items are jokes, items that are impossible to obtain."

"I take it that we want to win the contest?"

Like her grandfather, a shrug was beneath the Earl of Lilford, but he moved his shoulders restlessly. "We needn't play at all. We could simply return here in three hours."

"But what would we do in the interim?" Yasmin objected.

His eyes suddenly gleamed under heavy lids. She blinked. She must have misinterpreted what came to his mind.

"We should attempt to win," she said quickly. "The dowager duchess has gone to a great deal of trouble. To win we would merely need to go from Covent Garden Market to my grandfather's residence."

He raised an eyebrow.

"Number three," Yasmin said, pointing. "A hat worn by Napoleon, the erstwhile Emperor of France."

"That's right. You have one of his hats," Giles said, frowning.

"Exactly," Yasmin said, smiling. "My mother owns three. She gave me one when my father threatened to throw them on the rubbish heap. She is convinced that someday there will be whole societies devoted to the study of Napoleon and his campaigns. Academic congresses that do nothing but discuss him, the way they do Aristotle."

Giles snorted. "I doubt that very much."

"Yes, so do I," Yasmin said.

They waited in silence until Silvester's butler produced their outer garments.

"Lady Yasmin, do you wish for a chaperone?" the butler asked.

Only five maids waited in the entry although a chattering line of guests remained. The chance that Giles would bother to compromise her was approximately one thousand to one. She was about to assure the man that they would be fine without a maid when the butler spoke again.

"We are running out of chaperones, and I want to make certain that all . . . younger ladies are accompanied." The butler's eyes darted to her bodice and away. His implication was clear: a debauched woman such as herself had no need for a chaperone.

A gleeful thought shot into Yasmin's mind:

if she married Silvester, one of her first actions would be to dismiss the butler.

"That was an extremely ill-advised comment," Giles said, his voice rock hard. "Apparently, you don't realize that you may be speaking to the future Duchess of Huntington? His Grace's attentions have been extremely marked of late."

The butler's narrow mouth closed. He hadn't had any idea.

"Lady Yasmin is as vulnerable as any of those ladies. You offer her a tremendous insult."

"I had no intention of offending Her Ladyship," the butler said with a gulp. "Please accept my sincere apologies."

Yasmin was torn between pleasure that Giles was defending her, and surprise that he considered her Silvester's future bride. No wonder he had declared they shouldn't have kissed.

"We can do without a maid," she said. "Your name is Wickford, isn't it? Never mind, Wickford. I realize that you are in a difficult spot. The earl and I will contrive to engage in the hunt without improprieties."

"No, no," Wickford said, stammering.

"Now you offer me an insult," Giles said unpleasantly.

Wickford bowed so low that he folded in half like a sheet of parchment.

"That was not an insult," Yasmin said to Giles. "The truth is that I am perfectly capable of defending myself, whereas a younger woman may not be."

Giles did not reply, but he took her shawl away from Wickford and helped her put it on. "Is this all you have to wear?"

"It's a warm spring day," Yasmin said, looping the shawl around her shoulders in an elegant fashion that allowed the ends to drape almost to her knees.

"Please tell me if you feel a chill."

Yasmin looked up at him, raising an eyebrow. "Much though I enjoyed the moment when you removed your coat, Lord Lilford, I hardly think that the weather will have changed to that extent."

She caught sight of the butler's expression—no longer apologetic but smirking—and sighed inwardly. Another nail in the coffin of her reputation.

He would spread it far and wide that Yasmin had watched Giles undress.

CHAPTER TEN

Once in a hackney, they sat quietly until Yasmin couldn't take it any longer. She was not silent by nature.

"This will be a new experience for you. Didn't you tell me that you had never walked through Covent Market?"

"I have not," Giles said. He hesitated. "I apologize for the insult offered to you by that butler. I shall speak to the duke and have him turned away."

"Oh, I expect you frightened Wickford into future politeness," Yasmin said lightly. "I should clarify, though, that the Duke of Huntington has not proposed marriage, and if I read his mother's intentions correctly, she would prefer that Lady Stella have that honor."

They lapsed into silence again. Yasmin spent the time reminding herself that she planned to have nothing to do with Giles. She had been spinning fantasies about him, but none of them could come true. He was a hollow man, cold to the bone.

Silvester, on the other hand, was charming and warm. Almost cuddly. Perhaps she *would* marry

Silvester, just as Giles apparently thought she should. Or Viscount Templeton, who unfortunately had not been invited to the scavenger hunt.

They were drawing up to the market when Giles cleared his throat and said, "The Duke of Huntington will propose to you within a week or two. I've known him my entire life. He pretends to be frivolous, but he isn't. When he makes up his mind, he doesn't stop until he succeeds."

"Silvester told me that you consider him frivolous," Yasmin said, too surprised to censor herself.

"Not so. He and I are opposites."

Yasmin gave him a rueful smile. "He talks all the time, and you never speak? He's cheerful, and you're grumpy?"

"He's free," Giles said unexpectedly.

"What on earth do you mean?"

"He does and says whatever he wishes."

"I don't see why you can't say what you wish," Yasmin said, just as the carriage rocked to a halt.

"The duke's family is famous for its eccentricities," Giles said. "Mine is equally famous for less salubrious reasons."

"You feel that you need to mend the family reputation, whereas Silvester can simply cavort as he wishes?"

Giles nodded, then pushed open the door, jumped out, and helped her to step to the ground.

"You are an earl," Yasmin said. "You can surely do as you wish."

"A noble ancestry doesn't give carte blanche,"

he stated. "To the contrary, it binds you more to virtue."

She didn't have the virtue he required. He might as well have announced, *Only virgins need apply.*

Yasmin turned away. "I see my favorite flower seller. Hello, Lulu!" she called, waving her parasol.

The yellow-haired flower seller looked up from her cart. "Good day, Lady Yam!" she replied.

"No time to buy flowers," Giles said. "If we're snarled in traffic returning from your grandfather's house, we could be late to return."

Yasmin didn't feel like answering, let alone listening, to him, so she walked over to the flower seller.

"I saved one for you," Lulu said. Her bright face was mischievous. "Got one for Mr. and Mrs. Addison too."

"What do you have?" Yasmin asked.

Lulu pulled a bunch from under the flowers filling her cart. "This! For the hunt." It was a large boutonnière composed of a number of fluffy pink blossoms.

Giles appeared at Yasmin's shoulder.

"For you!" Yasmin said, turning to him. She had never seen the grim-faced earl with a boutonnière, let alone a pink one. "Lulu was kind enough to save us one of her last boutonnières."

"It's number twelve on the list," Lulu said importantly. "The gentleman must return wearing a button-ear that includes at least three flowers of one color." She held out the monstrous thing with a beaming smile.

"Thank you," Giles said, handing her a coin.

Yasmin took the posy and went up on her tip-toes to pin it to his lapel. "There," she said with satisfaction, patting the spray of flowers. She looked up and met his eyes. His expression . . . She stepped back, feeling heat rising in her cheeks.

Her heart was racing, and blood was thumping through her body. This emotion *wasn't* all on her side. His eyes held frank desire, and his "thank you" had a husky undertone that made her feel weak at the knees.

"You look a treat," Lulu advised. The flower seller turned to Lord Wade, who trotted over accompanied by Miss Yates clutching the scroll, a maid trailing behind them.

Yasmin's heart sank. Lord Wade was one of her admirers but not the kind she liked. He had an invidious habit of allowing his hand to brush over her hips or worse, her rear. Now his eyes skated over her bosom as he bowed. "I hadn't seen you standing there, Lady Yasmin." His greedy eyes reminded her of a turkey-cock scraping the ground for worms.

"We need a boutonnière!" Miss Yates told Lulu, ignoring Yasmin altogether.

"I'm very sorry, but that was my very last button-ear," Lulu reported. "The Dowager Duchess of Huntington and I had an agreement that I should sell ten and not a single one over that."

"Oh, please!" Miss Yates begged, clasping her hands together.

His Lordship pulled out a silver coin, but Lulu shook her head.

"This is twice the amount," Lord Wade pointed out. To Yasmin's disgust, he edged sideways so that his hip touched hers.

Yasmin pulled away so sharply that she bumped into Giles, who looked down at her in surprise.

"I could give Lord Wade my boutonnière," Giles offered.

Yasmin shook her head. "No need." She turned to Lulu. "Mr. and Mrs. Addison didn't join the scavenger hunt."

"Imagine!" the flower seller cried. "I might have one last button-ear!" She started digging under the jumble of flowers.

"I thought you would," Lord Wade said pompously. "A shilling is a powerful incentive."

"I won't take more than sixpence," Lulu said. "Me and Her Grace have an agreement."

"Best of luck to you," Yasmin said, taking Giles's arm.

Miss Yates sniffed loudly and deliberately turned away. "Lord Wade, allow me to pin on your boutonnière."

They were halfway back to St. Martin's Lane, where they could pick up a hackney, when Giles said abruptly, "That young lady was extraordinarily rude to you, not unlike the butler. Why do you allow it?"

Yasmin had been strolling along happily enough, but she flinched at that question.

"You stopped smiling," Giles observed. And then, "Why were you smiling?"

She waved a hand. "Because the market is so fascinating! Look at that man. He's selling piglets. Aren't they adorable?"

They walked over and surveyed four pink piglets.

"This one looks as if he's laughing at us," Yasmin said, scratching it between the ears.

Giles started to say something and thought better of it.

"Don't you dare say something about roast pork," Yasmin told him. "He might hear you. Oh, look. Miss Whisker is here today! She sells buttons, gorgeous buttons. I always find a beautiful button or two."

Or ten, but she didn't admit that. Giles already thought she was frivolous.

"I had no idea that people sold buttons," he observed as they threaded through the crowd to the button seller.

"Miss Whisker, this is the Earl of Lilford. I'm shocked to reveal it, but he has never bought a button."

Miss Whisker's smile was missing a few teeth, but it had great charm. "A few of my buttons have gone to the London Museum, me lord. My best are in this box. A shilling each."

"What on earth does one do with mismatched buttons?" Giles's tone was bewildered.

"I have a button box," Yasmin said. "I like them because they are beautiful."

"Buttons are made for use," Giles said. His expression cleared. "Do you use them as examples for a modiste?"

"No." Yasmin felt embarrassment creeping up her neck. "I just collect pretty ones. Some are tiny works of art. Look at this one." She held up a large brass button enameled with delicate posies and bordered by tiny brass dots.

"I suppose you could add it to a pelisse." Giles obviously thought she was cracked.

Yasmin told herself yet again that no one can command affection, and it was useless to bang one's head against the wall. "It has no purpose. It's merely beautiful."

Giles handed a shilling to Miss Whisker, who cackled and handed the button to Yasmin.

"You needn't!" Yasmin protested. Then something caught her eye. "I'll have this one." She dug in her pocket, handed over a coin, and gave the button to Giles. "For you."

The earl looked profoundly startled. "Me?"

"I adore buttons with painted scenes. It's a little boy feeding sparrows, and that would be his mother. I love her ruff and the feathery tree behind them. I would guess it's French. Metal with glass."

Giles's fingers closed around the button. "Thank you."

She felt a flash of embarrassment. "I know it's a

silly gift, especially for an earl. People likely give you ruby buttons."

"No one has given me a ruby button." He turned it over in his hand. "Actually, I don't think anyone has given me a present in years."

"That's—" Yasmin said, before she caught back the words. He was not a man who would welcome sympathy. "I suppose gifts are for children."

"We should make our way to your grandfather's house."

She turned to go, catching a glimpse of him handing Miss Whisker another coin, a shiny gold one this time. "That was kind of you," she said as they reached St. Martin's Lane. "I'm sure Miss Whisker finds it difficult to support herself."

A hackney pulled over the moment Giles stepped forward into the lane. Likely, providence just rearranged itself when he walked about. He would always find a hackney, even in the rain.

But when she told him that, he looked at her blankly. "I never ride in hackneys. I prefer my own carriage." As soon as the vehicle started, he returned to his previous topic. "Miss Yates treated you discourteously, Lady Yasmin."

Yasmin sighed. Thinking about being snubbed made her feel lesser. Besides, he was hardly one to speak, given the snubs that he'd given her on occasion.

"That's a strong way to describe it," she said. "Miss Yates is very young. I gather that her mother's third marriage is not a happy one, so perhaps her home life is not delightful." She rushed on, trying to change the subject again. "Delightful, of course, means filled with delight. That's one part of the English language that I admire so much: the way one can add three tiny letters and the meaning changes."

"It doesn't bother you," Giles said slowly.

Naturally, he refused to be distracted. It was likely a character trait.

"I am not responsible for Miss Yates's opinion of me. I cannot change it."

"But if you shifted your . . . your manner of dress, perhaps?"

"Are you trying to give me sartorial advice, Lord Lilford?"

"No."

But he was. Yasmin couldn't help a rueful laugh.

"When we give the dowager duchess Napoleon's hat, it will excite gossip about your mother," he pointed out.

"Perhaps," Yasmin agreed.

"I didn't like the way Lord Wade looked at you." His mouth was very firm. "It would be advisable to cover your bosom so that he couldn't ogle you in that manner."

"You're serious?"

"Entirely."

"He would ogle me no matter what I wore," Yasmin explained. "In his mind, there are two kinds of women, and thus he does not owe me respect."

"I disagree," Giles said. "You are a lady and as such, he ought to give you the respect that you deserve."

Yasmin looked at his stubborn face and couldn't help a wash of pleasure at his protectiveness. He was a gentleman, a true gentleman.

"I am not responsible for others' opinion of me," she said. "That's a lesson I learned long ago, when I was still a young woman."

"You *are* a young woman!"

"When I was a young girl, then. A young fool," she added with a rueful smile.

"Foolish how?"

"Trusting," she said lightly. "Eager to be in love and naïve enough to believe men's promises. At that age, illusions about love are as common as . . . as sawdust in a sawmill."

He frowned. "Your phrasing is very lively. But what you're saying is that young girls are vulnerable to lying men. Is that why you left France, Yasmin?"

She didn't answer.

"Is that why you have paid attention to my sister?"

She didn't answer that either.

CHAPTER ELEVEN

Giles could not take his eyes off the woman seated across from him in the hackney. Lady Yasmin's walking dress was not as low cut as her evening dresses but even so, the cut and fashion of it signaled that she was as flirtatious as his sister had labeled her—

Except that she *was* a lady, through and through. Flamboyant dress aside, Lady Yasmin had impeccable manners, charm, and a privileged lineage. She was ... *should have been* ... everything he sought in his future countess.

Yet, the gowns she chose to wear suggested otherwise. Even if his sister's insults stemmed from petty gossip, Lady Yasmin's clothing deepened the misgivings he already felt.

A thought darted into his head: The clothing she wore revealed too much of her creamy skin and hourglass figure, turning her into a sensual creature whom no man could call his own. He recoiled from the idea. When did he begin thinking that he could *own* any woman?

"Giles," Lady Yasmin said suddenly. "You're very kind to notice that my reputation is battered around the corners, but it is nothing you should be concerned about."

He blinked and asked, "Are we on a first-name basis?"

"Why not? You're hardly going to take advantage of our familiarity, as we already established."

More than anything he wanted to pull her into his lap and take advantage of any familiarities she would grant him.

"I promise not to address you so intimately when anyone might overhear us," Yasmin added.

Giles wanted nothing more than for her to call him by his first name in the same teasing, affectionate manner with which she addressed Silvester. Actually, no. He wanted her to call him Giles in a throaty whisper.

He shifted in the seat and clenched his jaw to counter the punch of desire, and the desire to punch. Namely, Silvester.

"I can see that my informality makes you uncomfortable," she said. "I apologize, Lord Lilford."

"No," he said abruptly. "I shall certainly address you as Yasmin. In private." He should have foregone her title days ago. Certainly after he heard her addressing Silvester by his given name.

He could see her waiting for him to continue, but he didn't know what to say.

"All right, then," she said finally. She plucked aside the hackney's greasy curtain and looked outside. "We're nearly at my grandfather's house."

An elderly butler ushered them into the Duke

of Portbellow's townhouse, creakily bowing to Giles as a footman took possession of Yasmin's shawl.

"May I introduce you to my grandfather's butler, Carson?" Yasmin asked. "Carson, this is the Earl of Lilford."

The butler bowed again.

Giles nodded, trying to remember the last time that someone introduced him to a butler. The only butler whom he knew was his own.

"May I bring you tea?" Carson asked Yasmin.

"Do we have time?" she asked Giles.

"Yes. We made good time." That wasn't precisely true, but he had made up his mind that he had to prevent Napoleon's hat from being flaunted before the dowager duchess's guests. Yasmin didn't understand how virulent London gossip could be.

If she presented that hat to Silvester's mother, it would force the duchess to take notice of Yasmin's connection to a man whom the British Empire considered an enemy. Even if Her Grace had wished to welcome Yasmin into her family, accepting the hat would put her own reputation in the line of fire.

Which led directly to one question: *Why* was Napoleon's hat on the list in the first place? In all London, no one except for Yasmin could possibly own one. How had anyone known that the hat was in Yasmin's possession?

The duke's drawing room ceilings were extraordinarily high, as high as those in St. James's

Palace. Steep windows had been made to appear even longer due to complicated curtain treatments that looped above the windows and dropped in heavy swaths of sapphire velvet to the floor. The walls were entirely covered with gold frames, the portraits within so darkened by age as to be practically indecipherable.

The floor was cluttered with eight or nine small tables, randomly placed to form an obstacle course. They were surrounded by chairs decorated with gilt paint that caught sparks of gold from the sunlight coming through the windows.

"The hat is over here," Yasmin said, heading toward one corner.

Giles followed her, threading his way among tables.

The skeleton in question wore a battered Napoleonic cocked hat, raffishly tilted over one eye. His only other garment was a British military coat; the gold epaulets on the shoulders suggested that the original owner was a major general.

"Is that coat from the King's Dragoon Guards?"

"I have no idea. One of my grandfather's many nephews was a lieutenant-colonel during the Battle of Waterloo," Yasmin told him. "This gentleman wears Napoleon's hat because my grandfather is certain that a just god will ensure Napoleon's passing in the near future."

"How will that make you feel?"

She glanced at him, looking surprised. "The emperor is an odious little man, and I won't mourn him any more than will most French people. He didn't destroy my parents' marriage, but it wasn't for want of trying. Hold my reticule, won't you?"

Yasmin handed him a little purse. It was as frivolous and lovely as she was, woven of silk and metal thread in a Cupid-and-heart design, with green silk trimming.

"Pretty," he said, turning it over. "I believe I saw you carrying this once before."

"Isn't it? I love that begonia silk. It's old, and the clasp is not reliable, but I still carry it with me everywhere."

"I thought begonias were flowers." He turned it over again.

"I meant the color," Yasmin explained. "Begonia is a special shade of pink. That purse is over one hundred years old."

He glanced up to find her on her tiptoes, reaching for the hat. "I'll get that for you."

"No need. I have it." She plucked it from the skull. "Here, why don't you wear it while we have tea?"

"Certainly not."

"So stuffy," Yasmin said, pouting laughingly as she stuck the hat on her head.

To his shock, Giles actually had to stop himself from snatching her into his arms and kissing her. "Which table do you prefer?" he said, looking away from her before he betrayed his ungentlemanly inclination.

"My grandfather is a pack rat, so most of his furniture is old and spindly." Yasmin headed off toward the other side of the room, where a daybed aligned with the wall. She sat down and patted the cushion beside her. "A man of your size might knock my grandfather's chairs into splinters."

Giles was still holding her reticule. "Did this purse belong to one of your father's female ancestors?"

"Oh, no! My father may be a *duc* now, but his grandparents were people of modest means." Yasmin reached out for her purse. "Napoleon gave this to my mother."

Giles blinked. "Had it belonged to Joséphine?"

"Certainly not! The former emperor bought it for *Maman* in a small shop near the Louvre, during the first week of their courtship, if you can call it that. She gave it to me, because she is not fond of antiques." She started fiddling with the purse. "Of course, my mother did accept other gifts from the emperor."

"May I remove the hat?" Giles asked, wishing Napoleon had been impotent and unable to entertain ladies at all.

She nodded. Giles carefully lifted away the hat with his left hand, dropping it on the floor. With his right, he tucked a lock of hair behind her ear, his fingers caressing her cheek.

Yasmin's eyes flew to his.

"May I kiss you?" he asked. "I'm sorry I didn't ask you last time."

He could have sworn that he saw desire in her eyes, but she gulped and looked away. "After what you said . . . I don't think that would be a good idea." Her fingers must have tightened on the purse, because it popped from her fingers and overturned, spilling its contents on the carpet.

Giles bent over at the same moment she did.

One small pot of lip color, a comb—and a condom. Sometimes known as a French letter. It lay on the floor, adorned with a yellow-colored ribbon, a frivolous scrap that informed him that Yasmin may take pleasure, but she protected herself from pregnancy and disease.

He pulled back his hand. "Forgive me."

"It's not my—" But she broke off, dropping the condom back into her bag, along with the other small items. No powder and no face paint, he noticed.

When she straightened, Yasmin's cheeks had turned scarlet.

Giles cleared his throat and tackled the subject head-on. "You needn't be embarrassed."

Yasmin gulped some air and said, "No?" in a wheezy voice.

"Absolutely not. Any man or woman who engages in intimate pleasure ought to use one of those to prevent the birth of unwanted children." She still looked so horrified that Giles astonished himself. "I may well be one of those children."

"*What?*"

"My mother was carrying a child when she married, and my father knew that it wasn't necessarily his child. My mother was of the opinion that I am the child of her lover, but there was no obvious sign either way. In novels, they solve the issue with a secret mole, but I have no such marker of fatherhood."

Yasmin's eyes widened.

"No one is aware of that."

"I won't tell a soul!"

Across the room, the butler opened the door and ushered in two footmen carrying heavy silver trays.

"I didn't want you to think that I would condemn you for engaging in intimacies. I would prefer that my own marriage be chaste, and I shall never commit adultery, but I understand the impulse."

Yasmin opened her mouth and shut it again. For the first time since he had met her, she seemed to be silenced.

The butler ordered one of the footmen to place a low table before the couch. He then directed the positioning of a number of delicacies while the second footman poured cups of tea. Giles regarded the feast rather grimly. In order to make certain that they missed the three-hour deadline for the scavenger hunt, he would have to eat all of the cake, though he didn't care for sweets. As well as drink many cups of tea, a beverage he took sparingly, if at all.

"Thank you very much, Carson," Yasmin said. "I didn't have a chance to ask this morning, but how is your nephew faring? Becky told me that you had a letter yesterday." She turned to Giles and explained, "Carson's nephew is serving in the army, stationed near Paris at the moment. We're all very proud of him."

"He is doing well," the old butler said, smiling broadly. "His letter asked for stockings because it's perishingly wet in France. Mrs. Carson started on a new pair last night."

"Excellent," Yasmin said. "His Lordship and I are going to Covent Garden after tea, and we shall buy some yarn. We'd like to do our part in supporting His Majesty's troops, wouldn't we, Giles?"

Giles was thinking about the fact that his family considered servants to be employees worthy of their hire. He had been taught to be respectful— but affectionate? His mother would have been perturbed by Yasmin's friendliness.

Yasmin's elbow hit his ribs. "Wouldn't we, Giles?"

"Of course," he said, having no idea what he had agreed to.

"We shall buy yarn in Covent Garden this afternoon for Mrs. Carson's knitting project," she informed him.

"You'll want to take something more than that light shawl, my lady," Carson said. "It's coming on to rain. I can feel it in my joints." He glanced over the table with the eye of an expert, then nodded to the footman. "That'll do. Ring if you want more tea."

"That'll do?" Yasmin laughed. "You've given us five desserts, Carson. We will make ourselves ill if we sample all of them."

"What are they?" Giles asked. "I love cakes," he added untruthfully.

Carson pointed to a cake that looked like a bishop's hat. "Nougat almond cake. Scones, of course. Apples à la Parisienne, Blancmange à la Vanille, and chocolate delight."

"Excellent," Giles said. "I'll have a piece of each."

Yasmin blinked at him. "You like sweets?"

"Why would I say it if not? I fully intend to have second helpings." He looked down at the plates Carson was arranging before him—the pieces so large that the butler offered five pieces of china— and felt ill already.

Yasmin laughed. "I'll wager you don't! Our cook is French, as you likely noticed. She puts cream in everything. Even after growing up in Paris, I can't manage more than one piece."

Ladies don't place wagers.

He dismissed the thought and put a huge bite of nougat into his mouth. His palate tried to reject it: thick, overly sweet, with an odd texture, but he swallowed it. "I'll take that wager."

"What could you possibly win, except to prove that you are a glutton?"

Carson was ushering the footmen out the door, leaving them alone.

"A kiss," Giles said flatly. He eyed the nougat and decided he would try something else before forcing down a second bite.

"I'm sorry?" Yasmin said.

"I would like to kiss you again."

Something suspicious, even hurt, went through her eyes.

Giles managed to swallow the silky sweet bite he'd put in his mouth and said, "Not because of the contents of your purse. Because of *this*." He drew her close, slowly enough so that she could easily resist—but she didn't. He bent his head, putting his lips on hers in the world's most awkward kiss.

Yasmin was still for a moment, then she shrugged, muttered something in French, and opened her mouth.

Since Giles had an organized mind, he invariably categorized kisses: welcome, unwelcome. Deep kisses, searching kisses, enflaming kisses, terrible kisses . . .

A new category was needed. Soul shattering. Life changing. His senses flamed to life as Yasmin's tongue met his; the combination of her taste and smell went straight to his head. He wrapped an arm around her narrow back and brought her body to his, kissing her again, his instincts driving him to devour her, mate with her, make her his.

He couldn't stop himself from thinking about her possessively, although the reasons why she could never be his were legion.

Legion.

Yasmin was not an appropriate countess. Yet, none of that mattered now, when he had her in his arms. She smelled of roses. Not bold red roses, but ruffled pale pink petals in early spring. Along with a touch of almond, and a hint of raspberry, and something mysterious that was purely Yasmin.

She made a sound in the back of her throat and threw an arm around his neck.

"Like that," he murmured. "Make that sound again. I adore that sound."

Yasmin's eyes were shining. Their next kiss was so deep and long that it broke his composure into pieces, leaving him shaken.

She shook her head. "Not yet." She pulled him toward her and caught his bottom lip in her teeth, sending a violent pulse of desire down his limbs.

Giles's voice was a low growl. "You want me. And God, I want you. I want you more than I've ever wanted a woman. You smell better than any woman I know."

That made her blink.

He leaned closer. "I'm going to kiss you again."

Sometime later, they drew back. "You took your prize before you won the wager," Yasmin said, her breath coming hard.

Giles had no idea what she was talking about. Then he remembered the desserts and the wager of a kiss. Yasmin was smiling at him: He felt as if he were a frozen person and she a fire. She was a warm haven, and he had been wandering in an icy field for most of his life.

He traced her lip with his finger. "I have dreamed of kissing you." He had dreamed of see-ing that desirous, joyous look in her eye.

Bloody hell, he was losing his mind. Giles

cleared his throat and pulled himself together. "I fully intend to eat the rest of the delicacies and win the wager. I love cakes."

"No, you don't," Yasmin said, shaking her head. "You hate them, don't you?"

He stilled, torn between denial and the truth. "How did you know?"

"You have perfected the art of avoiding expression." Her fingers plucked his sleeve, and she started pleating the fabric without noticing.

Giles stayed utterly still, as if he had coaxed a sparrow to land on his arm. She never touched him casually, the way she did Silvester. As if he were a friend.

"Yet I saw a flash of utter revulsion when you tasted the nougat."

He thought about what to say.

"No fibbing," Yasmin said. "You hate nougat, don't you?" Her giggle twirled around him like a warm breeze.

If he didn't eat the cakes, there was no reason not to return to Covent Garden. Yet he was certain that producing Napoleon's hat would destroy Yasmin's chance of marrying Silvester and becoming a duchess.

Becoming a *duchess*.

If Yasmin could become a duchess, she could bloody well become a countess. True, someone was trying to blacken her reputation, but as long as he kept the hat away from the scavenger hunt . . .

She could be a duchess.

He didn't want her to become a duchess, but a countess.

His countess.

Countess of Lilford.

The hell with reputation, his family's or hers. His mind reeled, but one thing was clear to him: there could be no presentation of Napoleon's hat. No, two things:

No Yasmin, Duchess of Huntington, either.

"I love cake," he repeated, forking up another bite of nougat. His tongue recoiled but he chewed the gooey mixture and swallowed it.

"Fibster! I won't allow you to eat any more," Yasmin said. She stood, grabbed his plate, and moved it to another little table. Then she moved the rest of the nougat cake as well.

"I wish to eat it," Giles said stubbornly. He fixed her with a stare.

"Ooo, the frozen glare," Yasmin said, giggling.

The look that terrified others slid off her. Didn't land. Had no effect.

She sat back down beside him and picked up her teacup, bright eyes meeting his over the rim of her cup. "Why are you trying?"

He put his fork down rather than dig into a different sweet confection. Instead, he took a sip of oversteeped tea, bitter to the palate. "Why did I eat the nougat cake?"

She nodded. "No more fibbing."

The truth, or part of the truth, sprang from his lips. "I don't want to return to Covent Garden. I want to stay here."

Her eyes widened.

"With you."

Slowly, he reached out, giving her time to shake her head, move backward, stop him. But she didn't. Instead, she leaned toward him. Still hesitant, he wrapped her in his arms and lifted her slightly, bringing her to his lap. She didn't say a word.

Their bodies interlocked with—to Giles's mind—an almost audible click. Her warm curves fit in his arms. The feeling made him dizzy, heady, almost mad. He shouldn't do this—and there was nothing else in the world he *could* do.

It felt right.

"May I kiss you again?" he asked, his voice hoarse with emotion that he didn't know how to explain to himself, let alone express aloud. "You are sweeter than cake. I would never eat cake again, if it was a choice between that and you."

Her face, for once, was rather solemn. "I believe that *I* shall kiss *you*," she announced. "May I?"

"Always," he said, the truth coming from his heart.

Her mouth fell open. "What?"

Giles leaned forward and kissed the curve of her jaw, not in the mood for conversation. He couldn't answer her query. He didn't know how. He was in uncharted waters, unplanned and unanticipated. A small voice in the back of his head was yammering at him, saying things about propriety and proper countesses, but he focused on the silky skin under his lips. "I adore the curve where your shoulder turns into your neck."

"I thought I got to kiss you next," he heard.

He brushed her earlobe with his lips and straightened. "I am not myself," he said, just so she knew.

"I realize that," Yasmin murmured. "For one thing, you are talking to me." She cupped his face in her hands and brought her mouth to his.

Their lips opened at the same moment. To Giles, the touch of their tongues felt like a sentence that he had never shaped into words. Fire blazed down his spine as her arms tightened around his neck, and his around her back. His cock throbbed and stiffened in fierce arousal.

"*Mon Dieu*," Yasmin breathed, and he felt a crack of triumph. This sophisticated woman had slipped into her mother tongue because of their kiss. *His* kiss. Not Silvester's or any of those other men who tripped over themselves with desire when she smiled at them.

His.

CHAPTER TWELVE

Yasmin's tongue teasingly darted around Giles's mouth. She kissed with the same effervescent joy with which she greeted life, he decided dimly, his fingers tightening on the curve of her hip because he didn't dare to relax his grip or his hand would slide upward toward her breasts.

One of her hands left his neck and landed on his front, fingers caressing his chest. Of course, she wasn't an innocent. So perhaps—

But gentlemanly instinct kept him from reciprocating that caress. Even stroking her back would be inflammatory. And she . . .

"What are we doing?" Yasmin asked as if she'd heard his thought. The French inflection in her voice was deepened by longing.

Giles couldn't stop himself from brushing a kiss on her forehead. "Making love," he murmured, realizing that was an experience he'd never had.

She pulled away.

"I'm not kissing you the way other men do," Giles told her. His arms tightened around her. "I want you, Yasmin."

Her brow furrowed. "You seem to be implying that I allow 'most' of my suitors to kiss me. I assure you that isn't the case."

He took a deep breath. "I want the same thing they do. I want to marry you."

"*What?*"

"Marry you," he repeated. "Would you do me the very great honor of becoming the Countess of Lilford?"

Yasmin's mouth actually fell open in an almost comic expression of surprise. "You don't!"

"I do."

"You don't even like me!"

"Yes, I do," he said, feeling the truth of it in his bones. "I tried not to like you, but I wasn't successful."

"Of course you tried not to like me," she murmured, looking fascinated. "You certainly didn't want to marry me, did you?"

"I didn't, but I do," Giles said. "In fact, I always *wanted* to marry you. I want it more than anything I've ever wanted in my life."

Yasmin leaned backward, away from him, as her eyes searched his face. "I find that hard to believe."

"That is my fault," Giles said. "I couldn't allow myself to woo you, even though I wanted to."

"Because of my mother's past or my own? There is a difference."

"My reasons are irrelevant. I couldn't stop myself from—"

"From desiring me," Yasmin said, her tone

rather stiff. Her facade slipped for a moment, and he saw hurt shining from her eyes. "You mistake yourself, my lord. There is no need to propose."

Giles felt a touch of frost somewhere in the area of his chest. Why *would* she want to marry him? He had been rude, cold, and dismissive.

"You don't like me," she said flatly.

"Only because I thought I couldn't have you."

"I find that hard to believe. My reputation precedes me always," she said, swallowing hard. "Men assume I am for sale. I am not certain that a marriage ring will change that."

"No man will *ever* assume that my countess is for sale."

A reluctant smile tugged at the corner of her mouth. "I've lived with that expectation for my entire adult life."

"Just as I have lived with the complexities of my parents' marriage and my father's death." He pulled her into an urgent kiss that tried to say everything he was failing to put into words. This time, he let his hands range down her back and then, because she was uttering inarticulate but agreeable sounds, he ran his hands up her waist until his fingertips just touched the curve of her breasts.

Improper sentences came to him unbidden, tumbling through his mind, babbling about her perfumed skin, except it was natural perfume. About the fact he'd like to lick her all over, nibble her like the finest delicacy ever made.

He barely stopped himself from talking and stilled his hands, knowing they were shaking.

"Giles." Her voice was velvety rough.

"Yes?" His equally so.

"Nom de Dieu, touch me!"

Giles looked into her eyes. "Not unless you marry me." His fingers slid up, just slightly, caressing the curves of her breasts.

"I can't marry you," Yasmin said, looking exasperated, her lids heavy. "You don't like me."

"I do like you." Giles had never had to seduce anyone; women fell into his hands, attracted by his money, if not his features.

"Pish," Yasmin said. "Just kiss me some more."

"No," Giles said, sliding his fingers down to her belly. "I love this curve," he murmured into her ear. "But I shan't kiss you again or touch your breasts."

She wiggled and then nipped his earlobe. "Are you actually saying that I have to promise to marry you before you'll kiss me again? Or . . . Or do anything else?"

"That's it," he said.

Yasmin muttered a few things in French.

He looked up and caught her intent gaze. "I like you in every way, Yasmin."

She looked doubtful.

"I am not used to having my word mistrusted."

"I'm not used to being blackmailed."

"It's only blackmail," he said softly, "if you want me as much as I want you. Which would be for life, Yasmin." He tipped up her chin. "I want you for life, not just on this settee, though I want that too. I want your smile next to me in the morning. I want your giggle over breakfast. I want your laughter. I want your chatter. God forgive me, I want your gossip."

Her mouth formed a perfect circle. Giles cleared his throat. "Of course, you may not feel the same about me. I could . . . I could court you."

Yasmin's eyes were fascinated. "You could? What would that look like?"

"We would waltz together more than once an evening."

"We do not waltz at all these days."

"I could take you to the theater."

"I strongly suspect that you view a performance of *Hamlet* with the same enthusiasm as a nougat almond cake."

"I can't stand the prince," he confessed.

"He's too emotional?" Yasmin surmised.

Giles shook his head. "We were actually studying 'To be or not to be' at Eton when the news arrived that my father had taken his life. Hamlet makes a philosophical mockery of something that rends a family apart."

Her face softened and she leaned forward, dropping a kiss on his lips, and whispered, "I'm sorry, Giles."

"It happened long ago."

"I'm fascinated by the shape of your bottom lip. Do you only dislike *Hamlet* or theater in general?"

He hesitated.

"Courtship does not involve forcing people to go to events that they dread."

"I could take you for rides in the park," he offered.

"It would be interesting to see society matrons fall into paroxysms of curiosity at the sight of the two of us in a curricle. Have you thought this through, Giles? You haven't been drinking, have you?"

There was just the faintest note of insecurity in her voice. He had the feeling that desire unnerved her.

Giles dusted a kiss on her mouth. "What man doesn't want to marry you, Yasmin?"

"Until twenty minutes ago, I would have said *you*."

"Would you—" He stopped. "Would you have any interest in marrying me?" He felt his gut tighten until his body was taut, waiting for her response. She was looking down at his hands. They circled her waist. From here, his hands seemed huge in comparison to her: his fingertips wide, clumsy, and male.

She stole a glance at him. "I can't pretend that I haven't imagined marriage to you."

Relief whipped through him.

"I gather I wasn't alone in feeling . . ." Yasmin, who had words for every occasion, seemed to have run out of them again.

"We have something between us, more than most couples," Giles told her. "More than I've experienced with another woman. In fact, I don't think I have ever felt anything for another woman." He paused, but it was better to get it out now. "Ladies seem to believe that I am brooding and mysterious, Yasmin, but I am not. In social situations, I often can't think what to say. I am a boring man."

"I see."

"So you might not wish to marry me," he said, making a clean breast of it. "I packed Lydia off to seminary because I didn't know what else to do with her."

"Do you loathe going into society?"

"No." He shook his head. "I like to dance with you. I would like to eat supper with you and your friends. But I spend my days at the House of Lords. We're debating a treason act at the moment that could change the judicial system."

"So when you're standing about looking mysteriously broody, you're actually thinking through the laws of the land?"

She kissed him again, which he thought might be a good sign.

"It's important," he said once they surfaced from that kiss. "There's a case coming up, labeled the Duchy of Lancaster Act, that will allow landed gentry and aristocracy to sell part of their lands if they put the profits toward improvement of the land. People don't seem to recognize how important that is. Words don't come easily to me, so even in the ballroom I think through speeches that I intend to give in Parliament."

Yasmin gave him a crooked smile. "Are you

not afraid that marrying me would reduce your influence in the House of Lords? That having a disgraceful Countess of Lilford would ruin your family name?"

He *had* been afraid of that. His father's warnings lay in the back of his head: The late earl had railed endlessly about rumors that lay in wait like the traps laid by poachers, ready to snap closed around someone's leg. Of course, his father had been thinking of his own history of theft, which did indeed surface, albeit years after the fact.

Frankly, if he survived the scandal of his father's suicide, he could survive anything.

"I do not care," he said with passionate truth.

Yasmin took a deep breath. "I see." She was fidgeting with his coat lapel. "I wouldn't be a very good political hostess. Such a wife would put on grand suppers, entertaining people of opposite parties. Talking knowledgeably to the prime minister. I am frivolous."

"I don't care to dine with the prime minister," Giles said.

"As long as you understand that I am not secretly intellectual. I read magazines that talk of *la mode*, never *The Times*. I adore lip color and silk underclothes."

"I love them on you. Not that I am asking to see your underclothes." His eyes devoured the curves of her breasts.

"Venetian lace," she told him impudently. "Embroidered with rosebuds, laced in front, to here." She traced a line from her waist up to her breasts.

He groaned, something that sounded like a curse.

"My point is that I won't be an asset. Countesses are supposed to be clever."

"I think you are the most intelligent woman I've ever known, and I've thought it since we met last year."

A startled laugh broke from her mouth. "That's absurd! I hate to admit this, Giles, but I'm not even sure that I know who the prime minister is!"

The fact was inconsequential to him. "For you, language is a game. I've watched as you've mastered English. I have the idea that at any moment your head swims with words, French and English, and you choose whichever you want as easily as . . . as a hen pecks grain."

"I'm a chicken?"

He winced. "I just meant that so many words present themselves to you at any moment."

Yasmin frowned at him.

"For example, how many words can you think of for the color yellow?"

"In French or English?"

"English."

"Gold and lemon."

He kissed her on her nose. "More than those."

"Daffodil, mustard, honey, jaundiced yellow."

He kissed her again, and Yasmin laughed before continuing. "Sandy, flaxen, creamy, citrine, primrose yellow, butter."

"I have only yellow," he said flatly. "Your hair, for example. I know the strands are different colors, but in my mind they are summed up as 'yellow.'"

"It does me no good to have all those words. My hair is still just my hair, and yes, it is yellow."

"Your vocabulary gives you delight, doesn't it? I've watched you learning words, storing them away. Last year, you sounded like a Frenchwoman, albeit one who was fluent in English. This year, you sound like an Englishwoman. Or, sometimes, like an American."

She nodded. "I suppose."

"I want to spend the rest of my life watching you learn more words. I don't care if you ever learn the prime minister's name. There will just be a new one in a year or two. I only want you. I don't care what society thinks if they see us in a curricle.

"I just want you to sit beside me."

CHAPTER THIRTEEN

Giles meant it.

After the welter of proposals Yasmin had received in the past year or so, she could separate those who were sincere from those who wanted her fortune.

"But you disapproved of me for good reason," she said, dropping her eyes to his chest because it was remarkably hard to admit one's faults. "I have a past, Giles. I am no maiden."

He kissed her eyebrow. "Look at me?"

She reluctantly looked up.

"As long as I am your present and your future, I don't give a damn about your past."

"No matter who I marry, some members of polite society will brand me a hussy, if not worse." She started twiddling with one of his buttons. A nice, if plain, button.

"The gossip will die in time," he said.

She shook her head at him. "I disagree. You'd have to accept that people will gossip about your countess. Given your strong dislike of gossip . . ." Her voice trailed away.

"I'll woo you until you are convinced. Marry

me, Yasmin." Giles brushed his lips against hers. "I want to make love to you." He lowered his voice to a husky whisper. "I would like to lean you backwards on this settee and love you properly. Will you allow me to make love to you?"

She gulped. "Even though—"

One thought was going through Yasmin's mind: he wanted to marry her, *even though he knew she wasn't a virgin*. Even though he thought the condom was hers, which would suggest she was sleeping with men willy-nilly. It wasn't hers, and Hippolyte had been her only lover. Yet Giles was willing to marry her, thinking that.

He truly didn't care if she had a scandalous past.

It was such a delightful thought that it made her head swim. He hovered over her, eyes blazing, waiting, and Yasmin opened her mouth without consciously making a decision and said the only thing she could say.

"I'll marry you, Giles. I will marry you."

She reached up and put her arms around his neck. His mouth came down, claiming hers. Did she ever dislike kisses?

He licked inside her mouth slowly, his hands gliding over her body, molding the light silk of her gown to every curve. His intimacies kept surprising her, if delightfully. His fingers ran over her breasts, slid around the inner curve of her thigh, slid under her garments and ran down the crease of her bottom.

"You startle like a virgin, Yasmin," Giles said.

Before she could answer, his head reared back. "That was an extraordinarily rude thing to say. I apologize." He kissed her fiercely until Yasmin let out a helpless whimper.

"May I touch you here?" His voice was dark and sweet as his hand paused on her knee.

"Ye-es," she breathed, her legs easing open.

"I love that," he rumbled in her ear. "I love your plump thighs, Yasmin. You've driven me mad in the last months. Watching you dance with other men. Watching you bend over. Sometimes I thought if you fidgeted and dropped that damn fan one more time, I would snatch you into my arms and to hell with the audience."

Yasmin almost giggled. Why on earth would he care if she bent over? But sensations were going through her body like streaks of heat, fogging her mind. He was kissing her again, and all the time his hand was sliding up her thigh until his fingers slipped under her silk underclothes and touched her—*there*.

"Are you . . .?" she gasped.

"Touching you between your legs," he whispered, when she didn't finish the question.

He tapped her with a finger, and she startled. "What do you call this in French?"

"Parties intimes," she whispered.

"That's a very proper-sounding phrase."

"Foufes or *foufoune."* Her voice was a thread of sound.

His fingers brushed her again. The caress was

rough but soft at the same time, or she was soft and wet . . . Her thoughts trailed off because he was crooning something about her pretty *fou-foune*, saying in a low rasp how wonderful she felt, and frankly, she didn't—

She didn't feel like complaining. Or stopping him.

"We *are* getting married," Giles said as if he heard her thinking. "You agreed, and I won't let you change your mind."

"You're always doing that," she said, embarrassed by how husky her voice sounded.

"What?" Giles's eyes were burning as he slipped a broad finger inside her.

It felt so good that Yasmin found herself wiggling, silenced. It was as if they were having two conversations at the same time, one that was silent and made her gasp. The other, conducted in fragments and questions.

"You guess what I'm thinking," she said in a rush, stopping with an audible gasp because his finger was caressing her. "Giles!"

"Do you like that?" His tongue ran across her lips. "I want to kiss you there, Yasmin. Has a man ever—"

"No!" she exclaimed. She knew about that sort of kissing, though Hippolyte had never offered it. Ladies in the French court had giggled about it, and even though English ladies were far more prim, her friend Cleo had made a laughing remark once.

"You're hot and wet," Giles said, his eyes meeting hers with a wicked glint. "May I lick you, Yasmin?"

May he?

May he what?

"Absolutely not," Yasmin cried. "Someone might enter the room at any moment!"

Giles withdrew his hand from under her skirts and sucked the same finger that had been inside her, a needy moan breaking from his throat. "Your taste is better than any cake. Your fragrance brings me to my knees."

"I thought you were so proper," she whispered, fascinated. "You never speak, but now you are speaking so much."

"I am proper," Giles said, coming to his feet. He walked away, threading through the tables. He looked over his shoulder. "I speak when I have something to say."

Yasmin's legs were throbbing, her heart pounding. It wasn't that she didn't recognize erotic desire or, for that matter, know how to satisfy herself. But this felt different.

The door was closed; Giles opened it, stuck his head through, and said something she couldn't hear. Then he put a hand around the door, pulled out the key, and locked the door from the inside.

She didn't move. She just lay on the settee, one hand over her head, her legs trembling like the debauched woman she was, allowing herself to feel embarrassingly hot and needy between her legs. Words drifted into her head and dissolved. Mostly she thought about pleasure.

How a woman could reach for pleasure if she wanted it . . . Yasmin wanted it. With this man, and only this man.

Giles returned, standing by the couch and looking down at her before he sank to his knees. "Will you marry me?"

She nodded.

"Will you allow me to make love to you?"

Yasmin felt a pulse deep in her stomach, a flare of emotion that responded to the desire in his eyes. She must have answered silently, because next thing she knew, he was back on the settee, braced on his elbows, kissing her deep and hard, one hand buried in her hair. A desperate sound broke from her throat, and she arched against him.

He responded with a satisfied hum. This time she didn't hesitate; her legs parted, and he actually ripped her silk smalls.

Then—

He stroked her again, hard and gentle at once, and one finger pushed deep. The pulse that had started between her legs flooded her body, so that her blood throbbed in tune to the thrust of his finger.

Giles didn't sound like a gentleman now. He was cursing under his breath, and the velvety purr of his voice was somehow as erotic as the rough caress of his finger. "Next time," he breathed in her ear. "This time like this, Yasmin."

She blinked at him, not understanding, and he bent his head to her lips. She began rocking against his hand, whimpering into his mouth.

"*Now*," he growled into her lips. "Come for me, Mina. I want you to moan, make that sound in the back of your throat. I want to make you blissful. I have dreamed about fondling you."

She thought of resisting—but what would be the point of that? Her body fell into the grip of need, wild joy arching through her, a sob breaking from her lips.

"Look at me," he commanded. And, low and fierce, "I want to see your eyes. You're so damned beautiful."

She gasped, unable to answer, pleasure washing over her skin, sinking deep into her bones, her whole body instinctively curling upward toward him and clinging as she trembled and shook. Finally, Yasmin fell back.

"You cussed," she whispered, a smile spreading over her face.

"I what?" Giles's voice was dark and rough. He was standing, doing something to his clothing. She felt too languid and happy to pay attention.

"Cussed," she repeated. "That's American slang. You cursed. Could we do *that* every day when we're married?"

Giles leaned over and nipped her lower lip. "Morning and night," he growled. "Every damn minute of every day and night."

She giggled.

"I adore your giggle."

He was pulling up her skirts, rearranging them around her waist.

She was thinking about the strange idea that he *liked* her giggle . . . She would have thought her giggle was, to him, part and parcel of being a frivolous ninny. But no . . .

Then he was braced over her again. "May I, Yasmin?"

Make love?

She bent one knee so she was in the position matching her favorite naughty etching, the one she kept hidden in the lining of her jewelry box.

"Yes," she whispered.

His hand landed on her knee. "You like it this way, dearest?"

Then he, well, part of him, touched her. Ran up her crease, and it felt so strange and good that Yasmin raised her head to look down.

He was large.

There was practically no relation to Hippolyte. Nor to her little toy.

Much larger.

"No worries," Giles murmured. "I'm fully gloved."

He was. The condom from her purse fit tightly over him.

His eyes followed hers, and one of his large hands smoothed the covering, holding himself tightly. "In French?"

"*Popol,*" she breathed.

"Cock."

Yasmin giggled. "Like 'cock-a-doodle-do'?" She

cleared her throat. "You are very large. Bigger than my toy."

Giles, who never smiled, was grinning, crinkles spreading from his eyes. "Toy?"

Yasmin felt herself turn red.

"Lord, I am so grateful you're experienced."

Yasmin felt a twinge of embarrassment. Just how many men did he think she had slept with? But her attention was caught by something more important. His *popol* was huge. Enormous, rigid, shoving deep inside her, filling her. She literally didn't have words to describe it.

Giles groaned, the sound escaping from somewhere deep in his chest.

Thankfully, it didn't hurt. But it was vaguely disgusting. She raised her head and looked down. Her heart sank. It wasn't a surprise because she'd suspected the truth long ago. She wasn't a woman who was going to enjoy intimacies.

Hippolyte and she had made love under the covers. In later years, without the rosy glow of love, she had realized he was a lackluster and selfish lover.

Giles withdrew with a sucking sound. She glanced down again and had to suppress a shudder. The condom had bunched up and was falling down his . . . his tool. It looked like chicken skin.

Giles let out a low curse, reared back, and pulled away. She came up on her elbows and watched as he pulled the condom up and tied the ribbon so tight that he must be at risk of cutting it in half.

"A messy business, this," he said with a rueful smile.

The words that came to Yasmin's mind were less pleasant than "messy." But she didn't feel like discussing it, any more than she did other intimate bodily functions, those that took place on a commode, in private.

He pushed himself back inside her, and Yasmin had to clench her teeth to stop herself from ordering him away. She shut her eyes, wondering how long it would take. His mouth brushed hers. "Would you like to stop?"

"No, no," she said. "Do continue." As if she was inviting him to keep dancing.

He didn't move; instead, he began kissing her carefully, slowly. Despite herself, her body relaxed into languid acceptance. Little prickles of desire flickered in her legs. Yet he was far too large. There was a noise that she did not like, a rubbing of that condom against her inner parts.

"I am going to withdraw, because I do not think you are enjoying this."

Yasmin nodded because frankly, this was the most uncomfortable experience of her life. The only thing she wanted was for it to be over.

He withdrew with that disgusting noise again. She squeezed her eyes shut because the last thing she wanted to see was that thing.

"Damnation," he swore.

Her eyes flew open. "What?"

"The infernal condom split." Sure enough, she could see the head of his tool, glistening and angry looking. And far too large. No wonder that sock-like thing split open.

Yasmin shuddered, then shifted and curled her legs to the side. "I see."

"Did I cause you discomfort? I know I am larger than some men."

That explained why his parts didn't match her memory or, for that matter, the illustrations in the cunning book she'd bought in Paris.

"Yes," Yasmin said baldly. "I noticed your size." She grabbed her skirts and pulled them down so she didn't feel so exposed. Her inner lips were wet. There was a strange empty feeling inside her that she didn't like either.

"Of course," Giles said. He took out a handkerchief and offered it to her. "Grateful though I am that you were prepared for such an encounter, Yasmin, I cannot celebrate the quality of your French condom. I would have thought that the French were experts, but it seems the English are better in that respect."

It was *not* her condom. Presumably, it was English.

She felt a hideous wave of embarrassment. Her inner thigh was wet. She needed a bath, and how was she going to explain her ripped smalls to her maid?

He was doing up his breeches, thankfully. Yasmin swung her legs off the daybed and stood.

"All right?" he asked.

"Of course." He had such a sweet expression in

his eyes, burning desire together with something that looked like affection.

Her eyes went to his waistline without conscious decision and sure enough, she could see the thick, long line of his cock under his placket, almost reaching his waist. *"Still?"* she asked faintly.

One side of his mouth tucked up. "Indeed."

"You're not—"

"Always, around you."

His tool wasn't the problem. In fact, she rather liked the look of him. But the act itself? Never. She would prefer to live with her grandfather and never marry. When was she going to inform him that she had changed her mind about marrying him?

Not now.

"Something went wrong besides the obvious," Giles said slowly. "Yasmin?"

"I think we should return to Covent Garden," she said brightly. "We did promise to buy some wool." She stopped. "Actually, no. You may deliver the hat, but I have to bathe."

He stepped closer. "I understand. May I have a goodbye kiss?"

"Of course." She came up on her toes and kissed his mouth, her lips clinging to his for a moment. Even that tiny gesture sent a shock of desire down her legs. She would have to stay well away from him until she got over this infatuation.

Giles's eyes were thoughtful. "I had something

more like this in mind." He tipped her chin up; the touch of his hand sent a prickle through her. He lowered his head so slowly that she had time to notice that his irises had turned silvery. No, green.

Her mouth instinctively opened, welcoming his tongue, his taste, the silky, sensual way their tongues slid together. The absolute opposite of the—the rest of it. Yasmin pushed the thought away. If this was their last kiss—because she'd have to tell him at their next meeting that she'd changed her mind about marriage—she might as well enjoy it.

He was the only man she'd met since Hippolyte whom she could even contemplate kissing so intimately without getting revolted. She stopped thinking about the past, wrapped her arms around his neck, and stepped closer until their bodies touched. Rather than disgust, she felt warm sensuality.

He drew back and before she stopped herself, she blurted out, "If only . . ."

His thumb rubbed across her cheekbone.

"If only?"

Yasmin gave him a sheepish smile. "I like kissing you."

"I feel the same about you."

The security and safety she heard in his deep voice filled her with longing. Lydia, his sister, was not pleasant, but all the same, he loved her. When Giles loved someone, he would protect them forever.

Yet marriage required *that*. Intimacies.

With that thought, she stepped away, ignoring the fact her heart was pounding and her breathing was ragged, trying to summon up a careless smile. "You should leave in order to arrive within the time limit."

"We have already lost the scavenger hunt," Giles said. His eyes were steadily fixed on her face.

She had no idea how much time had passed. "Perhaps it was best not to advertise my familial closeness to the emperor, as you suggested. Will you please let my grandfather know that I am safely home? This has been a most interesting afternoon." She walked toward the door, shivering with embarrassment. What a foolish thing to say.

When she reached out to unlock the door, a large hand stopped her from turning the key. Giles's eyes were urgent, searching hers. "Yasmin, what is wrong?"

She drew herself upright and raised her chin. "I do not wish to discuss it, Giles."

He opened his mouth, then shut it again. "May I pay you a visit later tonight? We do need to talk."

"My grandfather and I plan to have a quiet supper."

"May I take you for a drive tomorrow morning?"

Yasmin didn't want to be anywhere private with Giles. His kisses seemed to cloud her mind and lead to extraordinary gaps in judgment. Being seen with him would lead to gossip.

"Perhaps early in the morning. I would enjoy a drive in the park in your curricle," she said airily. In the open vehicle, she could refuse his proposal expeditiously and have done with it.

"I shall come promptly after breakfast."

She curtsied. "Good day, Lord Lilford."

Giles didn't bow, nor did he show any reaction to the fact she'd addressed him by his title. He brushed a kiss on her mouth. "I wish you a good day, dear."

Yasmin's heart thumped. She watched him go, struck by one thought: the woman who would be greeted by that quiet, deep voice morning and evening was so lucky.

But it would not be her.

CHAPTER FOURTEEN

Giles walked into his own house a half hour later, certain that Yasmin planned to reject his proposal. The debacle of the condom had changed her mind. He thought hard in the carriage, but until the moment of entry, so to speak, he could have sworn that she was enjoying herself.

It took time for lovers to learn each other's rhythms and pleasures, which meant that persuading her to marry him was a question of intimacies. The thought sent a burr of desire down his legs, even as his cock was still protesting the close confines of his breeches. Persuading Yasmin to accept his proposal—again—was a challenge for tomorrow.

Today he had to speak to Lydia. Learning from the butler that she had returned from the scavenger hunt, he strolled into the drawing room.

His sister was seated beside the window, plying her needle in a cross-stitch sampler she'd been working on for at least two years. She had changed into a demure muslin evening dress that he remembered from her first Season. He found himself smiling as he sat down opposite her.

"Doing it a little too brown, sis," he said teasingly. "You're the very picture of virtuous womanhood."

"Act as you mean to be," Lydia said, smiling back. "I had a good time with Lord Pettigrew this afternoon, and I think that his attentions are marked. Before you ask, I did not welcome a kiss, and he didn't offer one. The maid was never out of our presence."

"Who won the scavenger hunt?"

She snorted. "The whole thing was a cheat. Most of us had made it back to the house and were totting up how many things we found when the Duke of Huntington strolled in with Lady Stella."

"Accompanied by his mother's brother, the bishop?"

"Of course," she said, scowling. Lydia had always hated to lose at spillikins as a girl. Then she brightened. "Lord Pettigrew said that the hunt didn't matter because he loathed the idea of me wearing anything as ugly as a vulture crown. Lady Stella actually put it on her head. Can you imagine? She truly is the strangest creature. She looked a terrible figure of fun with a beak looming over her forehead."

"What was in the box?"

"No one knows! The duke opened it, burst into laughter, and refused to share the contents with anyone, including Lady Stella. She didn't look very pleased. I don't think they like each other at all, which is a shame because his mother would obviously like them to marry."

"I see," Giles said, thinking that this was his cue to bring up his marital plans. Lydia wasn't going to be happy, but she had to accept it.

"The dowager might wreak havoc on Lady Yasmin's ambition to be a duchess," Lydia said, picking up her sampler again and glancing at him under her lashes. She hadn't blackened them today, so they were the usual blonde that matched her hair.

"Speaking of which," he began.

But Lydia didn't hear him. "Where did you go? Everyone noticed when you and Lady Yasmin didn't return. I don't mind telling you that the Duke of Huntington was frightfully displeased. I heard him tell his mother that he was tired of her meddling. He was obviously referring to the way she paired him with Lady Stella and sent you away with Lady Yasmin."

"We didn't find enough objects to bother returning to Covent Garden."

"The list was not easy," Lydia said, clearly determined to be courteous. "Lord Pettigrew and I found only three, though we had a lovely time wandering through the market. I bought some darling buttons."

Giles twitched, but it wasn't the moment to mention Yasmin's button collection. He had a strong feeling that Lydia would not welcome any signs of affinity with his future wife.

"I asked Lady Yasmin to marry me."

Lydia gasped. "No." Her throat began working, but no sound emerged for a long moment. Then, "I shall *hate* you if you do this, Giles."

"That seems an extraordinary response," he said, startled.

"I shall marry and go away, and never speak to you again!" Her voice choked.

"Lydia." He moved to a chair from which he could take her hand. "I find it hard to believe that you are so deeply worried about my countess. My wife is my wife, after all. You will marry and live in another household."

"You don't understand!" The words burst out of her chest, and she dashed away a tear.

Giles was starting to have a very bad feeling. His sister was shaking visibly, and her eyes were bleak rather than enraged, glazed with tears. He tightened his grip on her hand. "Help me to understand."

"Mother told me." A sob struggled free, and she broke off. Giles fished out his handkerchief and handed it to her. "I ha-have no father," Lydia said, blotting her eyes. "My mother, our mother, was no better than a whore."

Bloody hell.

"Even if she made some unconventional choices, Mother deserved our respect," Giles said, thinking frantically about the best way to respond.

"She was *forced* to marry our father because she was carrying you," Lydia spat.

"I believe that may have been the case."

"That wouldn't be terrible, but she told me that the child might have been Father's—or some other man's! Doesn't . . . ? Don't you feel . . . ?"

She broke off again.

"I've never been much good at expressing feelings, Lydia. What do *you* feel?"

"I don't have a family," Lydia said brokenly. "I have a name, but it's a fraud. You have a title, but that may be a fraud as well. Our father was a thief, and our mother . . . Well, it hardly matters, does it? I did ask her, in case you're wondering, whether she stayed true to your father. She didn't. She refused to tell me the name of my father, and merely said that you might be our father's son. Or not, but either way you and I are only related through our mother."

"I am aware."

"Likely, they were footmen or grooms. We don't even look alike," Lydia said, starting to sob. "You're my only relative, and we're both frauds. All the time, in the seminary, I kept waiting for one of the girls to reveal it. Every minute I was wound as tightly as . . . as piano wire, waiting for the truth to come out."

"No one knows, Lydia," Giles said gently. He got up and fetched a glass of water from the sideboard. "I am not a fraud, because I was born within the bounds of a legal marriage, as were you. I do not doubt that I am the person intended to carry the title I was born to."

"Good for you," Lydia said bitterly. "I don't feel like that."

Giles handed over the glass of water, and she drank some, hiccupping.

"If you marry Lady Yasmin," she said in a scratchy voice, "you're marrying a woman just like Mother. Your children will likely be as fraudulent as we are. You'll never know if they're really yours."

"That is unjust and unfair," Giles said.

"Oh, really?" She looked at him over the rim of the glass, her eyes drenched and miserable. "Do you think your bride-to-be is a virgin? Because I don't think so."

"That is none of your business," Giles stated in his sternest voice.

"She's no better than she should be," Lydia retorted. "Everyone talked about it, when you left without a chaperone and didn't come back. They said you'd gone off to shake the sheets."

"I hope you did not join in this spiteful gossip?" Giles said, his voice hoarse with outrage.

His sister met his eyes. "Tell me that you weren't enjoying her favors, and I'll happily inform all the gossips that they are mistaken."

Giles never lied. His lips tightened.

Lydia's chin jutted forward. "Her children will be my nieces and nephews. I'll watch them, knowing that someday they will have to go through the same hell I went through. Do you know why I was such a dunce my first Season? Because I was terrified that someone—such as those girls from school—would notice that you and I don't look alike and figure out why. Neither of us resembles our supposed father."

Giles pushed away the question of Yasmin's virtue. His sister needed his attention. He took Lydia's hand again. "I'm so sorry that you were unhappy and unable to confide in me."

"I kept waiting for you to tell me about our parentage." More tears poured down her cheeks.

"I hoped you would never learn the truth," Giles admitted. "That was a mistake." He dropped her hand and wrapped an arm around his sister's narrow shoulders, guilt piercing him at the fragility of her shaking body.

"I didn't want to be presented at court under a false name!" she wailed.

"It is not a false name. You are Lady Lydia. Our father loved you."

"Not enough to stay in this world," she said bitterly. "He knew I wasn't his child. His wife betrayed him. He . . . he took his life because there was no one to keep him here."

"Not due to that reason," Giles said instantly. But he wrapped his other arm around her, pulled her against his shoulder, and started rubbing her back. She was so thin that he could feel every bump in her spine.

After a while, she straightened and blew her nose. "I'm sorry," she said shakily. "I know how much you dislike an excess of sensibility."

"I do not dislike it," Giles said. "I just seem incapable of deep feeling myself."

"Of expressing it, perhaps, but you feel it," Lydia retorted.

Giles was fairly sure he didn't. He certainly had

never entertained the idea that he didn't deserve his title. "I have more memories of Father than you do," he said, allowing her to slip backward into her seat again. "He was a troubled man, Lydia. He experienced deep misery well before his thefts were revealed to society. His constitution was not the fault of his wife nor his children."

Lydia sighed. "Right."

"I clearly remember when Mother announced that she was carrying a child. Our father was happy, rather than angry. They lived detached but civil lives, Lydia, in separate parts of the country house. He thought you were a beautiful baby. Thinking back, I don't think he gave a damn who the father was."

His sister managed a wavering smile.

"Remember all those lawsuits Mother launched to avenge him, suing those whose gossip made him unhappy? I think he was the love of her life, no matter how many men she may have slept with. More to the point, I do not think that Mother's choices can be applied to Yasmin."

"Her mother is just like our mother." Lydia sniffled and regained a little bit of her normal fieriness. "They both used adultery to gain a title. Well, Mother may not have been married to your father yet, but it amounts to the same thing."

Giles thought about Lydia's recent behavior but held his tongue.

"Oh, I'm a hypocrite," his sister said. "Disgustingly so. But Yasmin . . ." Her voice shook and she stopped to swallow. "Please, please don't marry someone like our mother," Lydia pleaded, clasping her hands together. "Did she say yes?"

"She is considering the matter," Giles said.

Lydia shook her head. "Only you would use such dry words to describe a proposal, Giles. If she accepts, of course, there is no recourse."

Giles nodded. "I wish to marry her, Lydia."

"You're not in love with her!"

"I don't think I'm capable of such an excess of sensibility." He managed a smile. "But I care for her, and I genuinely wish to marry her."

"Because you enjoy her skill in the bedchamber," Lydia retorted. "Don't you see what a mistake that is, Giles? To marry with a woman because you enjoy bedding her? You will end up living on opposite sides of the house, holding a baby with no resemblance to you."

"A dark vision," Giles said. "Unfair, I think."

"There's nothing to be done about it now," Lydia said bleakly. "I'm amazed that she didn't accept your proposal on the spot. Perhaps she's hoping to play you off against the Duke of Huntington and gain an even higher title." She pinned her eyes on Giles. "I shall pray that Yasmin refuses you, Giles. If only because one of us should marry for love."

"Love can come after marriage," Giles said.

"Perhaps," Lydia said wearily. "At least Lord Pettigrew is an honorable man. He won't flaunt his mistress in my face."

"Did you know he trained as a barrister?" Giles asked, remembering Yasmin's account of

Pettigrew. "So many gentlemen do nothing at all, Lydia. I understand that he practices occasionally, defending the indigent."

"Yes, he's marvelously virtuous." Lydia took a deep breath. "Luckily, I like dogs since that is his primary subject of conversation."

Giles's brows knit.

"No, it's quite all right. I need someone like him. He steadies me. When I am in the grip of an excess of sensibility, I mean. And in case you're wondering, I won't play him false, as Mother did."

"All right," Giles said. But it wasn't all right. He had neglected his sister, never realizing that she was in such pain. He had never known how to cope with her moods, so he had avoided them, which meant avoiding her.

"Why didn't you want a chaperone, Lydia?" he asked.

"It wasn't because I intended to kiss men in dark corners." She gave him a faint smile. "I wanted to be with you, Giles. You're the only family I have, the only person who is truly related to me by blood. When I marry and move away, I'll rarely see you, will I? Perhaps at Christmas, or for a fleeting visit when Parliament isn't in session. I wanted to be with you."

Remorse slugged Giles so hard that he might as well have taken a blow. "I'm sorry, Lydia."

"Why *should* you want to be with me?" she said, shrugging. "I am so much younger, and prone to crying. I'm not as intelligent as you. I tried reading *The Times* so we could discuss it at breakfast, but I could never think of anything to say."

"I feel like a beast. A terrible brother."

"I didn't mean that!" Her eyes met his. "The world is so much more interesting than I am. By refusing a chaperone, I ensured that you had to spend time with me. If I hadn't insisted on your company, you never would have met Lady Yasmin, so I am paid back for my selfishness."

Giles found his voice. "Yasmin is not a terrible woman."

"Neither was our mother. They are both selfish, lustful, and reckless." She got up and left the room before Giles could protest.

CHAPTER FIFTEEN

Yasmin lay sleepless for most of the night, her body alternately raging with heat at certain memories and chilled with disgust at others. In the morning, she chose her clothing very carefully. She didn't want to give Giles the slightest impression that she was interested in repeating that hurly-burly behavior.

Yasmin lay sleepless for most of the night, her body alternately raging with heat at certain memories and chilled with disgust at others. In the morning, she chose her clothing very carefully. She didn't want to give Giles the slightest impression that she was interested in repeating that hurly-burly behavior.

She chose a promenade gown with a tight band under the breasts. Unlike her favorite evening gowns, the bodice had a ruff that left just enough space for a circlet of pearls around her neck. The matching spencer was crimson colored, fashioned in a military style, with fringed epaulets on the shoulders. The sleeves came to points on the backs of her hands, and the trim of her gown featured the same jagged points.

Just the sort of gown that Giles would prefer she wear, actually. Not a bit of skin showing.

"*Very* elegant," her grandfather approved, as she walked into the breakfast chamber.

"Thank you, Your Grace," she said, allowing their butler to usher her to her seat.

"I trust your hat has a plume or two?"

"Three," Yasmin said, smiling at his enthusiasm. "It stands like a striped box on my head, and the three plumes nod to the right."

"Excellent. I do not approve of Quakerish simplicity in ladies' dress. I prefer feathers and jewels." He raised a languid hand. Carson turned to the sideboard, picked up a velvet box, and handed it to him.

"Grandfather," Yasmin exclaimed.

"You are about to entertain an offer of marriage from an earl," the duke remarked.

"How did you know that?" she asked. "I am about to *refuse* an offer of marriage from that earl, Grandfather."

"Lilford paid me a visit last night to ask for my permission. Very proper of him. Your response is up to you, of course. Yet you must be attired to your station, Yasmin. Let the earl know what he missed by failing to persuade you of his virtues."

The duke flipped open the top of the jewelry box to reveal a large sapphire hung from a string of smaller stones. "All sapphires," he said, taking out the necklace and handing it to Yasmin.

It was an exquisite piece, even the smaller jewels delicately cut.

"Belonged to my mother," her grandfather said. "I remember the queen herself praising it. My mother didn't offer it to Her Majesty, as perhaps she ought to have done under those circumstances. Yet as Her Grace commented on the way home, the queen had a treasure trove and no need for our sapphires."

"It's beautiful," Yasmin breathed. "I love the necklace, Grandfather."

"Then put it on." He took up his fork again. "I can't bear to see any woman past the age of twenty in pearls."

Yasmin winced. He didn't mean to remind her of her advanced age, but he was likely right. A moment later, the sapphire slid between her breasts and settled in just the right place.

Carson picked up the string of pearls she had set aside. "I shall have these returned to your chamber, my lady."

"That necklace looks as if it'd been made for you," her grandfather commented. "I gather from your attire that you will be going for a drive, rather than welcoming the earl in the drawing room?"

"I am," she affirmed.

She knew full well that Carson would have regaled her grandfather with the tale of yesterday's improprieties. That locked door.

"Lilford comes from a good family," her grandfather said. Then, considering, "Well, perhaps that's not the right term, but excellent ancestry and an ancient title. As I told him, I'd like you to marry a nobleman, and I'd prefer him over Huntington or Templeton."

"You told him that?"

"I didn't mince words. He had a suicidal father and a cracked mother, but only that generation was afflicted. The family of the Duke of Huntington, on the other hand, boasts eccentrics and worse going back centuries. My own father told me tales of outrageous behavior back in Queen Elizabeth's day. Lilford doesn't talk much, does he?"

Yasmin bit her tongue before she confessed that Giles said quite a lot at certain moments.

"He particularly didn't like the idea of Viscount Templeton," her grandfather said. "Said he was too old for you. I told him that a seasoned man was what you wanted."

"I do not wish to become the Countess of Lilford," Yasmin said.

"Very well." Her grandfather had a wicked twinkle. "Who would have thought it could be so amusing to live with one's granddaughter?"

"You don't think I should save the necklace for a happier occasion?"

"You'll do me a favor by wearing it, because Lilford won't bother to return and try to persuade me by increasing the jointure he offered. I didn't let him get into the particulars, said he had to win you from the viscount and duke first."

"Very well." Yasmin got up, went around the table, and kissed her grandfather's cheek. "I am so grateful to have you in my family."

He cleared his throat. "The feeling is mutual."

She hovered for a moment, her arms around his shoulders, and then whisked herself out of the room and ran up the stairs. As her maid was adjusting her hat so the plumes curled just so, and pinning the ruffles at her throat so they framed the sapphire, Yasmin gave herself a stern talking-to.

She would not marry Giles, no matter how enticing she found him, because he had no sense of humor. More importantly, all they had between them was desire, and she would disappoint him in the marital bed. He was a man of honor, who would not stray outside marriage. Yet she couldn't contemplate that sickening act more than once or twice a month.

If that.

To the best of her knowledge, one didn't bargain with a future husband over such matters.

Part of her revulsion was likely due to her history with Hippolyte. But realizing that intimacies were closely tied in her mind to humiliation didn't help. She simply didn't want to engage in those sorts of activities.

By the time a footman knocked on her bedchamber door, announcing the arrival of the Earl of Lilford, Yasmin was armed and ready. Her armor? The adorable military spencer, violet-colored boots, fringed gloves, and a sapphire necklace.

"Your parasol," her maid called as she was leaving.

Yasmin tucked it under her arm. Giles was waiting for her at the bottom of the stairs, discussing something with Carson, his rumpled hair shining in the morning sunlight coming in through the open door. She froze for a moment, swallowing hard before she remembered that she was not supposed to feel a wave of hunger.

It wasn't just the messiness of intimacy, she realized. It was the way lust drove her—both of them—to primitive behavior. She had groaned aloud in the drawing room, which made her wince to even remember. Giles had maddened her with his deep voice and rough breathing, saying things that she suspected no other gentleman said aloud.

He turned from Carson and looked up at her, his eyes blazing with desire.

She walked down the stairs, pulling on her gloves. "Good morning, Lord Lilford," she said, curtsying at the bottom of the stairs.

Giles bowed and raised her hand to his lips, kissing her fingers. "My lady."

From the corner of her eye, she saw Carson's knowing twinkle. She withdrew her fingers and gave the butler an admonishing look. "I have time only for the briefest of drives."

"Certainly," Giles replied without a flicker of an eyelash. "I am grateful that you are able to accompany me so early. I prefer London streets when they are relatively empty."

Once they were in the carriage, he distracted her by asking about her button collection, and Yasmin was so relieved not to talk about serious matters that she didn't notice where they were going until the vehicle drew to a halt.

Giles threw the reins to his groom and walked about the curricle, reaching up for her.

"The mounting block?" she asked, adding a touch of hauteur to her voice.

He gave her a wry smile that was so unusual, and delectable, that she instinctively leaned toward him. His arms closed around her, but he didn't place her on the ground. Instead, he tipped her to the side and scooped her against his chest. The smell of starched linen and delectable man surrounded her.

Giles began climbing the steps of a large townhouse.

She narrowed her eyes at him. "Where are we?"

The front door opened. "My house. Hopefully, your house, once we are married."

"Your ... your house? I can't go into your house! I don't have a maid with me, so it would be vastly improper."

"You are my fiancée," Giles said. He strode into the entry, and a butler closed the door behind him.

A flash of alarm went up Yasmin's back. "No!" She peered around his arm at the man in black livery. "I am *not* his fiancée!"

"Just so, my lady," the butler said. He opened a door to the left.

"Tea for my fiancée," Giles said, walking through.

"Put me down," Yasmin said sharply.

"Certainly," Giles said, placing her on her feet. "Lady Yasmin, may I introduce my butler, Duckworthy? He does an admirable job of running this household as well as the country estate."

"Lady Yasmin," Duckworthy said, bowing low.

"Duckworthy," Yasmin said, politely smiling at him, even though she would never be mistress of the household.

Once the door closed behind the butler, Yasmin

frowned at Giles. "Very clever of you to introduce me, thereby cutting off my protests."

"You are to be his future mistress, so of course I introduced you."

Yasmin peeled off her gloves, placing them on a side table. Then she walked over to a couch and sat down. "Please join me." She saw that his rigid tool was outlined by his breeches again. "*Not* for that."

Giles bowed. "Certainly not."

"Doesn't it hurt to bow, given your condition?" she asked, curious.

"Not at all." He sat down. "Sometimes it's uncomfortable if I have to sit next to you for long periods of time. An entire dinner, for example."

Her mouth fell open.

"The longing moves through a man like lightning," he said as if he were describing a sprained ankle. "I throb whenever you laugh, or eat a bite of food, or glance at me. I watch your lips move, and I can't think of anything else."

Yasmin couldn't stop herself from glancing below his waist again. The sight made her oddly proud and mortified at the same time. "That sounds like a most uncomfortable condition. As well as embarrassing."

"Why have you changed your mind about marrying me, Yasmin?" Giles asked.

"I can only describe what happened in the drawing room yesterday as a fit of madness. In truth, I'm frightfully prudish."

Had she thought he didn't have a sense of

humor? Apparently, it only made an appearance when she was trying to speak from the heart, because he was clearly amused. Yasmin felt a stab of resentment.

"I did not enjoy our encounter," she said defiantly. "It led me to decide not to marry you."

Amusement disappeared from his face as if it had never been.

"I apologize for misleading you," she continued. "I understand that you believed me a far more interesting woman than I am. That French letter was not mine."

He raised an eyebrow.

"I have decided not to marry," she added, before he could ask any questions.

"Never?"

"I expect not," she admitted, peaceful with that decision. "I am enormously fond of my grandfather, and I shall live with him until he passes away. Luckily for me, I have no need for a husband's support, as my mother and grandmother both endowed me with funds."

"You enjoyed kissing me."

Her eyes flashed to his face, but he didn't look annoyed, just inquisitive, as if they were discussing a preference for Ceylon over Assam tea. She cleared her throat. "Kissing you is pleasant."

"For me—" Giles stopped and started again. "For me, kissing you is one of the most sensual experiences of my life. In fact, it is probably the most erotic thing I have ever experienced."

"If I were inclined to further intimacies, I

would—" She ran out of words. The right words. "But I am not."

Giles took her hand and turned it over, tracing a circle in her palm with his forefinger. "You might choose me under certain circumstances?"

"Kisses are not sufficient for marriage."

His lips curled into a faint smile. "They could be."

Yasmin blinked at him. "What are you saying?"

"I would happily just kiss you, if that is all you would allow."

Her palm was tingling, so she pulled her hand away. "Nonsense! You need an heir for your title and all the rest of it. I am not a fool. A woman has no choice in such matters within the bonds of marriage."

The look in his eyes made her falter. "You think that I would force you—would force any woman?"

"No!"

He raised an eyebrow. "Then?"

"You could talk your wife into doing something she didn't want to do." She didn't know how to explain that a mere look at him made her melt, as if she wouldn't mind leaning backward on this settee, just as she had yesterday—but no.

No.

"What if I promised never to engage in intimacies that you didn't directly request?"

Feelings were cascading through Yasmin: embarrassment, mortification, irritation . . . desire. He was so irritatingly desirable, especially when he fixed his eyes on her face.

"It's more than that," she said, summoning up conclusions she had reached during the night. "I don't think you want to marry me. Frankly, Giles, you don't even like me! Desire is not enough, and it would eventually destroy us."

He glanced down at their linked hands. "You're wrong, Yasmin. I do like you. I won't marry any woman, if not you."

"You—you have danced with me only once a night for the last months," she pointed out. "I have surmised from your frowns that you find me improper, empty-headed, and prone to chattering too much. You told me that you need to bind yourself to virtue, and my past will always be between us."

"I danced with you only once a night because that's all I would allow myself."

"You certainly weren't courting me," Yasmin stated.

"No." Giles's lips curled into a smile again. "I didn't think I could have you. But then I realized that if a duke could marry you, why not me?"

Yasmin bit her lip. "So you only realized I was marriageable once Silvester offered competition?"

Giles nodded. "I had told myself that I had to marry a woman of obvious moral fiber."

"I think we've talked enough," Yasmin said, jumping to her feet. "No matter what you think of me, I consider myself a good person."

He stood. "It wasn't *you*. Just the circumstances."

"Bollocks! I was not good enough to be your

countess when I was a dissipated creature beneath your notice. But when you realized I might become an immoral duchess, you decided I could be an immoral countess!" Her cheeks were hot, and tears were pricking at the backs of her eyes, but she kept her head high. "I would not marry you, not if you are the last man who ever proposes to me. I think better of myself, even if you don't!"

"I'm not making myself clear. I was thinking of children, of the children I may have someday."

"You are *entirely* clear. You believe my children will be ashamed of me." Pain seared her heart, but it was a familiar feeling. She straightened her back and put on a calm expression. "Due to my mother's love life, or my own? That would be the love life that you assume I have had."

A pulse throbbed in his forehead. "You must admit, Yasmin, that you have done nothing to dispel the incorrect assumptions of polite society as a whole. You dress in a flagrantly sensual manner, and you carry a condom in your reticule. Moreover, it has a weak catch. If the condom had spilled on the ballroom floor, it would have been your last ball. Even your grandfather could not overcome the scandal that would have ensued."

"A crime," Yasmin snapped. "I picked it up and admittedly, I forgot that it was in my purse. As I told you, it was not mine."

"How could you possibly *forget*?" His voice wasn't exactly scathing, but close.

"When I brought it home, I didn't want my maid to see it," she said stiffly. "Yesterday I snatched up that bag without thinking. So if the condom had been seen, and I had been judged unable to attend future balls, it would have been a miscarriage of justice."

"But that miscarriage of justice would have occurred. Frankly, if you had handed Napoleon's hat to the Dowager Duchess of Huntington, a similar scandal would have erupted. It's as if you are thumbing your nose at society, Yasmin."

"My friends would have stood by me. I would hope you know from my response yesterday that I do not cheerfully bed multiple men. Yet, you still have complaints about my conduct and my dress."

She snatched her reticule from the settee. "If you'll excuse me, I'll ask Duckworthy to summon a hackney."

"Yasmin!"

She didn't look at him, just headed across the room, head high. But at the door, she turned around. "I can tell you, Lord Lilford, that a life ruled by fear of a soiled reputation is no life at all. Perhaps you will find your perfect countess. I hope for your sake that she doesn't have feet of clay."

He was beside her, one hand braced against the closed door.

"Let me out!" she said hotly.

"I didn't explain myself."

Yasmin curled her lip. "Don't you think that I've noticed this year, all last year, when you ignored my attempts to be funny, my attempts to be your friend, my stupid, stupid attempts to make you desire me?"

"I had to—"

"Bollocks!" she cried again, interrupting him. "No one made you behave in such a demeaning manner or look at me as if I were a fool. You *chose* to behave that way, Giles. You wanted me to feel small and improper."

His face was white, his jaw set. "I did not want you to feel small. I would never want to hurt your feelings, Yasmin. I apologize."

"Open the door." She turned away from him and faced the door.

"Won't you allow me to explain?"

"Why?" Despite herself, she looked back at him. "Don't you see how wrong it would be for *me*, for my sense of self, to marry you? Of all the people in London, including those matrons who snub me, you made me feel the most belittled." She dashed a tear from her eye.

"I didn't mean to." There was a harsh, desperate note in his voice.

She shook her head. "I allowed it to happen. I made myself vulnerable to your opinion, didn't I? I cared what you thought, and that was beyond foolish. I shan't make that mistake again. Yet I was always surprised."

He shook his head. "By what?"

"Surprised that you wanted to dance with me. Surprised when you would sit beside me, even if you dismissed everything I had to say. Surprised that you allowed me to try to make you laugh." She shook her head. "I suspect you were surprised too. You would have been much more comfortable if I had kept a distance."

He didn't answer.

"Wouldn't you?"

Giles shook his head. "No. I forced myself to stay away from you."

"You must have been shocked to find yourself on that settee yesterday," she concluded, dark fury coursing through her. "How lucky you are that I have changed my mind and set you free. You and your sister will share the experience of sidestepping marriages with people whom you despise."

She pulled at the door, so Giles moved his hand away.

"I don't despise you. Please allow me to drive you home."

"No." Yasmin swept past him.

"Then I shall summon my carriage to take you home."

She refused to look at him as a footman scuttled off to find Duckworthy, and another footman ran around to the mews. She met his eyes only when he extended a hand to assist her onto the mounting block and into the carriage. "Goodbye, Lord Lilford."

Giles was stark white, his cheekbones standing out. "I've broken everything." His voice was raw and ragged. "Please allow me to try to explain one more time, Yasmin. Please."

"I think it's best if we forget about this mistake."

"How can I forget it? We made love!"

Of course, the despair in his eyes made sense. Giles was so proper that he would be agonized by the idea of debauching a lady.

"I choose not to give you my hand in marriage, which is my prerogative. Good afternoon."

He bowed and closed the carriage door.

CHAPTER SIXTEEN

Giles walked back into his drawing room, feeling as if someone had slammed an anvil onto his head. He'd mucked it up. Entirely. Yasmin had charged him with his own despicable behavior, and he couldn't defend himself, because she was right.

He *had* thought she was debauched. He *had* decided she was ineligible to be his countess. He had demeaned her in thought and behavior. It was irrelevant that he was trying to fend off an attraction to her so deep that he felt buffeted by it.

The fact was that he'd done it.

He'd made Yasmin feel small. He'd belittled the woman whom he desired above all other women: not despite her chatter, and her sensuality, and her sense of humor. He desired her *for* those things.

He sank into a chair and dropped his head into his hands. He had no idea how to make her understand. Nor did he think that she was wrong to say that she could find a better husband. He was like poison. He'd belittled her, and now he'd seduced her as well. Given her response to yesterday's intimacy, she wasn't used to *affaires*, no matter her reputation.

A staggering wave of despair went through him. He hadn't felt like this when his mother died. In fact, he considered himself immune to deep emotions. He'd realized that years ago, when his father took his life, and he had had to mimic the sad faces of others at the graveside.

He heard the door open. "No tea," he growled.

"Thank you very much for your opinion!" his sister chirped. "Yes, we will have tea," she said, presumably to Duckworthy.

He didn't look up.

Lydia sat down beside him in a flurry of skirts that made it clear she was still wearing her "young debutante" as opposed to "sensual matron" wardrobe. "What's the matter? You look uncharacteristically disheveled."

"She refused my proposal." His voice came out leaden.

"Lady Yasmin?"

"You needn't sound so astonished," Giles said, straightening his back. "No matter what you think, Yasmin has most of the eligible men in London at her feet. If there's a man who isn't, it's because she hasn't bothered to look at him."

Lydia leaned in, as if to hug him, then changed her mind and patted his knee. They didn't hug in their family. "I know you desire her, but—"

"I feel more than mere desire," Giles bit out.

"I see." After a moment, Lydia said, her voice

awkward, "Why on earth won't she marry you, Giles? Did she find out about Mother?"

"Our parentage had nothing to do with it."

Lydia's brows drew together. "But she does know?"

"I told her myself. Don't worry. She won't share the truth."

"I see." Silence again. "Are you quite certain that didn't enter into her decision, Giles?"

"Yes. She refuses to marry me because I belittled and disrespected her. She deserves better than me. She's right." He dropped his head into his hands again.

"Oh." A hand rubbed his sleeve, trying to comfort. "I'm sorry, Giles. She's making a mistake."

He snorted. "No, she's not."

"She always danced with you, Giles. And she . . . she *liked* dancing with you."

The words filtered into Giles's brain slowly. "We desire each other. She succumbed to that, briefly, then thought better of it overnight."

"I used to kiss boys during the waltz you shared. Did you realize that?"

He shook his head, not giving a damn.

"I was free to do as I wished during the first waltz because you never looked away from her face. Other people glanced around the room while dancing, but your gaze never shifted. It may be true that she does not feel the same," Lydia said, her voice not unkind. "She *did* glance around the room. That's how she noticed that I was sneaking away."

Giles took a deep breath, trying to clear his mind. A dull pain reverberated in his chest.

"Perhaps she wanted you to propose simply because you had belittled her," Lydia said thoughtfully. "I suspect there's pleasure in bringing a man to his knees who has made his aversion apparent. It's not unlike what I was doing, for slightly different reasons."

"I didn't mean to show my . . . my aversion."

"Yet, you did," his sister said as blunt as ever. "You danced with Lady Yasmin only once an evening, so everyone assumed it was merely a matter of courtesy. You curled your lip when she giggled. I never wanted you to be around her, because I could see how much you wanted her. But everyone else?" She shrugged. "They think you despise her. Apparently, she told Algernon Dunlap in your presence that you disliked her, and you didn't counter it."

"What?" Giles racked his memory. "I didn't counter it?"

Yasmin had indeed said something like that, just before they walked in the garden and kissed for the first time. He had ignored it.

What if Lydia was right? If Yasmin had been compelled to make him *like* her simply because he had disparaged her?

Suddenly, her comment after their first kiss jumped into his mind: "You needn't like someone to desire them."

Lydia sighed. "I'm sorry. She's not good for

you, and you're not good for her, but that doesn't help when one has been rejected."

He stood. "It's quite all right, Lydia. If you'll forgive me, I shall not wait for tea."

A patter of feet followed him up the stairs. "Giles!" his sister protested.

At the top of the steps, he took a deep breath. If Yasmin didn't want to marry him, it was hardly a reason to be uncivil to his younger sister. "Please forgive me, Lydia. I am not myself today."

"I blame her," Lydia said, her voice shaking. "You are never—She has hurt you!"

"Not on purpose," he said curtly. "I am shamed by my behavior, which she had to point out, and you have affirmed. I was attempting to ignore my feelings for her. I did so in an unpleasant fashion. I caused her pain."

"You're better off with a different woman," Lydia declared. "I know you don't want to hear that, Giles, but it's true."

He bit back an answer that would shred her. "I criticized *your* behavior on the grounds it might damage your reputation," he said instead. "That was laughable, given the damage I was doing to another woman. I apologize, Lydia."

"You were only trying to protect me," his sister said.

"Perhaps. I was protecting myself when I treated Yasmin as less than a lady. That was unacceptable."

"We all make mistakes," Lydia said. "You too,

Giles. Granted, this is the first mistake that I can recall you making in the years I've known you."

He frowned at her.

"You're perfect," Lydia said flatly. "Always perfect. It's as if we are from different families, rather than merely different fathers. I fart, I stumble, I make an exhibition of myself. I can't help wanting revenge even though it's unladylike. I rather liked kissing strange men."

"I am not perfect," Giles stated. "I just told you—"

"You were trying to be perfect," Lydia interrupted. "You were trying to avoid the temptation to attach yourself to the wrong woman. You are a much better person than I am."

"I don't think so," Giles said. "But thank you for your opinion, Lydia." He leaned down to put a kiss on her cheek before he strode down the corridor to his room.

He didn't break a window or dash the water pitcher into the fireplace, though those actions occurred to him. Instead, he closed the door and tried to imagine a life without Yasmin. A life in which he knew they weren't together because he had hurt her.

It was inconceivable.

So he sat down and began to think in a concentrated way, the way he had learned to do when the issue at hand in the House of Lords was truly important.

He needed a campaign to win Yasmin's hand in

marriage, and unfortunately, his campaign would spring from a position of weakness rather than strength. After a few minutes of hard thought, he amended his goal: he needed to win her hand in marriage without doing anything nefarious, such as kidnapping her or seducing her again.

An hour later, his valet entered. Giles threw him a look, and the man backed out without a word.

He had planned—and won—campaigns that seemed impossible before. No one thought the anti-slavery bill would pass Lords after the eleventh such bill failed in 1805. He had partnered with Quakers to meticulously, craftily, plan a new campaign, and abolition of slavery passed in 1807.

Failure was simply a preface to winning.

The key to winning any campaign was giving ground. He was going to have to explain himself to Yasmin. He couldn't make up for his behavior, but he could explain it.

A point in his favor was that she liked to kiss him. Moreover, he was a different man when he was with her. When she looked at him with desire, words eagerly tumbled out of his mouth, words he had never uttered to any woman, and never would again, if he didn't win Yasmin's hand in marriage.

He sent away Lydia when she came knocking at his door.

Only late at night, after he had fashioned a coherent campaign, did he ring his valet and ask for a meal, which he ate in his bedchamber, going over his strategy again and again, testing each turning point.

He wouldn't launch it for a week. They both needed to calm down.

The hardest question: Was marriage to him right for Yasmin?

He thought so. After all, she had always danced with him. Always. She had tried to make him laugh, and even if he hadn't shown it, he loved the frivolities she shared with him, the way she shone with joy on finding a special button. Finally, she had allowed him to seduce her, obviously a novel experience, even if she hadn't been a virgin.

He was unsparing with himself, sitting over that solitary tray.

Either he married Yasmin, or this tray would be his future. He would watch Yasmin dance into the future with the Duke of Huntington or Viscount Templeton.

Watch her surrounded by laughing, mischievous children; watch her bright hair fade and her beauty deepen. Watch her husband love her more every year; watch her become even more joyous.

While he deservedly sat in a room with a solitary tray of food.

CHAPTER SEVENTEEN

Two days later
MR. AND MRS. ADDISON'S TOWNHOUSE

*Y*asmin walked into Cleo's house to pay a morning call, her heart sinking when she heard the chatter of voices. She should have sent a message the evening before, asking her friend to refuse visitors. Instead, she'd spent yet another night tossing in her bed, her mind spinning in miserable circles.

Giles would never come back to her. She had shamed him, rightly or wrongly, and he was gone forever.

No more waltzes with Giles. No more squabbles.

That was what she wanted. Except . . .

She couldn't sleep. In fact, she may never sleep again. Even thinking of him made aching, desperate hunger flood her body, keeping her awake, staring at the ceiling. Lust was overwhelming.

You didn't have to like someone to desire them, and she desired Giles.

A wave of sadness twisted her stomach. Her rejection of the earl was as good as saying that she, at the age of twenty-five, was giving up . . . all of that. An erotic life. A love life. A family of her own. If she couldn't imagine the act with Giles, she certainly couldn't do it with anyone else, even Viscount Templeton. No matter how cuddly he was, she shuddered at the thought.

The Addisons' drawing room was crowded with gentlewomen. Cleo sprang to her feet and walked to meet her after Yasmin was announced.

"Good morning," Yasmin said. She dropped into a curtsy—and swayed.

"Darling, what is the matter?" Cleo hissed, catching her arm.

"I haven't been sleeping."

"Shall I send my guests home?"

Yasmin managed a faint smile. "Of course not. That would ensure a scandal."

"Come sit beside me," Cleo said, towing her across the room. Yasmin sank down on the settee, registering numbly that the worst possible pair— Mrs. Turing and Lady Dunlap—were seated opposite. United in their loathing of Yasmin, they dared not give her the cut direct in front of Cleo. Instead, they nodded frigidly.

For once in her life, Yasmin turned her head away and cut *them*.

Why should she be endlessly polite to poisonous women who were so eager to hurt her feelings?

"Have a scone and some tea," Cleo said. "You look exquisite as always, but if you'll forgive me, darling, you are not yourself. You are too thin."

"I'd rather not have a scone, thank you. I feel nauseated this morning."

"The last time I was queasy was when I was carrying my dear son Edwin," Mrs. Turing muttered to her companion.

Yasmin's head was spinning with sadness, but she was tired, bone-tired, of nasty whispers. She met the woman's mean eyes and lost her head. "Are you insinuating that I might have conceived a child with your poetry-writing son, Mrs. Turing?"

"God forbid!"

"I have never encouraged his poetry, nor have I *ever* found myself alone in a room with him, no matter how much he attempted to inveigle me."

"Thank goodness," Mrs. Turing said, her sour smile growing larger.

"You and I both know that I wouldn't be the bride in that scenario!" Yasmin flashed back.

Too late, she heard indrawn breaths around them.

And: "I knew it!"

Yasmin turned her head slowly and realized for the first time that Lydia was in the room. Not only that, but she had leaped from her chair.

"I told my brother that you could not keep a secret. I told him that you were a liar!"

Yasmin sucked in a breath, not sure what to say. Mrs. Turing seemed equally frozen. The matron definitely didn't want Edwin to be forced to marry Lydia—which he would be if people realized they had been alone together.

Cleo frowned at Lydia. "My dear friend Yasmin is no liar. I must ask that you apologize, Lady Lydia. I am sure that you did not mean what you just said."

Lydia's mouth clamped shut, and her eyes showed bleak horror. She had realized, Yasmin thought dully, that *she* was the only one who would suffer if the righteous ladies of London society realized that Edwin Turing had played the voluptuary with her, and that even his own mother knew of it.

"You don't understand," Lydia said with a gasp.

"Lady Lydia has no reason to apologize," Yasmin said, intervening. "The truth is that I entered a drawing room to find Mr. Turing proposing marriage to Lady Lydia on his knees, in the most romantic fashion, as one would expect from him. I hasten to add that they were properly chaperoned. The young lady refused him."

Lydia swallowed hard. Her cheeks had turned purple.

"He wept," Yasmin continued with a touch of disdain. "Cried with all the fervor of his poetic temperament. I did promise that I would never reveal the event, and I apologize for blurting out the truth. I am particularly sorry to mention your son's disappointment in such a public setting," Yasmin said, looking at Mrs. Turing. "I hope that he has recovered his former good spirits."

"You know young men!" Mrs. Turing tittered. "He was saddened . . . but . . ." Her voice ran out.

"I'm sure he will find a bride in time," Cleo put in.

From the corner of her eye, Yasmin could see two ladies whispering to each other. The story didn't hang together, but no one had the temerity to interrupt and ask for clarification.

"A happy marriage is a gift," Cleo continued. She was holding Yasmin's hand tightly in her own. "I consider myself the luckiest woman on earth to have found Mr. Addison. You may not know this, but he disliked me intensely on our first meeting."

Instantly, the room stopped thinking about the implications of Lydia's angry comment and focused on Cleo.

"How *did* you meet?" Yasmin managed.

Cleo looked around the room, smiling, holding her audience. "You will all be terribly shocked. Horrified, even."

As one, the ladies caught their breaths.

"I had purchased Quimby's Emporium from under my dear Mr. Addison's nose," Cleo said merrily. "He bribed a footman to lend him a suit of livery and showed up at my door with a decanter of brandy. It was very good brandy."

"I don't understand," one lady said. "Were you living with your grandfather?"

"Oh, no," Cleo said cheerfully. "I had a suite at the Fauberg's Hotel. Jake walked straight into my dining room. I scarcely noticed him at first. My maid was in another chamber . . ."

As their hostess spun a tale that had her guests

alternately fascinated and horrified, Yasmin tried to still her thumping heart. She glanced under her lashes at Lydia. The young lady's face was white and strained, but rather than gratitude for Yasmin's creativity, her eyes shone with hostility.

Despair filled Yasmin's breast. If people thought too hard about Turing's supposedly romantic proposal, comparing it to Lydia's first exclamation, the story would fall to pieces. The girl's reputation would be ruined if the gathered matrons realized that Yasmin had found her alone in a room with Turing. Lord Pettigrew would back away without a second look.

Giles would never forgive her. At that thought, her nausea strengthened until she felt truly ill. "Forgive me," she murmured, letting go of Cleo's hand, rising and walking toward the door.

To her horror, Lydia started to her feet and followed. When they were out of earshot of the seated guests, Yasmin turned to face her. "I apologize."

"If you tell a soul what my brother told you about our mother, I won't ever find a husband," Lydia said in a low voice. "Lord Pettigrew asked me to marry him last night. He wouldn't have me if he knew the truth."

"I wouldn't!" Yasmin protested.

Lydia's mouth curled with disgust. "As you promised that you would never reveal my assignation with Mr. Turing?"

"Keep your voice down," Yasmin breathed. She leaned forward and kissed both of Lydia's cheeks as one does in France. "What a delightful compliment!" she said in a carrying voice.

"Stay away from my brother," Lydia hissed. "It would destroy him to marry a woman like you. He's a good person." Her voice dropped. "*Please*, Yasmin."

Yasmin's heart was beating hard, but she kept her head high. "I already refused his proposal of marriage. You have nothing to worry about."

Lydia didn't say goodbye; she wheeled about and walked back to the group. Not a lady glanced up; they were enthralled by the disgraceful implications of Cleo's story. No scandal would injure *her* reputation; the Addisons' elevated status partly stemmed from their dismissal of social absurdities.

More than anything, Yasmin longed to go to bed and sleep for a week. Instead, she made her way to a retiring chamber. She wasn't *ill*, not really. She was gut-sick from misery.

In the small room, she sank onto a tufted hassock and thought about crying. Somehow, she never cried anymore, even when she wanted to, but she took out a handkerchief. A maid took one look and trotted away. It didn't take Cleo long to empty her drawing room and come sit at Yasmin's side, gathering up her hands.

"I can't marry him," Yasmin said with despair. "But he's the only man I want to marry, the only man I can imagine marrying."

"The Earl of Lilford?"

"Yes. His sister just begged me not to marry

him, because it would destroy him. Because I'm such an . . . an awful person."

"That's rich, coming from her," Cleo muttered.

"You see, he wants me, but he doesn't like me. So he fights the desire, but sometimes it gets the better of him. Earlier this week he proposed to me. Obviously, he told her."

Cleo scowled. "Just how much 'better' did it get?"

"Enough." Yasmin squinted at her friend. "I've never heard you growl like that."

"I learned it from my husband. It's wise to marry a man whom one's bedded," Cleo said with all the practicality of a woman who ran a business concern that spread from the United Kingdom to Germany. "Expediently, if possible."

"We didn't—He didn't—" Yasmin waved the handkerchief. "There was a condom."

"Excellent!" Cleo cried. "A woman after my own heart."

A flood of sadness welled up inside Yasmin's chest. "He doesn't like me."

"Jake decided I was an upstart English witch," Cleo said, wrapping an arm around Yasmin's shoulder. "He told Merry that I had a witchy chin."

Yasmin took a shuddering breath. "If Giles found me undesirable, this would be easier. I want him so much, but . . ."

"Take him," Cleo advised. "You can work everything else out later."

"He's very private. I blurted out that thing that happened with Lydia."

"I collect that his sister had an amorous encounter with Turing. What a squabby little libertine that man is."

"I promised not to tell."

"*You* didn't tell. Lydia did," Cleo said firmly. "Everyone knows Turing is a loose fish. I shall not be at home to Mrs. Turing or Lady Dunlap in the future. While I pity Mrs. Turing, she shows a lack of refinement and a contemptible disregard for good manners."

Yasmin had twisted her handkerchief so tightly that its delicate lace border would never be the same. "She merely doesn't want her son to marry Lydia. Or me, obviously."

"She should be so lucky," Cleo snorted. "You would be the making of that man."

"No, I wouldn't. Because I don't *like* Turing and I don't *want* him either."

Cleo frowned. "I should hope not. I suggest you tell Lilford the truth, just in case Lydia embroiders her story, accusing you of God knows what. She's clearly a loose cannon. I could do it, if you wish."

"No, please don't." Yasmin shuddered at the thought of her friend clashing with Giles. Cleo didn't suffer fools, not that Giles was a fool, but—

"I'd like to tell him a thing or two," Cleo said moodily. "I don't care for the way he looks at you with distaste, given that any fool could tell he's in love with you."

"Not love, desire," Yasmin corrected.

Cleo rolled her eyes. "Once a man becomes so obsessed that he can't look aside, the words don't matter. Do you think that Jake started out thinking that he loved me? He spent a good amount of time telling himself that all we shared was lust. As," she added fairly, "did I."

"I do have to tell Giles what just happened," Yasmin said.

"You can offer a counterbalance to the lovely Lydia's account." Cleo's arm tightened. "His sister alone is a good reason not to marry the man, Yasmin. Can you imagine Christmas dinners with her for years and years to come?"

"I'm not going to marry Giles," Yasmin said tonelessly. "I'm going to give him proof that I'm as bird-witted as he already believes. Lydia thinks that I can't stop myself from tattling, but that's not true."

One tear escaped and slid down her cheek. "I'm so tired, Cleo."

"Tell the earl tomorrow. Another day," her friend said, kissing her cheek. "You are the most intelligent, exquisite lady in all London, Yasmin, and if that idiot doesn't know it, *he's* the bird-witted fool, not you. You are loyal and loving, and I couldn't wish for a better friend."

Yasmin gave her a wavering smile. "Thank you. I think . . . I'll go home and send him a message."

"Instruct him to pay you a call tomorrow, when you've had a chance to sleep."

CHAPTER EIGHTEEN

Giles looked up when his butler entered his study. "No interruptions, Duckworthy." He could scarcely concentrate as it was, and he was due to give a speech in Parliament the following morning.

"A missive has arrived that you would wish to read immediately," his butler announced, presenting a silver tray.

Giles had never seen Yasmin's handwriting, yet he knew instantly whose it was. Elegant copperplate in dark blue ink, rather than customary black. He ripped the folded sheet open.

She wished to see him tomorrow morning or perhaps the next day, whenever he had time to spare.

His campaign to win her hand reeled through his head. He planned to request the first waltz in precisely five days. His plan branched thereafter, depending on whether she refused his request, or wouldn't speak to him while dancing, etcetera.

"I took the liberty of sending Jacobs for your curricle," Duckworthy said while Giles was still staring at the sheet of paper.

Giles was waiting in the street, tapping his whip against his leg, when his curricle swept around the corner from the mews. "With me," he bit out, and his groom dashed around to jump on the back.

It was challenging to drive at speed when London streets were crowded, but it took all his concentration, which was to the good. If he began to think about why Yasmin had summoned him, he ran the risk of collision.

At the Duke of Portbellow's mansion, he tossed the reins to his groom and told him to drive back to his stables. Once in the door, he handed his coat to Carson. "Lady Yasmin?"

"She's in the morning room, Lord—"

Giles jerked open the door. He strode into the room and looked about.

Yasmin was asleep.

She was seated in a large armchair turned to face the fireplace. When he walked across the room, she didn't stir. Her head leaned against one wing of the chair, her hair rumpled like gleaming silk, her eyelashes lying on her cheek like a golden fringe.

He crouched down in front of her, his fingers clenched against the urge to touch her. Instead, he looked at her carefully. When she was awake, he found himself absorbed by her eyes, cataloguing the way they sparkled when she giggled, the way they shone with joy when they spun in a waltz.

Now her cheeks were white. She looked thinner, almost drawn. Her eyes had faint blue circles beneath them. What had his girl done to herself in the past few days?

Without hesitation, he leaned forward and scooped her up, tucking her against his chest. Yasmin's indefinable perfume drifted to his nose, and his whole body relaxed. One of her hands curled confidingly against him, but her eyelashes didn't even flutter. Instead, she muttered something and turned her head into his chest.

He realized he was smiling.

Giles rarely smiled: the expression resulted from emotions that he'd eschewed long ago as undignified and unnecessary. Yet his mouth was curving without sardonic or sarcastic intent.

He headed for the door. Thankfully, Carson was no idiot. The butler backed away into the corridor.

Yasmin's grandfather emerged from the opposite room. "Good morning, Lord Lilford."

Giles nodded warily. He didn't intend to put Yasmin down if her grandfather asked him to, but he'd rather not have a confrontation.

"My granddaughter has been acting like someone with a broken heart," the duke said gruffly.

"She summoned me." He couldn't help the sprig of hope in his heart. Perhaps Yasmin had changed her mind about not marrying him.

Her grandfather quirked an eyebrow. "At breakfast she informed me that she would be hovering at my deathbed, devoted and unmarried. I didn't tell her that I have no plan to die before I meet my great-grandchildren."

Giles nodded. "Where shall I bring her?"

"You may carry her upstairs. Top of the stairs, second to the right."

Yasmin's bedchamber was papered in cream silk, hand-painted with sprays of rosy dogwood blossoms. The bed was made up with pale pink linen, with mounds of fluffy pillows that seemed utterly unnecessary to Giles, and yet utterly delightful. Next to the fireplace was a haphazard stack of books; beside it was a wide bowl full of buttons and another that seemed to be filled with twists of silk. Glancing at the window, he realized that it was covered with strings decorated with silk twists. Like kite strings, only far prettier and more delicate.

The room was so feminine, unlike his bedchamber, that he froze for a moment, looking around, then back down at the woman in his arms.

Yasmin lived a life that was purposefully beautiful, a strange, interesting thought.

As a man who would inherit an ancient title and seat in the House of Lords, he had been trained to live a life that was purposefully discreet and devoted to duty. His own preferences had been irrelevant; his parents' scandals combined with his ancestry shaped everything he did.

He walked across the room and sank into one of two cream-colored armchairs. Yasmin sighed and nestled against him, so he rested his chin on her hair and thought about that inheritance. A comment of Lydia's had been niggling the back of his mind.

Perhaps, without realizing it, his obsession with the reputation of his future wife *did* spring from the fact that he may not have the requisite blue blood. For most aristocrats, duty stemmed from knowledge of their ancestry.

Perhaps Silvester was free to act as he wished, because he had his late father's nose.

Yasmin didn't open her eyes for long minutes.

She drifted awake, aware only that she was happy.

Happy?

She had never been more *unhappy* than in the past few days. Her eyes flew open. There was no mistaking the safe, strong circle of Giles's embrace.

"*Sacré bleu!*" she exclaimed, looking up at him, her eyes widening. "We're in my bedchamber! What are you doing here?" Under her bottom, she felt iron-hard legs and that ever-present erection, the one that caused him no pain, or so he said.

"I carried you upstairs," Giles said, his arms tightening. His expression was composed, but his eyes were . . . longing? Of course he *did* want her. "Your chamber is very peaceful. Very like you, Yasmin."

She blinked at him. "You shouldn't be in here."

"I expect your grandfather feels that ship

sailed when I locked the drawing room door last week. After I found you asleep, I carried you here—on his instructions."

"Oh." Yasmin frowned at the wallpaper, trying to decide what she should say. Or do. Everything in her wanted to sink back against his chest and close her eyes, but that was the coward's way out. "You were supposed to come tomorrow or the next day, after I am more rested."

"You are not being compromised," Giles said, dropping a kiss on her head. "I would never force you to marry me."

"You'd have no luck with that," Yasmin replied, trying to pull herself together. Abruptly, she remembered why she had asked him to pay her a call. "Did you talk to Lydia?"

His brows drew together. "About what?"

Yasmin sighed and then reached for the arm of the chair, pulling herself upright. Giles's arms slid away and she stood, feeling unpleasantly crumpled. "I did something that will make you very angry."

Giles came to his feet. "I doubt that."

"I was at Cleo's house this morning, and Mrs. Turing provoked me. I don't have any excuse for this, but I blurted out the fact that if her son was forced into marriage, it wouldn't be with me."

He nodded.

"I told," she added.

"Why should I be angry? From what I understand, any number of young ladies have experienced Turing's unwelcome advances." His brow tightened. "Or welcome advances, in the case of my sister."

"I promised never to tell," Yasmin said, leaning against the back of the armchair on the other side of the fireplace. She was still so tired.

"Perhaps I don't understand. Did you inform the assembled ladies that you found my sister Lydia alone with Turing?"

Yasmin bit her lip. "No. But I'm afraid that Lydia was there as well, and she spoke before thinking."

Giles closed his eyes for a moment. "I'm going to have that intolerable poet as my brother-in-law?"

"Hopefully not," Yasmin said. "I informed everyone that I had walked in on Turing proposing marriage to Lydia in a most poetic vein, and that when she rejected him, he wept. I said that we had agreed to never speak of his shame, and I apologized to his mother for breaking my promise."

Giles's mouth eased. "Not a bad story."

"Mrs. Turing was displeased with the characterization of her son as a lovelorn fool, but she had to go along with it or expose him as a seducer of young maidens."

"The story will hold."

"Yet I blurted it out, Giles. You must be worried that I'll do the same as regards your parentage, but I swear that I won't. I am not a gossip. That is, I am a gossip, but I dislike trading in scandal. Lydia is afraid, but I *promise*. Not that you'll think my promises are worth much after this."

Giles stepped forward and put his hands on the back of the chair, on either side of her. She could feel the warmth of his body. "I am not afraid."

Yasmin made herself keep going. "Even though I lived up to all your worst ideas about me? I'm a gossip who shared hurtful information."

"I often told myself that I disliked you."

She flinched, keeping her eyes on his. "So you said."

"It was because I like you so much. I want to hear all your gossip."

Yasmin took a deep breath. "You needn't—"

"I don't just desire you. I like you," he interrupted. "I like this room, with all its feminine fripperies. It's a *happy* room. My parents were never happy, Yasmin. My father was melancholic by nature, and my mother was angry. I have no idea whether they were constitutionally like that, or developed those characteristics over time. But they were *never happy*." His voice was jagged.

Truthful.

"From the moment I met you, I felt like a moth drawn to a flame, and it had nothing to do with desire. Desirable women are everywhere. But you? Your courage and joy and pure love of life? The way you tease and giggle and dance through the day?"

She sounded very frivolous. Yasmin pushed the thought away. She *was* frivolous. It didn't have to be a criticism. "You may think you like frivolities, but what if you get tired of someone who is not more useful?"

"I don't want a *useful* wife. I want you. Only you. I want to be the only one who kisses you."

Yasmin cleared her throat. "Actually, I haven't kissed very many men, Giles."

"May I?" His voice was low and strained.

She swallowed hard. All the time she had been flirting with Giles, trying to get him to drop his proper demeanor, she had been counting on the man *behind* the facade. A man whom only she would know, who had saved himself for her.

Now she saw that man in his eyes.

"I know you don't wish for further intimacies," Giles offered. "I remember, Yasmin. I will never forget that, nor ask you to do something you don't care for."

The subject was embarrassing; she didn't want to discuss it. She'd been wretchedly unhappy for the past few days, unable to sleep. Brokenhearted, her grandfather had called it. She remembered feeling terrible when Hippolyte betrayed her, but this heartache had been more acute.

Now, she looked up at Giles's clear, grave eyes and couldn't stop the happiness that bubbled up inside her.

She leaned in and kissed him, rather than the other way around.

Giles's arms wound around Yasmin, and heat

coursed through her, healing the cracks in her heart. When she drew back to take a breath, his mouth slid along the line of her jaw, and teeth gently tugged at her earlobe. It felt so good, and yet so silly that she burst into giggles.

"What are you doing?" she asked.

Giles came back to her mouth. "You make me want to bite you."

She shook her head, tapping his strong jaw with a finger. "Are you certain, Giles? I want to marry someone who knows I am not like my mother."

"I trust you."

"Even though I blurted out your sister's secret?"

"*She* blurted out the truth in a rage, which is characteristic of Lydia," Giles said. There was a painful edge to his voice. "I learned that my sister knows more of our mother than I thought, and the truth has hurt her."

She frowned at him. "What do you mean?"

"My mother was carrying me when she married, as I told you. Thereafter, she took other lovers to bed. My sister and I have different fathers, and in her case, he was certainly not the late Earl of Lilford."

"Goodness," Yasmin said faintly.

"I didn't realize that my mother had informed Lydia of her parentage, but now I think that the reason my sister almost ruined herself lies in my family's past." He took a breath. "As do my own convictions. I was raised to believe that my countess had to be the most prudent, virtuous woman in all London, so that her children would not experience that particular shame."

He had both her hands again. "Yet I truly don't care about the name I inherited. If we never have children, so be it. I will care if you take another man to your bed, because that will break me. *That* is the only thing that would destroy me."

CHAPTER NINETEEN

The only sound in Yasmin's bedchamber was a lonely sparrow chirping outside the window. Somewhere in the bowels of the house, comforting sounds suggested that a meal was being prepared.

"I don't know how to trust your feelings about me," she said haltingly. "What will happen to your title without an heir?"

"I promise you, I *promise* you, that if you agree to marry me, I will simply kiss you for all the days of our life, if that is your wish."

"I've never heard of such a marriage."

The corner of his mouth curled up. "No one knows what goes on in a couple's intimate life. My parents are a good example. My father did not mind the fact that my mother conceived children with other men. In fact, I think he may have encouraged it."

Yasmin didn't know how to reply.

"It was not a point of contention between them. They did argue at times, but not over that. I clearly remember my father's joy on holding my baby sister for the first time."

"He truly didn't care?"

Giles shook his head. "He had no interest in his legacy. I remember him as despondent and self-effacing. My mother was carrying a child when they married, and he knew there was a good chance that his heir wouldn't be his. I don't care about an heir either, Yasmin."

"You think so now, but you may change your mind."

"It might be best if we didn't have children. My father was too unhappy to be a good parent, so I have no idea how a father behaves."

Yasmin instinctively leaned in, her hand sliding from his chest around his back. "I'm sorry about his misery."

"Shame and guilt are terrible bedfellows." Giles caught up her right hand and put a kiss on her palm. "I can curb my desire, and I will. No matter who my father is, I am a man of honor."

Yasmin took a gulping breath. The uncompromising honesty in his voice was convincing. She could have Giles, the man whom she had danced with, was entranced by, had dreamed about.

Her eyes flashed down, below his waist.

His mouth quirked up. "That's irrelevant." He flattened her palm against his chest. "Marry me, Yasmin. Please."

She could feel the thump of his heart under her fingers. It didn't make her uncomfortable, any more than did the hungry desire in his eyes.

"We would have a platonic marriage, though you would be welcome to kiss me at any time, day or night," Giles said, his voice deepening with a hungry edge.

A sizzle of heat went down Yasmin's back.

"In private or public," he offered, a gleam of amusement in his eyes.

"Kiss you on the ballroom floor? The very proper Earl of Lilford?"

"Anywhere."

She leaned forward and brushed her mouth against his. "Here? In my bedchamber? 'Twould be a scandal if anyone knew."

"Only if you want to."

"I do want to kiss," she breathed.

His tongue flicked her lip, and she opened her mouth with a gasp.

It felt like hours later when Yasmin finally pulled herself away. True to his word, Giles hadn't touched her, which meant—annoyingly—that she wished he would.

He had talked, though: his deep, rumbling voice told her that she made him ache with desire, that he wanted to breakfast with her, that she smelled like elderflowers with a hint of raspberry, that he wanted to see her grow old. That, and his kisses, made her muddled and hot, so much so that alarm pulsed through her.

"We should probably leave my bedchamber," she murmured. "I can't imagine what the household thinks of us."

"Will you marry me?" Giles's big hands were at her waist, and his eyes were dark with lust. His voice had that aching tone he never used in public, that she heard only when they were together alone.

How could she not marry him? "Are you in love with me?" she asked, blurting out the question.

He froze.

A stab of pain went through her. He wasn't in love with her, but she was agonizingly in love with him. The silence in the room was deafening. "Do you consider the question inexcusably gauche?" she asked, trying to give her voice a flippant air.

Giles cleared his throat. "Being in love is not a condition to which Englishmen are prone. I would like to marry you, Yasmin. I want you and no one else to be my countess."

All of Hippolyte's false promises ran through her mind. The fact that Giles readily admitted to not loving her was actually a positive. He would never lie. Perhaps he loved her and he didn't know it. Or perhaps he would come to love her in time.

"Yes, I will marry you," she told him, for the second time. "But not immediately."

Joy lightened his eyes, and she was quite certain she'd done the right thing. "Excellent! I shall court you."

"You want to *court* me?"

"With roses and champagne. Dancing with you twice and openly scowling at other men who touch your hand. Walking with you in the garden and kissing you within sight of chaperones. Bringing you gifts. Letting everyone in the world know that I am at your feet. I've had to pretend otherwise for a year, and I've had enough."

Yasmin cleared her throat. "I don't think your sister will be happy." Giles was so certain, so passionate, that her heart was pounding in her throat. It felt like some sort of dream: this particular man saying that he wanted to marry her.

His brows drew together. "Lydia does pose a problem."

Yasmin flattened her hand against his chest. "I don't think you should openly court me until your sister is married. She mentioned this morning that she'd accepted a proposal of marriage from Lord Pettigrew."

"They plan to marry at the close of the Season."

"I don't want to cast a shadow on her betrothal or her wedding, for that matter."

"I might lose you." Giles's voice came out in a growl, a delicious, hungry growl.

"You won't lose me!" Yasmin said, laughing again.

"Every unmarried man in London wants to marry you, Yasmin. Silvester, damn his eyes, is not a bad man, though Viscount Templeton is too old for you."

Yasmin dropped a kiss on the corner of his mouth and gave him a naughty twinkle. "I am very fond of Silvester, and the viscount is very cuddly."

Giles looked revolted. "My sister must accept my choice for a countess," he stated, all the arrogance of his ancestry in his voice. "My wife is *not* her choice."

"But Lydia is newly betrothed. What follows an engagement is a series of parties in her honor. It's one of the happiest times of a young lady's life. You have to admit, Giles, that if you suddenly began wooing me, rather than acting as if you despise me, all of society will be transfixed."

"I never despised you." He captured her mouth again and kissed her until she was clinging to his shoulders, her heart racing.

"You did," Yasmin managed. "You used to look across the ballroom at me with the nastiest expression, as if I were a small rodent."

His eyes glittered. "A small, sexy rodent." They kissed until she was more than clinging: one hand was deep in his hair, and the other stroking the broad planes of his chest.

"Worse than a rodent," Yasmin said somewhat breathlessly. "Something beneath notice." She returned to her earlier point. "People are already obsessed with the fact that you and I were paired for the scavenger hunt. If you begin courting me, we shall be the only subject of conversation. Your sister will be ignored, and you would be paying attention to me, rather than her." She shook her head. "Her loving brother should usher her into society as a betrothed woman—and make certain that she does nothing rash."

"Now that the betrothal has been—" Giles broke off, his eyes narrowed. "There's something else, isn't there?"

"No, of course not!" Yasmin protested. "What could you mean?"

He blinked. "You're not a very good liar, are you?"

Yasmin bit her lip.

"That wasn't your condom," Giles stated, working it out for himself. "It was *Lydia's*, wasn't it?" His spine stiffened. "My sister was planning to sleep with Turing. Or with Pepper." His voice was biting.

"Planning is not the same as doing," Yasmin offered. "You won't need to repair the family name on her account."

"Because *you* saved the family name by picking up that condom," he said. "I owe you so much."

She rubbed her cheek against his chest. "I couldn't let you see it. Or Turing, for that matter."

"He might have gossiped," Giles agreed. His eyes were dark with fury. "Lydia has said despicable things about you."

That was no surprise. Yasmin sighed. "Giles, you'll have to become accustomed to that sort of comment. I already told you there was a scandal in my past."

"She claimed you were a light woman who had slept with any number of men."

"*That* was not true."

"All the time she was carrying a condom in her purse." Giles pulled back, strode a few steps, and swung around. "My sister actively tried to ruin your reputation, even though she herself was debauched."

"That is taking the very worst interpretation of the condom," Yasmin said uncomfortably. "Lydia is very young."

"Hardly an excuse for breaking every principle that she was taught in her life!"

"But was she taught those principles? You just told me that your mother freely interpreted her marriage vows," Yasmin pointed out. "As did my mother, I hasten to add. I don't mean to be critical."

"Lydia is a young *lady*."

"So was your mother when she married your father shortly after entertaining a lover. As is my mother, who took a lover during marriage. It's quite likely that Lydia does not agree with the strict rules governing society. I've observed that women in our situation—those whose mothers were less conventional—often follow in their mothers' steps."

Giles took a step toward her. "Is that what led to the scandal you mentioned, in France?"

She nodded. "Something like that. To return to the next few months, I can imagine a number of ways by which Lydia could destroy her future. She needs her older brother at her side, making certain the engagement succeeds. I do believe she will be happy with Lord Pettigrew."

"So do I," Giles said, wrapping his arms around her. "So we'll have a secret betrothal. It sounds like an old-fashioned play, like *A Man of Mode*."

Yasmin came up on her toes and brushed a kiss on his lips. "No courting me in public."

"I will agree as long as you allow me to pay you private visits. I can't stay away from you, Yasmin. I might challenge Silvester to a duel merely for touching your hand."

"I can't believe you're so worried about losing me!"

"I know loss," Giles said, his expression bleak. "My father was there one day, gone the next. My mother was ranting about a judge at breakfast, dead by dinner." His arms tightened around her.

"I'm sorry," Yasmin whispered. She reached up to put a kiss on his lips, which led to another round of kissing that didn't end for long moments. "Oh, my goodness," she gasped.

"I shall pay you a visit every evening, if I don't see you during the day," Giles decreed, his jaw set.

"Only if my grandfather agrees."

"Your grandfather allowed me to carry you into your bedchamber," Giles pointed out. "He didn't challenge me to a duel when his butler informed him of the locked drawing room door. Your grandfather wants me to marry you."

"True." Yasmin leaned into him, loving the warm strength of his body. She barely stopped her hand from dropping from his chest to below his waist. Just . . . just to feel.

She sprang away, startled by the sweet ache she felt between her legs.

"You'll have to learn to ignore it," Giles said ruefully, one side of his mouth hitching up.

Yasmin felt heat spilling into her cheeks, but she didn't know what to say.

He leaned in and took one more kiss. "Tomorrow."

CHAPTER TWENTY

The following afternoon, Yasmin walked into a tea party only to discover that her fiancé had accompanied his sister there.

Not that anyone would guess they were betrothed.

Giles bowed stiffly before her, intoning, "Lady Yasmin." He promptly turned about and sat beside his sister. For her part, Lydia threw Yasmin a triumphant look, and it took all of Yasmin's inner strength to curve her lips into a gracious smile.

An hour or so later, when she walked upstairs to visit the ladies' withdrawing room, feeling forlorn and a bit lonely, she saw her fiancé. "Saw" wasn't the right word. Giles came up the stairs behind her, his legs eating up the steps.

His expression had changed from austere to hungry.

"Oh," Yasmin breathed.

He backed her into someone's bedchamber and shut the door smartly behind them. "Giles!"

"No talking," he growled. "May I kiss you?"

"Always," she gasped, her heart speeding up.

He spun her against the door, his mouth descending on her parted lips in a feverish kiss that sent heat coursing through her body.

She pushed back his coat so that she could spread her hands over his chest, her fingers stroking slabs of muscle barely disguised by a linen shirt.

Giles was kissing the side of her neck, making grumbling noises in the back of his throat that made her thighs shake. "I can't stop thinking about you," he growled. "The way you smell, and the taste of your mouth and your skin, the way you moan in the back of your throat."

"Giles."

He looked up.

Her gown was sophisticated, dissolute, suggestive: the neckline barely skimmed her nipples. Yasmin looked him straight in the eye and yanked her bodice down. She was wearing a French corset, the kind that hoisted her bosom into the air without covering it.

Giles's lips drifted over her breasts in a display of tenderness that was endearing, but not *enough*.

Her hands slid under his shirt, and she pulled it free of his waistband.

"More," she ordered. And then added, "Please."

"Your wish is my command." Giles moved back, wrenched off his coat, and pulled off his shirt.

"Thunderation," Yasmin said blankly. Her eyes drifted over the planes of muscle that narrowed to his waist, the arrow of hair disappearing into his breaches. She reached out, spreading her fingers over his chest. He was breathing heavily, as if he'd been running.

"Touch me," he commanded, his voice dark and low. "Touch me, Mina. Put your hands on me."

She felt the sleek point of a nipple under her thumb and his body jerked. She returned to the spot again, listening to his breathing coming harder. Then she pulled back her hands, running them under her breasts so they plumped up. "Kiss me again," she invited. "Not the sweet kind."

How could she have thought Giles was composed? His mouth fastened on her nipple, pushing her hand away. That caress wasn't like anything she'd felt before. The lips that looked carved and disdainful suckled her nipple until she gave a little scream. He nipped her, and laughed low in his throat.

Her round breasts looked small in his hand even though they were larger than most women's. She could feel herself, her *foufoune*, growing plump and slick, which would have distracted her, but her body was focused on what he was doing.

A moan came from her throat, a sound she'd never made before, husky and accompanied by a shiver. Her fingernails curled into his chest, pricking.

"I love that sound," Giles said under his breath. "It makes me think that you want me almost as much as I want you."

His head lifted from her breast. Breathing hard, his eyes met hers.

"Don't stop," she whispered.

"We must. We've been here too long."

Giles pulled up her bodice; Yasmin winced as cloth brushed her nipples. He turned, grabbed his shirt, and pulled it over his head, shoving it into his breeches. With his coat on, and a sweep of his hand through his hair, he looked exactly the same.

She looked below his waistline. Not precisely the same.

"I am planning to pay a visit to Quimby's Emporium," Giles said conversationally.

She blinked. "Why?"

"Reputedly, they will construct unfashionable clothing, if requested. I need a coat that will hide the bulge in my crotch. I'm shocking matrons who know where to look."

Yasmin slapped a hand over her mouth, but giggles escaped. "I keep promising to accompany Cleo to Quimby's, so perhaps I shall see you there!"

He had a hand on the door, but he turned. "I love your laughter."

He was gone.

The next day they kissed in a dark corner of Lord Breckenridge's house. The following day was Sunday, and she accompanied her grandfather to the church. Though Giles lived in the parish, she'd rarely seen him at a service.

But today the Lilford pew was occupied by Giles and Lydia, who looked sweetly pious, with a pale yellow bonnet, a handsome prayer book, and a satisfied expression. Yasmin spent the service thinking about the fact that disliking one's future sister-in-law wasn't charitable.

After the service, Giles sauntered up and explained that Lydia had decided to accompany a friend to Gunter's Tea Shop to try the fashionable lavender ice, and would Lady Yasmin care to see the tombstone of one of his ancestors?

Her grandfather laughed and turned away, claiming the attention of those parishioners who remained in the chapel. Yasmin put her fingers on Giles's arm and walked away from the chattering voices, down the stairs to the crypt. "Did anyone watch us leave?" she whispered.

"I doubt it. Your grandfather is a wily accomplice."

The crypt was cool and dark, sunlight filtering through narrow slits. The walls were fashioned in vaulted bays, each containing a marble tomb.

"My ancestor," Giles said, leading her to the second on the right. The sarcophagus was carved with angels blowing trumpets. "Margaret was the first Countess of Lilford."

"Is her husband here as well?"

He shook his head. "Rumor has it that he mistreated her, so she buried him in a pauper's grave, but records were not reliable in 1467. We do have her will, bequeathing her clavichord to her daughter. So we know that she loved music, if not her husband."

Giles plucked Yasmin up, sat her down on the flat marble surface, and kissed her.

"Perhaps we oughtn't," she whispered a few minutes later. She was already breathing quickly, pleasure turning her shaky and hot. "It's not polite, here on Margaret's tomb."

Giles laughed. Actually laughed! "Would that bodice pull down like your other one?"

She demonstrated, and his laugh turned to a groan. His hair slipped through her fingers like silk, and then she couldn't think anymore because he was sucking her nipple so hard that her back arched toward him. She gasped and then bit her lip so that no sound would go up the stone steps. If her skirt hadn't been so narrow she would have wrapped her legs around his waist, if only to relieve the intolerable feeling of emptiness between her legs.

"What?" Giles asked her, his voice dark.

"More," she whispered.

"Next time," he said, straightening, pulling up her gown.

Yasmin looked down at her body in shock. Her nipples were standing out against the light cotton of her bodice. Her thighs were clenched together in a useless attempt to assuage the ache between her legs.

"Darling," Giles said, stepping close and brushing her lips with his. "Think about what you want to ask me for, the next time we see each other."

Yasmin's hand shot out and grabbed his coat. "Don't go."

One of his eyebrows rose. "I must, as must you. Your grandfather can only be expected to hold the stage for so long. We mustn't draw attention to ourselves."

She sagged, and then slid off Margaret's sarcophagus, swaying before Giles caught her elbow. Hunger was an ache that seemed to have settled in her bones. But frustration flickered there too, because Giles was composed, as if nothing had happened between them. He was like a box that she wanted to pry open.

"Tonight," she managed. "Please pay us a visit."

He who never smiled, grinned at her and held out his arm. "I'm afraid I am unable to visit this evening. Shall we?"

"I shall get you back for this!" Yasmin promised in a low voice, on the way back up the stairs.

"I have no doubt," Giles said, rich enjoyment in his voice. They were about to emerge into the sunlit chapel. He bent his head and nipped her earlobe, making her breath catch. "Think of what you want to ask me, Yasmin. Your wish is my command."

She frowned. "My command is your wish?"

"Exactly."

CHAPTER TWENTY-ONE

The next evening, Yasmin dressed for a dinner party at the Addisons' house with particular care. Lydia, Giles, and Lord Pettigrew were also invited, part of the celebrations that followed the announcement of Lydia's betrothal.

Yasmin was determined to drive Giles wild with desire. He had been entirely in control after the church service, driving her to embarrassing emotions—on a *tomb*. A little growl broke from her throat at the thought.

Not acceptable.

These days, he was like a big game cat, stalking her, deciding when he would corner her for a few kisses, leaving her raging with desire while he sauntered away.

She didn't have to accept that. She could fight ack.

"The new round robe of blossom-colored ," she told her maid. A half hour later, she at herself with satisfaction. The bodice fit ove, with a narrow skirt and a demi-train n the back.

kline is uncommonly low," her maid

observed. "Would you like to tuck a fichu into the bodice, my lady?"

"No, thank you," Yasmin said. "Where is that crimson lip color that I purchased in Fitzroy Market?"

Giles, for his part, had impatiently thrown on evening wear and was ranging around his drawing room, nursing a glass of sherry while waiting for Lydia to descend and Pettigrew to join them.

His future brother-in-law seemed to have no idea how challenging life with his future wife might become. Thankfully, his mother took after him, never noticing Lydia rolling her eyes. Giles had brought it up over breakfast.

Of course, Lydia had flared up. "What about you? You always look as if you have a toothache. Like a bad novel, where the author describes someone as having a brow that's dark with displeasure. That's you."

"I will endeavor to look more cheerful," Giles had said. "I would appreciate it if *you* could be more respectful to your future mother-in-law."

"I am polite! Last night I didn't say a word when she went on and on about the English Channel. She needs to pluck her eyebrows. They are far too heavy. But I didn't say that, did I?"

Giles ground his teeth. "Your future husband will not take it well if you offered grooming suggestions to his mother."

"I heard of a tincture called Liquid Bloom of Roses," Lydia snapped. "Perhaps I shall give it to her for Christmas. That way I could make a point without being insulting." She had marched off.

Luckily, Pettigrew seemed to like Lydia, though Giles suspected that the man was far more interested in the bloodhounds born earlier that week than his fiancée.

They were late to the Addisons' house. As the butler took their outer garments, Jake Addison wandered into the entry, bowed, and then slapped Giles on the back in an American way that Giles ought to despise but somehow didn't.

"Good to see you," Jake said.

Lydia took Lord Pettigrew's arm and they disappeared into the drawing room.

Giles bowed. "It is always a pleasure."

"My wife tells me that you're winning the contest between yourself and the Duke of Huntington. Likely you know, but Viscount Templeton is topping the bets at White's."

I've won, Giles thought.

He kept his mouth shut. He'd always believed that jealousy was experienced by mediocre minds. Unfortunately, from his first meeting with Yasmin, he'd learned of his own mediocrity: jealousy was his daily companion.

"Yasmin means a good deal to myself and my wife," Jake said.

Giles suddenly realized that the American didn't have a carefree look in his eye. In fact, he seemed rather dangerous. "Are you threatening me?" he asked, curious. They both boxed in Gentleman Jackson's Boxing Saloon, but they'd never engaged in a bout.

"I was simply informing you how very, very fond Cleo is of Lady Yasmin. We wouldn't want to see Yasmin's heart broken. Or her spirit crushed."

"I would never do such a thing," Giles stated.

"She does not have an ascetic temperament," Jake said. "Like yours."

"I cherish her as she is," Giles growled.

"Excellent!" Jake said, slapping him on the back again.

Giles followed his host into the drawing room, thinking that he didn't care for American manners. He wouldn't dream of commenting on the Addisons' relationship.

When dinner was called, he was happy to discover that Mrs. Addison—Cleo—was apparently ignoring the "secret" part of his courtship, because he found himself seated beside Yasmin. Under the cover of the table linen, a small hand slipped into his.

"Good evening, Lord Lilford," Yasmin said, smiling at him.

His fiancée was so damned beautiful that for a moment he couldn't breathe. Her hair darkened to the color of aged amber in the candlelight, and her eyes danced with happiness. Presumably, to see him.

That was a first. His mistresses never shone with pleasure at his presence. They were good women, kind women, but he had never encouraged friendship. Somehow Yasmin was breaking down his reserve.

"I've missed you," he said under his breath.

She twinkled at him. "I hope your sister is enjoying all the excitement attached to her betrothal? Is everything going well?"

Yasmin would be his *wife*. He could be honest. "Luckily, the Pettigrews don't seem to register Lydia's critiques," he said, choosing his words carefully.

"How fortunate," Yasmin said. "Some people never do notice criticism. As opposed to those of us who are overly sensitive to slights."

"You?"

Her mouth twisted. "I'd love to say that I wasn't, but I am."

"Yet you act as if they don't matter."

"Some things truly don't bother me much, as when a lady gives me the cut direct, or a gentleman ogles me." She gave him a swift elbow. "I was very bothered when a gloomy earl curled his lip at me."

He looked at her smiling face. "Why did you have anything to do with me if that is how you felt?"

"I couldn't look away from you." Her smile was impish.

Giles stared at the curve of her delicate earlobe for a moment. He wanted to kiss it. Nip it. "What do you mean, you couldn't look away from me?"

"Just that. At first, I considered you to be the sum total of all the people who have despised me."

He felt sick and must have looked it because a small hand locked around his again.

"Not like that! I mean that I tried hard to tell myself that other people's opinions don't matter. And yet I failed to convince myself with regard to you. There you were, scowling at me from the margins of the ballroom, and still I saved the first waltz for you week after week. I couldn't stop myself."

Giles smiled ruefully. "I was the same. I was looking for a wife to placate ancestors who've been dead for years, but I couldn't stay away from you." His muscles tensed from the effort to stop himself from gathering her into his arms.

"Don't look at me like that," she said in a low voice.

"I'm incapable of looking at you in any other way."

Her eyelashes flickered, and then she wrapped her arms around her middle and let out a low moan. The table went silent.

"Something is wrong," Yasmin said plaintively. She sounded as fragile and pained as a bird with a broken wing, though her eyes glinted with laughter under her lashes. "I feel ill. I believe it was the chicken. Did it look pink to anyone else? Perhaps it was the white sauce."

A woman opposite dropped her fork.

A foot sharply collided with Giles's shin. "Ah, the chicken," he said lamely.

Yasmin gracefully slid sideways and collapsed against his shoulder. Her long lashes lay against her cheeks.

"I will escort Lady Yasmin to another chamber," Giles said. He tipped her body into the curve of his arm and rose, managing to avoid looking toward the head of the table, where Lydia was seated beside her fiancé.

Cleo joined them in the entry. Yasmin scarcely lifted her head from his chest, as if she were too ill to move. But her voice betrayed her. "Hello, darling."

Their hostess rolled her eyes. "My chef won't thank you for this, Yasmin. Mrs. Patchett appears to be warming up to a bout of hysterics. My guests will likely inform most of London that they've been poisoned."

"Forgive me?" Yasmin asked.

"You do look as limp as a mackerel," Cleo said, poking her in the side. "Who knew you were such a good actress?"

Yasmin's lips moved.

"I saw that!" Cleo crowed. "Very improper, darling. Lord Lilford, will you please carry Yasmin upstairs?"

"I think it would be better to accompany her home," Giles said.

Yasmin frowned. "My grandfather might worry."

"He didn't rise from his seat, so I think it's safe to assume that he sampled the chicken without ill effect and judged you not to be terribly ill," Cleo pointed out. "Lord Pettigrew may use one of our carriages to escort Lady Lydia home later. I shall send a maid to chaperone the betrothed couple."

"Your vehicle is just round the corner, Lord Lilford," the butler put in.

"Excellent." Giles walked through the door feeling happier than he had in a week. "Very good idea," he said, once they were outside, waiting for the carriage to appear.

Yasmin's head lay against his chest, but she tapped him on the chin with a slender finger. "Lydia will be afraid that I am trying to entrap you."

"She had been spending hours conjuring up terrifying pictures of my future if I marry the wrong woman. She is haunted by the idea that I might have married, for example, a woman who sells commodes."

"Do you agree?"

"Actually, I think it would be marvelous to have another source of income, though we have no need for it, if you are disinclined."

"I could probably sell a commode here or there, but I couldn't run a company. I'm only good at making useless things."

"Your kite strings are lovely."

Yasmin frowned at him. "What are you referring to?"

"Those silk threads with bright twists in different colors, hanging in your window. They reminded me of the flags I used to tie to kite strings when I was a boy."

Her eyes cleared. "They're made of extra scraps of silk from Cleo's Emporium. She loathes waste, so she gives me a bag of them now and then. Quite, quite useless, Giles."

"But exquisite, like you." He lifted her into his carriage, and jumped in after her.

She smiled at him. "We're going to cover her drawing room in them for next year's Trent ball. The theme is—"

Giles caught Yasmin in his arms, his mouth crashing down on hers.

In moments, Yasmin felt tender and hot, her whole being shamelessly focusing on enticing him to do more than kiss her.

Touch her. Stroke her.

"Do you know what I thought about in bed last night?" Yasmin asked, tearing her mouth away from his.

Giles's eyes opened, reluctantly, she thought, but they were blazing. Her breath hitched.

"You, when we were on the settee in the drawing room, when you held me, with one hand," she said, her voice uncertain. She was being frightfully bold.

"I held you *here*," Giles said. His right hand slipped under her skirts and cupped her between her legs.

It felt so good that she dropped her head back against his shoulder. The deep well of longing in his eyes made her blood burn hotter. She could feel a flush rising in her cheeks and her breasts, the whole of her skin prickling to life.

"Shall I just hold you?" he asked, his voice low and teasing, like someone with a sense of humor.

"Or?" His fingers flexed, once, and she bit back a moan. "Tell me how it feels," he crooned and flexed his fingers again. "What should I do next, Mina?"

"*Mina?* You called me that before."

His eyes were heavy lidded. "When *I* am in my bed, alone at night, I think of you as Mina. It's your name, and it's almost 'mine.'"

They were kissing again, but all the time his fingers were holding her tight, until she found herself rocking against his hold, trying to make pleasure thrum through her body.

In the back of her mind, a voice was reminding her that she didn't want the messy part. But *this* part . . .

This part was not messy. This part was enthralling. Giles was whispering, his voice gravelly and low in her ear, calling her Mina, saying that he loved the sounds she made, the little whimpers, that it was all he could think about, in bed and out.

All of a sudden, he pulled away, moving his hand, pulling her skirt over her knees, picking her up like a rag doll, and placing her on the opposite seat.

"No," she gasped.

"We have arrived." Thankfully, Giles didn't look unmoved, or she would have had to murder him. Slashes of color made his cheekbones look even more prominent.

Carson greeted them at the door.

"My fiancée isn't well," Giles said coolly. "I shall escort her upstairs."

A bolt of embarrassment went through Yasmin, but when she glanced at Carson, his face looked concerned and respectful. Not as if she were a hussy, but as if she were a countess whose husband loved her and had brought her home early from a dinner party.

Loved her?

She pushed the idea away.

Theirs was not a mere convenient arrangement, but not a love match either. Giles hadn't even given her a betrothal ring, after all. He'd scarcely wooed her; one moment they were grappling on the settee and the next, they were secretly betrothed.

Her relationship with Hippolyte had been secret too, but the Frenchman had lured her with promises of love and adoration. Giles had never lied to her.

Yasmin walked up the stairs aware that all the delicious, bawdy heat was leaking out of her. What was she doing? She was the one who said that they wouldn't bed each other, and then she acted like a strumpet.

He had the right to expect—

Except she knew deep down that Giles would never make a demand, no matter how strumpet-like her behavior might be. He would wait for her to decide.

He followed her into the bedchamber and closed the door behind him. And latched it, she noticed.

"I would like to try making love again. Not now," she added hastily.

He walked over to her. "There's no rush, Yasmin. We are not yet married."

"But we are betrothed."

"True." He waited, eyes patient and warm and lustful all at once.

"Did you expect me to change my mind?"

"I hoped you would. When you asked me to hold you in the carriage, I felt hopeful." His eyes drifted down to her crumpled skirt.

Yasmin smoothed the creases, knowing her fingers were trembling. She cleared her throat.

"Would you like me to leave?" Giles asked.

It was only at that moment that Yasmin realized how much she had expected humiliation as a response to revealing desire. The way Hippolyte had made her desire him, and then laughed about it to the French court. Shamed her for going to that cottage with him. She fidgeted. "Before, you seemed to consider me such a wanton."

Giles's jaw tightened. "I believed gossip, even when I was scolding my sister for repeating it. I find that ironic given what happened to my father."

Yasmin stepped forward into his arms and pressed her lips to his chin. To the right of his lips. To the left of his lips.

A sound escaped his mouth, hardly more than a sigh. She kissed the sound, the echo of longing that she felt in the strong hands curving around her back. His mouth opened and then they were clinging together as arousal roared through her limbs.

She pulled away to breathe, hearing words tumble from Giles's lips, raw and hoarse, telling her that he was on fire, that her breasts were . . . She let the sound of his voice sink into her skin, leaving the meaning to the side.

Giles loved it when she showed desire for him. She just had to believe him.

She took one step back, bringing him with her. And then another step and another, until she pulled him down to the bed on top of her.

He caught himself just as he was about to sprawl on top of her, pushed himself up on his arms, and asked, "Yasmin?"

"Why am I sometimes Mina and sometimes Yasmin?" she asked, smiling at him. A thick lock of hair had fallen over his forehead, and she pushed it back.

"Mina when I have no control. The moment I saw you in this gown, I felt like a wild man."

"It *is* nice, isn't it?" She beamed at him.

"Nice? It's designed to make a man fall on his knees and beg." His thumb rubbed along her jaw. "I've spent my life avoiding the kind of strong emotions that drove my parents, but here I am on my knees. So to speak."

She blinked at him, suddenly getting it. He was a box she wanted to pry open, a castle whose parapet she wanted to scale . . . When he called her Mina, she was inside the walls.

"I want to make love," she whispered, after more kisses. He'd been calling her Mina.

Giles's eyes glowed with a deep happiness.

"May I have permission to ravish you?" he asked, his tone oddly formal.

"As long as there's no condom involved," Yasmin specified.

His brows drew together. "We might conceive a child."

"I like babies. I do not like that chicken skin thing with a ribbon."

After that, it seemed a minute until her new gown was off, and her corset and chemise had disappeared as well. Giles unwrapped her as if she were the most precious gift he'd ever been given, and all the time he talked. Apparently, she, Mina, was a peach that he wanted to eat every day of his life.

Yasmin lay on the bed smiling, because the man who rarely spoke was throwing out compliments as if he couldn't stop. His words, and his voice, were the most delightful things she'd heard. Ever.

When Giles undressed?

Wrenched off his boots, pulled down his breeches and smalls, throwing them on a chair with his crumpled shirt? He was more heavy boned and muscled than she had imagined. When he turned around, his rear . . .

Was she supposed to think a man's arse was beautiful? Likely not. She wasn't sure. Probably not. But her eyes gobbled up his rounded muscled globes and the little hollows on the sides.

From the front he was so much *more* than any erotic drawing she'd seen that she closed her eyes for a moment. His cock stood up proudly, and without that wrinkled condom covering it, she thought she'd like to touch him.

So she did.

Giles sucked in a breath and then eased onto the bed, knees on either side of her. Her hand slipped away and circled his neck because he was kissing her again, deep and sweet.

"Are you going to lie on top of me now?" she asked.

"I want to taste you first."

Her heart was already beating quickly, but at that it started hammering. Her legs were trembling too, but before she had time to think about it, he slid down her body.

"Did we latch the door?" she asked suddenly.

He kissed her inner thigh. "We did."

"You don't suppose anyone is upstairs?"

"I don't. Carson will keep the maids away."

He licked her then, and a breathy moan came out of her mouth before she could stop it. In truth, she didn't try to stop herself from crying out, or rocking her hips, or any of the embarrassing, lustful things she did.

Giles talked throughout, telling her that her gasps were the most erotic sound he'd heard in his life. She squeezed her eyes shut and followed the sound of his voice through a wildfire that raged in her blood. All her muscles tensed when she felt one of his fingers inside her, then another.

White sensation sparked through her legs, and her hips arched, shoving against his mouth and his hand, against the feeling that was too much for her body. She cried out in sheer pleasure. Utter joy.

She came back to herself slowly, with Giles hovering over her, elbows on either side of her head. He was kissing her face and talking about beauty, not the color of her eyes, or the shape of her mouth. Beauty in the way she surrendered and let herself go.

When Yasmin finally found words, her voice sounded higher than normal, airy. "What next?" she asked, surprising herself. It wasn't enough, not when she'd scarcely got to touch Giles. "May I touch you?"

He looked down at her with feverish eyes, and said, "Whatever you want, Mina."

"Will you lie down?"

He did. She knelt beside him and spread her hands on his chest, tracing the bones and planes of muscles that knitted together so beautifully. His stomach was arranged in tight rows that she couldn't stop caressing.

He propped up his head on one arm, but the other hand came down and tugged her fingers to his nipple. When she caressed him there, she saw his stomach muscles tighten. And when she replaced her fingers with her lips, his eyes squeezed shut.

But he didn't speak, which fascinated her so much that she tried her best to enchant him into words. She ran her hand down his stomach to his cock, and acquainted herself with its thick strength, the way it jerked in her hand as a shuddering groan broke from his lips. The head felt softer, smoother, hotter, than the rest.

She could see a pulsing beat in his throat but still he said nothing, even when she put her lips there and kissed him, let her tongue roll over the rounded top until his gasps were greedy and loud. Then he reached out for her and said, "Mina."

Only that word. The name he had given her, but his voice was hoarse and sent fire cascading through her limbs again.

She arranged herself next to him, propping herself up on one elbow. "Shall we try again?"

He rolled, dropping a hungry kiss on her throat and another on her jaw. Yasmin's heart was beating a frenzied rhythm. She thought Giles would move on top of her directly, but instead he kept toying with her, kissing, nipping here and there, swiping her nipples with his tongue.

Abruptly he began talking again, his throaty voice telling her how much he loved the hungry sounds she was making. Her mind blurred, and when he finally moved over her and paused, she pushed up her hips demandingly.

"I love the drowsy look in your eyes," Giles said, kissing her.

"I want you," she said, surprised by the raw note in her voice.

"I'll do my best," Giles said. He cupped her face with his hands and kissed her hard.

Rational thought melted away because the

hard, smooth length of him slid inside with no squelching noise from the condom. His harsh breathing as he sank deeper was fuel to the fire raging in her limbs.

"Is it painful, Mina?" Giles asked, his voice a full octave lower than normal.

She shook her head. "You feel large. And hot," she added. He pushed forward, sending a bolt of lightning down her legs. Her eyes widened. *"Mon Dieu!"*

"I'm going to take that as a compliment," Giles said with a slow-burning smile.

"You're smiling," Yasmin said, tracing his lips with one finger.

He flexed his hips, and carnal heat exploded in her. His mouth plundered hers, and after that they didn't discuss vocabulary. Even Giles stopped saying more than throaty curses as he braced on his elbows, breathing hard, ravishing her with thrust after thrust.

Yasmin's mind blurred, and she let herself simply *feel*. No thinking. No judging. It occurred to her to curl her legs around Giles's hips, so she did. She ran a hand down his back and then rounded his arse, her fingers trailing a caress over flexing muscles. His body jerked in reaction, and she pulled her hand away.

"I'm sorry!"

He lifted his head from her breast. "I'm *yours*, Mina. Yours. Touch me again. Please touch me again."

Giles's thrusts were slow and steady, every flex

of his hips making her quiver, leaving her body taut and waiting. She wrapped her arms around him, surrendering to a stroking motion that made her cling.

With a groan, he pulled her hips up, and a strangled moan tore from her throat.

"Yes," he breathed. With a last thrust, he sent Yasmin tumbling again into burning heat, a scream escaping her.

Afterward, they lay beside each other, Yasmin's heart thundering in her ears. Her body pricked with sweat and heat, and yet the clearest sensation was in her hand, her left hand. Giles's big hand was curled around hers. She could feel his strong fingers. Her whole body was thrumming with warm satisfaction, but those two interlocked hands?

They felt like safety.

She had lost her composure. She'd behaved like a strumpet. It hadn't been disgusting. *He wasn't disgusted.* The sentences filtered through her mind dazedly, slowly.

Finally Giles propped himself up and brushed damp hair off Yasmin's forehead. "That was more than I ever could have imagined. Than I did picture."

"You imagined making love to me?"

One side of his mouth crooked up with slumbrous amusement. "From the moment I saw you. I'm sure they have a phrase for it in French."

"Coup de Foudre?" Yasmin asked. "A thunderbolt."

His brow furrowed. "I must have the definition wrong."

Could he mean "love at first sight"? Yasmin swallowed. Surely not. Giles wouldn't lower himself to such an undisciplined emotion.

"From that moment I wanted you," he explained. "More than I've ever wanted a woman before."

Thank goodness she hadn't blurted out the word "love." She'd heard that particular claim from several men: something about her beauty and her tarnished reputation made her more desirable than most women.

So she didn't answer, just lay quietly, shoulder to shoulder.

"I said something wrong, didn't I?" Giles asked.

"Of course not," she replied, summoning up a smile. So Giles had the same reaction to her as so many men before him. More importantly, he was the first man other than Hippolyte whom *she'd* ever wanted.

Their relationship—their marriage—would be the better for it. Somewhere deep inside, she must have recognized that she could be intimate with him even as they quarreled. "I am feeling quite proud of myself," she said, changing the subject.

He leaned down and placed a kiss on her lips. "Because you are *magnifique*?"

Yasmin blinked. "In bed?"

"Yes."

"In that case . . . could we do it again?" Her

face turned pink at the expression in his eyes. "I'll take that as a yes."

"I want to come into you in the middle of your orgasm," Giles said.

Again he kissed his way down her body. It was easier for Yasmin to let pleasure take over this time. At his first lap, she arched up with a gasp. Giles crooned to her, a flood of unintelligible, hoarse words. He drove her to the edge by bringing a broad finger into play, making her whole body catch fire.

She was frozen there, on the brink of the wave, when Giles commanded gruffly, "Now, Mina."

She let go with a cry.

With one swift movement, he came over her and thrust inside her pulsating body. Yasmin opened her eyes in time to see the wild look in his eyes as he rode *her* storm. Before she could catch her breath, urgent, deep strokes drove her toward another peak.

CHAPTER TWENTY-TWO

The weeks that followed were the happiest of Yasmin's life. Lydia pranced around London with her brother on one arm and her fiancé on the other, celebrating her status as a newly betrothed lady.

Yasmin and Giles often found themselves at the same event. He would bow before her, intoning, "Lady Yasmin," in a particularly flat voice.

She would curtsy and walk away, giving her hips an extra wiggle, knowing that he was watching. Flirtation had always been a charming pastime; now it took on an entirely different resonance. If Giles wasn't in the room, she didn't bother.

But if he was?

She lit up like a firework, the kind that sent off sparks—and those sparks singed any unmarried man in her vicinity. Gentlemen were knocking down her grandfather's front door, offering marriage, having no idea that every enticing glance was meant for Giles. Was directed at her secret fiancé. Viscount Templeton proposed on one knee, so fervently that Yasmin felt terrible refusing him.

That was the daytime.

At night?

After Lydia was in bed, and her grandfather retired upstairs? A rap on the front door would be answered by a murmured greeting from Carson, and the sound of a man walking quickly up the stairs. Finally Giles would walk into Yasmin's bedchamber.

Some days she was reading a book. Others she was just out of the bath, pink and damp. Once he appeared when she was still in the bath, and her maid was dismissed with a quick nod. No matter what, the moment their eyes met, her body would flare into life, tingling from head to foot. By the time he was halfway across the room, her heart would be pounding, her thighs clenched.

Then he'd wrap his arms around her, the scent of clean-smelling male as entrancing as the smolder of raw desire in his eyes.

"Mina," Giles would murmur, and the day suddenly brightened.

The happiest moments were when Giles, unable to stop himself, broke into words. Yasmin would succumb to a hoarse narration that made her feel desired for herself, for her emotions, not for her beauty.

One Friday night, she was curled against his damp shoulder, her fingers tracing patterns in his hair-roughened chest, when Giles said, "I wish you wouldn't flirt so much, Yasmin. Does that make me a beast?"

She laughed and stretched to kiss his mouth. "There's no need to worry about me finding another man," she told him merrily. "I'm so tired after your nightly visits that I've stopped breakfasting with my grandfather. Finally, I know why married ladies are allowed to breakfast with a tray in bed. It's because they didn't get any sleep!"

"I have no fear of you being unfaithful," he said, kissing her cheek.

"I don't flirt if you aren't in the room," she confessed. "I can't help wanting you to look at me, Giles. It's as if you're only half-mine. There's something so *delicious* about the way you look at me across the ballroom."

He reached out and crushed her to his chest, kissing her fiercely. "You're driving me mad, Yasmin. I want you to look only at me."

Yasmin pulled her head back. "I *am* looking at you."

"Please." He nipped the tender curve where her neck and shoulder met. "I can see that you are having fun, but I fear I might actually do damage to one of those men."

Yasmin thought about it. "I suppose it's horridly inappropriate for me to feel rather thrilled by that?"

"Peers cannot engage in fisticuffs on the ballroom floor. If society knew you were my fiancée, men wouldn't be so overtly lustful."

"I hope not," Yasmin said doubtfully. "I think it might be the human condition, Giles. Or the male condition, anyway. For example, Cleo loathes Lord Wade as much as I do. He doesn't care that she's married."

Giles's eyes narrowed. "The man who ogled you at the market."

"It's not the ogling," Yasmin said. "He brushes against me when he's walking past. And Cleo as well."

"I'll slay him." There was something about Giles's tone that promised violence.

"No need," Yasmin said. "I refuse to dance with him." She nestled closer. "I'm practicing my *countess stare*."

A smile pricked his mouth. "Indeed?"

"It has to be fierce to match yours," Yasmin pointed out.

"My ancestors were rather dour," Giles said. "My father told me once that the earls all look so bad-tempered because the smell of linseed and paint is unbearable."

"What on earth do you mean?"

"My father had a particularly acute sense of smell." He dipped his head and took her nipple into his mouth.

Yasmin gasped as he moved above her, his tool sliding over her wet folds and breaching her as her legs curled around him. He smelled like soap and something indefinable that was *him*, the unique person whom she loved.

She arched her back, thrusting her breast into his mouth, loving the way it made him start thrusting faster and harder, a muted groan escaping. This time was less frenzied. There was time to run her hand through Giles's hair, to catch his eyes with hers, to moan into his mouth. When he rolled over, she practiced her new skill of balancing on top of a man.

Her hand clutched the slabs of Giles's chest. Her hair had fallen down her back, her breasts were held in his hands, his thumbs roughly caressing her nipples. "I love this," she gasped. "My favorite position."

"You said the same thing last night when you were bent over a chair," Giles murmured, his eyes gleaming, his hips flexing up to meet her.

"I liked that too," Yasmin said, giggling.

He pulled her down and kissed her laughing mouth. "I've never imagined anything as wonderful as the sound of your happiness." Giles dragged his mouth along her cheek, the abrasion of his stubble making her breath catch.

"I can't help it," Yasmin gasped. "I feel as if I'm melting, and it's such a strange feeling, but so . . ." She couldn't find the right word. "I feel free," she decided, finally. Heat was building in her limbs, and she couldn't pay attention to language.

It wasn't until later that Giles picked up the thread of conversation. "What do you mean by feeling free?"

"I didn't like kissing."

"Why not?"

She wrinkled her nose. "A man puts his lips on you, and he thinks you will be overcome by craving for their tongue, and it's all so unlikely and disgusting!"

"But not with me," Giles said with deep satisfaction. He wanted to prove it, so he kissed her
until she lost her head.

"I'm exhausted," she murmured sometime
later. "I need to sleep."

"I should leave."

Her arms tightened. "I wish you wouldn't. I
wish you'd spend the night here and drink hot
chocolate in bed with me tomorrow morning."

Giles dropped a kiss on her mouth. "Soon. We
set Lydia's wedding date, by the way."

Yasmin blinked at him. "That's marvelous.
Next week?"

He laughed. *Laughed.*

The sound was still unfamiliar to Yasmin.

"Not quite," he told her. "Lord Pettigrew, the
future Marquess of Chichester, will be married
with pomp and ceremony in St. Paul's Cathedral,
which requires preparation. But I have readied
the announcement of our betrothal for the London papers. I cannot wait to tell the world that
you are mine." A trace of desperation crossed his
face. "Every damn time I watch you dancing with
another man I feel as if I'm losing my mind."

"I can develop a sprained ankle if you wish,"
Yasmin said, tracing his bottom lip with a finger.

"What an ass I am," he said ruefully. "You enjoy dancing, and dance you shall."

"I wish we could waltz."

He shook his head. "Lydia will accept reality
once she is married. I intend to give her a letter to

open when she returns to England after her wedding trip. This time with her is my wedding present. Not that she hasn't noticed me watching you. She's still briskly enumerating all your faults."

Yasmin flinched.

"You do give her cause, the way men fall at your feet."

She searched for the right answer, couldn't find it. "I don't have to dance," she offered again.

Giles shook his head, then swung out of bed and pulled on his breeches. She watched as he bent over to haul on his boots. Not even the slightest belly fat bulged over his waistband. "Our bodies are so different."

He glanced at her. "Thank God."

"I have a rounded tummy," Yasmin said, pursuing her train of thought.

"It will be more rounded," Giles said.

She blinked at him.

He bent over the bed, bracing his arms on either side of her head. "Are your courses regular?"

"Never," she said promptly. "There's no reason to worry. It takes ages to have a child. Just look at my mother having only me. She tried to have another with the emperor."

Giles shook his head. "My point is that you, my dear future countess, may already be carrying a child."

"I would know," Yasmin said. "I would be nauseated, or dizzy, or any number of other symptoms that women discuss."

"Excellent," Giles said.

"You don't want a child?" Yasmin's eyes searched his face.

"Not yet." He dropped a kiss on her forehead and went to the door.

She watched the door shut behind him, thinking about how in love she was with her grumpy, ethical earl.

Totally, wildly in love. The feeling was nothing like what she felt for Hippolyte. She knew Giles's faults and loved him for them.

For being himself.

CHAPTER TWENTY-THREE

One week later
LORD AND LADY MELTON'S MUSICAL SOIRÉE

As guest of honor, the Duke of Portbellow was ushered to the front row of Lady Melton's musical soirée, which meant that Yasmin was unable to turn her head and see whether Giles and Lydia had arrived yet.

"You seem rather subdued," her grandfather observed in an intermission. "What did you think of this guitar? An absurd instrument, like a violin that belched."

"Hush, Grandfather!" Yasmin said. "Mr. Rossini might hear you."

"I prefer Handel. Or Haydn, on the violin."

She patted his arm. "It'll be supper time after a quartet performing Beethoven."

"Thank goodness," the duke said with satisfaction twenty minutes later, after the musical portion of the evening concluded. "I've arranged for us to eat a bite with young Pettigrew. He's got prize hounds, you know. I mean to have one off him."

"Do you still hunt, Grandfather?"

"Every gentleman hunts!" her grandfather said indignantly. But as they walked to the dining room, he added, "I thought a dog might be company when you leave."

Yasmin hugged his arm closer, lowering her voice to say, "I won't go far. Giles's estate runs next to yours."

"But that future husband of yours is endlessly in town, racketing around the House of Lords, raising trouble," the duke said. "When he stopped by last night, did he tell you about the speech he gave yesterday?"

"We didn't get to the subject," Yasmin said, and broke into a storm of giggles at her grandfather's wry chuckle.

"I don't miss being young," he said, leading her across a dining room dotted with small tables. "I do miss your grandmother. She had more *joie de vivre* than I did, so the early years of our marriage were a constant surprise. I have a feeling that your earl already finds himself similarly startled."

"Oh, dear," Yasmin said under her breath as she realized Lord Pettigrew was—naturally enough—seated with his fiancée, Lydia. She looked about wildly and caught Giles's eye just as he seated himself at a table across the room. He had apparently asked Lady Stella for the supper dance.

The duke turned his head. "Hmm?"

"Lady Lydia is not fond of me," Yasmin reminded him under her breath.

"Young fool," His Grace said, barreling forward. "Here we are!"

Lydia and Lord Pettigrew came to their feet, His Lordship bowing with the respect due to an elderly still-powerful peer, and Lydia dropping a curtsy that expressed dissatisfaction verging on disrespect.

A footman had sprung forward and pulled out a chair for Yasmin. Her grandfather's attention had been caught by an acquaintance at the next table.

"What an exquisite gown you are wearing, Lady Lydia," Yasmin said.

"My mother has noted that my fiancée's elegance sets an example for her sex," Lord Pettigrew said, beaming.

Lydia looked Yasmin over, her eyes lingering on her bodice. "Thank you, Lord Pettigrew," she said to her fiancé. "Of course, not everyone can be a good example; some must serve as a warning."

"Quite so," Lord Pettigrew said heartily, turning to the duke, who was seating himself. "I understand that you'd like one of my hounds, Your Grace. Were you looking for one with scenting ability alone, or would you care for one that loves water as well?"

"I've actually thought about cold-hardiness," the duke said. "Some of my happiest memories involve hunting roe deer after a snowfall."

"Of course," Lord Pettigrew said, his face brightening. "Now . . ."

Lydia caught Yasmin's eye. Would it be unkind

to label it a "beady eye"? Yes, it would. But there was something about the fixed way Lydia was staring that made her blue eyes seem small.

"Lady Yasmin, would you mind if I were blunt?"

Yasmin *did* mind. Her grandfather and Lord Pettigrew were deep into a lively discussion of hunting after a heavy snowfall, so there was no help to be found there. As it happened, Lydia didn't wait for her response.

"You can be at no loss to understand what I wish to say," Lydia proclaimed in a low voice.

Yasmin practiced her countess glare while raising an eyebrow.

Lydia flinched, so it must have been effective.

"I was very glad to hear that you declined my brother's offer of marriage. That alliance would have been—" Lydia broke off.

"A disgrace?" Yasmin suggested.

"I did not say that," Lydia retorted. She took in a deep breath. "Your arts and allurements are such that my brother has been drawn in, yet the alliance would be most imprudent. The infamous aspects of your . . . your background would forever mar the family name."

A bolt of fury went straight up Yasmin's spine. "But your imprudent actions would not?"

"They are hardly in the same category," Lydia asserted, her voice rising. "I love my brother. He deserves better. You would never be welcome in my family!"

The duke's head whipped around. "I am most

displeased by your impertinence," His Grace barked.

Lydia paled.

"My fiancée misspoke," Lord Pettigrew said, his voice even. "We would both welcome Lady Yasmin to the family, should that be the outcome of Lord Lilford's proposal."

"Lady Yasmin has refused his proposal!" Lydia retorted.

Yasmin lost her head. "I must tell you, Lady Lydia, that I make no promises about what I shall do, should he ask again. I am resolved to act in accordance with my happiness, rather than the honor of an ancient title or concern for your family's reputation."

"Ask again?" Lydia squeaked. "My brother hasn't come near you in days, in case you didn't notice!"

"But my arts and allurement . . ." Yasmin said sweetly. "I feel certain that I could curl a finger and bring him back to me."

The Duke of Portbellow broke into a chuckle. "I never imagined it would be so interesting to live with a granddaughter," he said to Lord Pettigrew. "That's why I want a dog, you know. I'll miss Yasmin when she flies the coop."

Lord Pettigrew was a man who was not quick on the uptake, but now he was visibly perturbed. He rose from his chair, a firm hand bringing his future wife with him. "If you will excuse us, I'm afraid that my fiancée has offered some opinions that are as untrue as they are ill-judged. I would be grateful to both of you if you would forgive her rashness on the grounds of her youth."

"Lady Lydia's impulsive comments will not cause me a moment's concern," Yasmin said.

Lydia's eyes flashed, and a flush replaced her pallor.

"We are grateful," Lord Pettigrew replied. "My fiancée has much to learn. I assure you that her instincts, no matter how impolite, stem from deep love of her brother."

"Your protectiveness is ill placed," the duke said to Lydia. "The earl can take care of himself."

Yasmin rose and dropped a curtsy. "Good evening, Lady Lydia. Lord Pettigrew."

Her grandfather grunted. "You'll have to forgive me for not rising. An old hunting accident."

"Just so," Lord Pettigrew said. "I will be honored to send Your Grace the best of the new litter of puppies." With that he bowed yet again and drew Lydia swiftly through the dining room and out the door.

"The lad will be the making of that young harridan," the duke said, cheerfully signaling for more wine. "She'll be a pesky sister-in-law, I must say."

Yasmin finished her glass, discovering her fingers were trembling.

"Lady Lydia is the image of her mother," His Grace said. "The woman couldn't bear to lose an argument. Have you ever read about a hyena?"

Yasmin shook her head.

"Strange animal found in the wilds of Africa. I came across a couple in that zoo in the Tower of London. The keeper told me that the female hunters are aggressive. They lead the pack."

"Lydia will be furious when she discovers that Giles and I mean to marry," Yasmin said bleakly.

"It'll be good for her," the duke said with finality. "She's no leader of the pack, that one. She's too impulsive, and she can't hold her tongue."

A chair scraped and Yasmin started as Giles dropped into the seat.

"My sister has been borne away by Pettigrew, supposedly suffering from a headache. From his glowering demeanor, I'd guess that Lydia has managed to upset even that most placid of peers."

"She is a hoity-toity Holy Willie," the duke said. "Spiteful, thoughtless, and hypocritical. If you'll forgive the insult to your sister, Lilford." At a tilt of His Grace's chin, a footman sprang forward and poured Giles some wine, filling Yasmin's glass as well.

"She takes after my mother," Giles said. "More to the point, Lydia has gone home. Lady Melton has announced that the quartet will play a few waltzes, Lady Yasmin. May I request your hand for the first?"

The rest of the evening was delightful. Everyone in the ballroom eyed them waltzing and chattered about it, but Yasmin didn't care. She just wanted to keep circling the floor in Giles's arms, his legs brushing hers with every turn they took.

At some point, she leaned back in his arms and laughed at him. "This is my favorite waltz of all we have shared."

"Why?"

"Because of the way you're looking at me," she said under her breath.

"As if I want to ravish you?"

She cleared her throat. "Lord Lilford, I must ask you to behave with more dignity." She burst into giggles.

"When you laugh, I fear that your breasts might escape your bodice," Giles said a moment or two later.

Yasmin frowned at him. "Are you saying I am too voluptuous for this gown?"

"I can see into your bodice," he said, the raw hunger in his eyes soothing to her spirits. "Lush breasts, hoisted into the air by your corset."

"That's one way to put it," she said rather dryly.

"I just don't want other men to enjoy them."

She sighed. "Since you've brought up my clothing several times, Giles, I am assuming that you would like me to attire myself more genteelly. I use that word 'genteelly' deliberately, by the way, because those at the top of society have no need to pay attention to the small-minded impulses of the prudish."

The waltz drew to a close. "May I escort you for a walk in the gardens?" Giles asked.

They had already created a stir, but they needed to talk frankly.

"You want me to be a wallflower," Yasmin said

when they were far enough from the house so that no one could hear them. When he didn't speak, she threw him a look. "I am not a wallflower. It's not in me. Frankly, that has nothing to do with my clothing."

Her fiancé's face took on the dismissive expression that she hated. "You are exaggerating. I don't want you to be a wallflower. I'm merely frustrated. The Countess of Lilford will be a leader in society, but that doesn't mean all the men in the room should be able to imagine her in their bed."

"I've said this repeatedly. I am not a leader," Yasmin said flatly. "I never will be, except perhaps when it comes to fashion, which I understand better than you do."

Giles opened his mouth and shut it again.

Yasmin decided to wait. She'd learned that if the silence grew too long, Giles allowed himself to elaborate.

"You are not merely fashionable," he observed. "Your dresses are regularly the most outrageous in the room."

"Cleo's gowns are quite revealing."

"Mrs. Addison carries herself differently. No man would interpret her clothing as an invitation."

Yasmin swallowed hard and let her hands curl into fists, creasing her gloves. "I am too— inviting?"

"I dislike having to keep an eye on my future countess to make sure that no one misinterprets her demeanor."

"Don't do this," Yasmin said desperately.

"We're merely having a conversation," Giles said patiently. "I would never order you to comply with my wishes. But I do wish that fewer men lusted after my betrothed."

"That's not really the problem, is it? You think I welcome their lust, that I want it."

"I think you enjoy attention."

Yasmin swallowed. Horrible memories of being labelled a strumpet washed over her. She tried to banish them. She and Giles were going to marry. Marriage involved compromise.

"I suppose I can change my style of dress," she said reluctantly. "I will go to Quimby's tomorrow and ask—I will ask them to make me a wallflower." Her heart hurt, so much that she felt as if her chest was closing in on her.

Giles touched her cheek. "Please don't look like that, Yasmin."

She forced a smile. "I am learning to be a countess, I promise. But Giles, changing my clothing won't work."

"When you actually are my countess, I won't feel so possessive."

Yasmin wasn't sure about that. She was realizing that her future husband, whom she loved despite his cranky nature, had very few people in his life. His father and mother had been uninterested. His sister and he loved each other but they weren't intimate. He had acquaintances, not friends.

She was the first person who was truly his. She

glanced back at the house but no one was within view, so she came up on her toes and kissed him gently. "I will buy a wallflower wardrobe, I promise. I will try to be more countesslike."

"Not countesslike," Giles said, closing his arms around her and putting his cheek against her hair. "*Mine*, Yasmin. Be mine."

"I *am* yours."

Quite likely, men like Lord Wade would fade away once an earl with a possessive edge in his voice declared himself ready to defend her honor. She sighed. "Wallflower it is, but *only* until we are married." She poked him in the chest. "I won't put up with interference in my wardrobe after that, even if my skirts are so drenched that I leave a snail trail behind me!"

Giles started laughing. "A snail trail?"

She didn't answer because Giles had lost his head and was kissing her so fiercely that the only thing she wanted was to be *without* clothing.

His hands ran up the front of her bodice and with one gentle tug, exposed her nipple. "I'll miss this," he murmured.

A sharp thought went through Yasmin's mind. What did he imagine she would be wearing? The kind of garment that Quaker women wore, with only a glimpse of skin visible?

Then she realized that her betrothed was looking at her with more than just lust in his eyes. There was a flickering touch of wonder there too. He looked at her as if she was the only interesting person in the world.

In his world.

Yasmin suddenly felt as if a cloud had moved away from the sun. Who cared what her fiancé thought about her garments? Giles was merely trying to say, in his masculine fashion, that he liked her. Or more than liked her.

Loved her, perhaps.

CHAPTER TWENTY-FOUR

The next morning, Cleo accompanied Yasmin to Quimby's Emporium. They walked into an open area with curtained dressing rooms to one side and a huge mirror situated before a low platform.

Mrs. Quimby bustled over to them, dropping a curtsy before Cleo—who was her partner in the emporium—and Yasmin.

"We're here to order Lady Yasmin a prudish gown," Cleo said, smiling at her. "Yasmin, this is my dear friend and co-proprietor, Martha Quimby."

"Good morning, Lady Yasmin," Mrs. Quimby said, dropping another curtsy. "Prudish will be a pleasure. I spent yesterday measuring debutantes, most of whom believe they should dress like a young matron, exposing every asset they have. They're imitating you and the Duchess of Trent," she told Cleo.

Cleo shrugged and settled onto a couch, drawing Yasmin down beside her. "Martha, do join us."

"I'd like to order a demure ball gown," Yasmin said when they were all seated. "More than demure, in fact. A gown that *hides* my assets, as you called them. My fiancé thinks my clothing is too improper."

Mrs. Quimby blinked at her. "Indeed?"

"I want to be turned into a wallflower," Yasmin supplemented. "If not a wallflower, a nun."

Cleo broke out laughing. "I remember saying the same thing to you," she told Martha Quimby.

The proprietress was smiling. "As it happens, I might have just the gown for you, Lady Yasmin, so you wouldn't even have to order one. It has yards and yards of fabric, and will cover you from your earlobes to your feet. But it is a *terrible* gown. Dreadful! I should pay you to take it. In fact, if you do take it, you'll have to promise never to disclose its origins."

Yasmin hesitated. "I don't want to make fun of Giles's request."

"I think it sounds perfect," Cleo said. "You can't do better than a neckline that sweeps your earlobes, Yasmin!"

Mrs. Quimby came to her feet. "If you'll give me a moment, I'll fetch the gown. *If* you can countenance wearing it in public, we can do any necessary alterations immediately, and the gown will be delivered to you tomorrow morning."

"I believe that's the future," Cleo said to Yasmin.

Yasmin had slipped back into thinking about Giles. He loved her; she was almost certain. And she was madly in love with him, which explained why she was considering winding a bolt of fabric around her body. "What is?" she asked belatedly.

"Walking into an emporium, choosing a gown, and having it delivered in a day, or perhaps even altered on the spot."

"That would be astonishing," Yasmin said. But she couldn't help returning to Giles. "I'm truly worried. What if he thinks I'm mocking his request?"

Cleo shrugged. "I made Jake wear flowered vests and golden breeches. Frankly, if Giles jumps to such a negative conclusion, perhaps you should rethink the connection, Yasmin. Do you really want a husband who believes he can control your wardrobe?"

"No," Yasmin said. "Certainly not. I'm just worried that he doesn't understand. Men don't dance with me merely because of my neckline."

"They dance with you because you are endlessly enchanting," her friend said, dropping a kiss on her cheek.

"That's very sweet of you, but they also assess my reputation and think that I might be available for intimacies," Yasmin said somewhat miserably. "If Giles sees me in a Quakerish gown and realizes that men still throng around, he might change his mind about marrying me."

Cleo frowned. "Why?"

"Because he will always have a scandalous countess," Yasmin explained. "I've tried to warn him, but he doesn't believe me. My reputation is unaffected by what I wear."

"In that case, the more fabric, the better," Cleo pointed out. "Make your point, Yasmin, and thereafter inform the man that further meddling in your wardrobe is not acceptable. I allowed Jake to order me a few garments from Quimby's before we married, but thereafter I revoked his rights to interfere."

Ten minutes later, Yasmin walked from the dressing room, and Cleo began giggling before Yasmin even stepped up on the platform before the large mirror.

The gown was made from heavy purple-and-yellow-striped silk that frothed into ruffles below the waist. Orange silk crossed over the bodice, and a white bodice sewn beneath rose into flared collar points at the neck.

It was certainly demure. There was no chance that anyone might glimpse the line of her leg. Yasmin occupied twice as much space as she might normally, thanks to a ruffled petticoat.

"You look like a rooster dressed for a costume ball!" Cleo went into a fit of laughter.

Mrs. Quimby stood back, arms over her chest. "The gown is still a monstrosity," she observed. "You'd be a pleasure to dress, Lady Yasmin, if you weren't set on being a wallflower."

Yasmin had never seen a garment like the one she was wearing. "These sleeves are unusual," she observed, plucking the puffs that marched down her arm. The puffs of gold silk were tied with red cords, giving her arms a vague resemblance to a puffy caterpillar.

"Miss Racking drew the pattern herself," Mrs. Quimby said gloomily. "When her mama saw it, she refused to accept the gown, saying that I should have ripped up the design. The Racking fortune comes from textile mills, so the girl thought the more fabric, the better. She was wearing her dowry, in effect."

"The trim is worse than the sleeves," Cleo said, chortling with laughter. The hem was adorned with a series of scalloped ruffles, each half-moon marked by an orange net flower. "On a happier note, this gown is guaranteed to make you a wallflower."

"Possibly," Yasmin said, twisting gently so the gown belled at the bottom. For all its design flaws, it was beautifully constructed.

Mrs. Quimby's mouth twitched, and Yasmin had the feeling she was biting back a harsh comment. "The gown is as good as a chastity belt," she said instead.

Unfortunately, the very next day, Yasmin's grandfather had an attack of gout that kept them home. Even more disappointingly, Giles sent a hastily written note saying that concerns about his sister's betrothal would prevent him from visiting. Apparently, Lord Pettigrew was expressing some doubts, and Giles was escorting Lydia to the family home outside London, where hopefully the cracks in their relationship could be smoothed over.

They would return to the city for the ball that Lord Pettigrew's parents, the Marquess and Marchioness of Chichester, were giving in honor of their son's betrothal . . . if the betrothal survived.

By the time the ball came about, a week later,

Yasmin was itching to see her fiancé. That wasn't a very romantic way of putting it, but she felt as if she was losing her mind, lying in bed at night thinking about the angles of Giles's cheekbones, the clean lines of his jaw . . . the rest of him.

Especially the unruly part that refused to obey him. The part he wanted to cover up with a long coat. Every time she thought of its velvety strength, her fingers curled as if they were caressing something hard and hot.

When Yasmin descended the stairs attired for the betrothal ball, her plan nearly came awry.

"I won't be seen with you!" His Grace declared, scowling. "You look like the upstart offspring of a grocer trying to elbow her way into society."

"The fortune of the lady who designed this gown stems from textiles, not lettuce," Yasmin said, adjusting the little orange reticule that Mrs. Quimby had given her. "Perhaps I won't be recognized."

"Oh, they'll recognize you," the duke retorted. "They'll think you're dicked in the nob. I don't have an overly high opinion of my consequence—"

"Yes, you do," Yasmin said, cutting him off. "Giles wants me to dress like a wallflower, Grandfather."

"That won't work." It took a moment to sink in, then His Grace's eyes sparked with mischief. "Oh, ho! So we're teaching your future husband a lesson, are we?"

"Do you think it's too mean?" Yasmin asked.

"Not at all! The boy thinks if you dress like a

Puritan, men won't be on their knees before you?" The duke snorted inelegantly.

"Do you think that if I wear my pearls over the white gauze it would be too preachy?"

"Absolutely not," His Grace said, chortling. "Carson, fetch my granddaughter's pearls. On second thought, where's that double strand that my wife wore to church? Let's wrap her in pearls."

"I have pearl-headed pins in my hair," Yasmin told him.

He squinted at her. "I can't see them. What happened to your hair? It seems to be a different color."

"A dusting of powder," Yasmin said. "To bring down the gold tones."

The duke hooted. "Why didn't I summon you from France when you caused your first scandal? Time wasted, time lost."

"I'm somewhat worried that Giles will be annoyed," Yasmin admitted.

"Hasn't much of a sense of humor," the duke said, nodding.

"He's developing one," Yasmin said, hoping that was true. "He has strict notions of the way a Countess of Lilford should be viewed by society. I'm hoping to show him that clothing does not make the man. Or woman. He says that my wardrobe—no, more than that, my behavior—is not appropriate for a countess."

"Balderdash! A countess can wear whatever she wants. You'll take them all by storm," His Grace said, cackling with glee. "If anyone can carry off that gown, it's you, Granddaughter. Then I suppose you'll wear your Frenchified gowns again."

"My wardrobe gives me confidence." She shrugged. "I see no reason to placate the sterner elements of English society, as they will never approve of me."

"Your disregard for the rabble's opinion stems from the blood of dukes in your veins," His Grace said, smiling at her again.

"Any show of weakness is fatal," Yasmin said, sharing her favorite maxim.

"Precisely. A duchess has no weaknesses."

CHAPTER TWENTY-FIVE

The Marquess of Chichester's Ball in honor of
the betrothal of his son, Lord Pettigrew, to Lady
Lydia Renwick, sister of the Earl of Lilford

As Yasmin and her grandfather walked into the Chichester ball, she was aware of a thrumming excitement deep inside, based entirely on the fact she was desperate to see Giles. True, he would not dance with her, given that the ball was in honor of his sister.

But hopefully they could steal time in a corner.

The moment her grandfather walked over to join one of his friends, Yasmin was surrounded by a flock of suitors.

"A new style," the Honorable Algernon Dunlap said, trying to look knowledgeable about women's fashion. Despite his mother's fierce disapproval, he continued to trail after Yasmin, rattling off ill-conceived compliments. "The collar flatters your swanlike neck."

Lord Hulsey elbowed him to the side. "Lady Yasmin, may I have the first waltz?" He didn't notice her gown.

Yasmin smiled and held out her dance card,

which was pounced on by two gentlemen and ended up losing its little attached pencil.

"They're all talking about *her*," Lydia hissed at Giles sometime later.

"Who?" Giles asked. Usually he would have spent some time inconspicuously watching his fiancée, but this evening he was focused on saving his sister's betrothal. Lord Pettigrew was slow to anger, but after being forced to notice Lydia's discourteousness to Yasmin, he had become visibly guarded.

Giles was grimly determined to make sure the wedding went through, because not only would a broken engagement be crushing for his sister, but in the event that it was cancelled, she and Yasmin would have to live together.

By dint of carefully steering Lydia away from dangerous topics of conversation, Giles felt the breach was almost healed. His sister wasn't a terrible person. She was impulsive and quick-tempered, but she had a genuine affection for Lord Pettigrew. Perhaps even more important for the success of that particular marriage, she loved dogs. Several days in the country, spending virtually all their time in the stables with the new puppies, had gone a long way toward settling Lord Pettigrew's nerves.

"You know who," Lydia said crossly. "Lady Yasmin, of course. Did you see what she's wearing?"

"I wasn't aware she had arrived."

Lydia gave him a sharp look. "She's mocking all of us. Wearing the most absurd gown. Her sleeves resemble bulbous purple caterpillars."

The wallflower wardrobe was making its debut, apparently. "How can that reflect on you?" Giles inquired.

"No one wears sleeves in this weather! We dress to entice," Lydia said with the long-suffering sigh of a younger sister. "The truth is that Lady Yasmin could wear a grain sack, and men would all ask her to dance before any of us."

"You have made an excellent match," he pointed out. "You have no need for other admirers, Lydia."

"It's just the principle of the thing," Lydia grumbled.

"The principle of what?" Lord Pettigrew said, appearing at their shoulders.

"I was saying that Lady Yasmin put on that wretched purple gown in order to make fun of the rest of us," Lydia said. She put a hand on her fiancé's arm. "I am so glad that you have never succumbed to her charms, Lord Pettigrew. I cannot bear the fact her grandfather thrust her upon us, with all her bedraggled charms."

Her fiancé's brows puckered. "I say, Lydia, that seems quite harsh. As I told you, my mother thinks quite well of Lady Yasmin. Did you know that she—"

"I don't care what she does," Lydia interrupted.

Pettigrew studied her face and then turned his

eyes to Giles. "I don't understand what Lady Yasmin is doing to mock other ladies."

"It's what she's wearing," Lydia explained again. "She's bundled herself up from the chin to toes, and managed to gather all the men around her anyway." She brightened. "Except for you two. I haven't allowed her to bewitch every man in London."

Pettigrew opened his mouth, but Giles shook his head, and the man subsided.

"Shall we dance?" Lydia said, giving her fiancé a glowing smile. "One good thing is that she looks a true fright in that ghastly gown. She's just gone into the ballroom with Viscount Templeton, so we might as well enjoy the full spectacle."

Toward the end of the evening, Yasmin finally stopped dancing long enough to drop onto a couch beside Silvester. "I haven't seen you in ages," she cried. "Why didn't you ask me to dance?"

"Your dance card was full by the time I arrived." The duke raised an eyebrow. "Let me guess. A modiste thumped you on the head and forced you into her creation? I'm surprised there's room on this sofa for both of us, given the size of your skirts, not to mention your arms."

"You don't care for my ruffles?" Yasmin asked. "These bulges are the very latest style." She patted her sleeves.

"In what country are they fashionable?" Silvester asked. "Mongolia? Why do they stand out in that fashion?" He pinched one of the bulges and thoughtfully wiggled it back and forth. "You could hide jewelry in here."

"Why would I do such a thing?"

"Jewelry heist," Silvester suggested. "Snatch a diamond bracelet and store it in your sleeves."

"Each bunch is padded with tulle, so I have no room for ill-gotten gains. During the bouncy parts of the cotillion, I feared they might bonk someone on the shoulder."

"How many strings of pearls are you wearing?"

"Four," she said, dimpling at him. "Mine and my grandmother's."

"You have a distinct resemblance to a winning racehorse decked out in a wreath of white flowers," Silvester said thoughtfully. "I would hazard a guess that you are offering a corrective to a grumpy peer."

"Something like that." Yasmin hesitated.

"No need to warn me of your pending nuptials," he said with a sigh. "I saw it coming. Though I will point out, darling, that at least *I* realize your charm is intrinsic and cannot be dimmed by the yards of fabric covering your admittedly glorious bosom."

Yasmin gave him a stern look.

"Before you moralize, I assure you that I am also looking for generosity of spirit and spiritual virtue in a wife."

"Are you actually telling me that the size of a lady's breasts will come into play when you decide whom to marry?"

"Do you want to know the answer if you won't care for it?"

Yasmin sighed. "No."

"Look, here comes your earl, looking like a thundercloud. Are you sure that you don't want to kiss my cheek?" Silvester tapped his face. "Right here would do the trick."

Giles appeared from the crowd and bowed before them.

Yasmin held out her hand for a kiss, so that he could appreciate the full impact of her bunched sleeves.

Naturally Giles didn't let on by a flicker of an eyelash what he thought of her gown, simply touched the back of her glove to his lips. "Good evening, Lady Yasmin. Duke."

"I suppose you've come to tear her away to dance," Silvester said, rising to his feet. He bowed and departed.

Giles caught Yasmin's hand, bringing her to her feet.

"I'm afraid I promised the next dance to Lord Boodle," she said, dimpling at him. "I didn't expect you to acknowledge my presence."

"Will you allow me to escort you home?"

Yasmin blinked at him. "My grandfather—"

"I already spoke to him."

"I don't usually leave a ball this early."

Giles's eyes caught hers. "Please." His voice was curt, even angry. But surely, that was desperation in his eyes?

She had the dizzying feeling that she would never be able to refuse Giles when he brought the word "please" into play, which didn't bode well for their marriage. Earls needed to hear "no" at home, since the world so rarely refused them anything.

Then she blinked because Giles's intent was suddenly clear. He was on the verge of kissing her in front of a crowded ballroom, and the devil take the hindmost.

She quickly stepped back and tumbled onto the couch in a flurry of ruffled skirts. By the time she got herself upright, Giles looked more bemused than lustful.

He held out his hand again. "Your sister?" Yasmin inquired once she was upright and he began marching through the room without glancing left or right.

"Taken care of," Giles said.

Yasmin smiled at all the fascinated faces they passed. She felt feverish, a sweet ache in the pit of her stomach, her heart speeding from a grave polonaise to a merry waltz.

Giles must have already warned the butler, because they walked straight into the night to find his carriage waiting. He silently handed her into the vehicle. Yasmin waited until the door was closed, and the carriage jolted into movement, before she said, "May we kiss now?" She pouted at him because this was *so much fun*.

"No, because when you are in my arms, I plan to rip that dress down the middle," her future husband stated in the calm way that he might say that the grain tax was too high or the sun was setting.

Yasmin's heart notched up. Her nipples tightened, not that Giles could see through four layers of fabric. They sat staring at each other as the carriage made its way through the streets of Mayfair.

"Do you plan to rip my gown because it is ugly?" she asked finally, unable to sit silently any longer.

His eyes strayed over her. "You are *more* enticing when you cover yourself up, Yasmin. You knew that, didn't you?"

"I knew that scandalously low bosoms and dampened skirts didn't make a real difference. People think they can interpret character by what someone wears, but that is never true."

The carriage stopped. Giles flung open the door and leaped down, pulling her after him. Right there in the street, where the duke's neighbors could easily see, he pulled her into his arms and caught her in a fierce kiss. "Mina," he said, low and deep in his throat.

Giles was in the grip of some sort of primitive male desire. Yasmin laughed, took his hand, and drew him past Carson waiting at the door, straight up the stairs into her room.

"You'll have to help me with all these buttons," she said, smiling at Giles over her shoulder. "Unless you truly mean to rip it open."

"I always mean what I say." He reached out and wrenched the back of her dress in two. "I don't want to see this gown again."

Yasmin couldn't help giggling. She held out her arm. "In that case, will you do the honors?"

He rent the seam of one puffy sleeve, and pulled it free, then the other, tossing them against the wall.

Yasmin didn't care about the dress, didn't care about anything other than the look in Giles's eyes. "Now, will you please help me with these pearls?"

"Why so many strings?" he asked, his fingers working nimbly at her throat.

"I am drawing attention away from my bosom. Silvester compared it to the wreath that bedecks a winning horse."

The last string of pearls clattered as Giles flung it onto her dressing table with its fellows. He unlaced her corset and let it fall. Her chemise was made of whisper-thin silk edged in Valencia lace.

Then Giles lifted her up, one arm under her arse.

With a laugh, Yasmin wrapped her legs around his waist and leaned into his kiss.

CHAPTER TWENTY-SIX

Long minutes later, when they were lying beside each other, trying to catch their breath, Yasmin asked drowsily, "Did you come up with the idea of ripping my gown in the ballroom? Because, though it was vastly entertaining, I'd hate to make a regular practice of it."

Giles turned his head. She blinked, because his eyes weren't tender and affectionate, but cool. Not that they were ever precisely warm . . . The thoughts tumbled through her mind. "Are you all right?" she asked cautiously.

"Of course. Why do you ask?"

She was probably misreading his expression. He naturally had a brooding aspect to his face, after all. The legacy of being the fifth earl, she thought.

"The idea came to me while watching men cluster around you."

"I dressed as a wallflower," Yasmin said, pushing herself up on the pillows. She didn't like the edge in his voice.

"You made a mockery of my request," Giles

said, staring at the ceiling rather than at her. "You were not dignified."

His flat statement was followed by silence as Yasmin thought about how to reply. "I didn't mean it that way," she offered.

"You delivered a lesson," Giles replied. "A remarkably succinct one."

"I just don't believe that clothing is important," Yasmin said, stumbling into speech. "I choose my gowns—my usual wardrobe—with that in mind."

"You choose your gowns to flout society's opinion of you," Giles said. "They judge you a strumpet, so you dress like one."

"My gowns make me feel confident. Mrs. Quimby already had that dress when I asked for a demure garment." Yasmin steadied her voice. She'd be *damned* if she'd plead with him.

"I asked you to act like a countess, to be dignified. You were the opposite of dignified. Surrounded by men, dressed like a member of a traveling circus, cutting a figure."

Angry sentences caught at the back of Yasmin's throat. She pushed herself higher up on the pillows and wrenched at the sheet, pulling it up to her waist. He was lying on it so she couldn't get it over her breasts.

"Everyone was talking of you," Giles repeated with a savage note. "So yes, I had the foolish notion that if I destroyed that gown in a truly intimate moment with me and me alone, it would make a difference."

Clearly it hadn't. Yasmin felt a pulse of shame.

"This evening, I had to not only watch my betrothed besieged by fortune hunters and roués, but also to witness society matrons cackling over your absurd sleeves."

Yasmin took a deep breath. "Giles, they always—"

"They do *not* 'always,'" he interrupted. "You step into a ballroom, and all eyes are on you, Yasmin. You proved your point. Every man in that ballroom desired you. *Lusted* after you, as if your dress was a barber's pole, advertising your wares. That was your intent, wasn't it?"

She managed to catch hold of her dressing gown, hanging from a bedpost, and pulled it over her breasts.

"I merely asked you to be dignified," he said in a dull voice. "To avoid attention until my sister married. Do you know that she and Pettigrew had a squabble about *you* this evening? That young fool tried to defend you."

"I gather *you* did not defend me."

Silence bristled in the room.

"I think I should wash," Yasmin said, sliding out from under the sheets, managing to swathe herself in the dressing gown. "You ought to leave. This conversation is hurtful."

Giles stood up. "We need to talk, Yasmin."

"You have been talking." She tied the dressing gown tightly about her waist. "I can summarize, if you wish. I am not dignified enough to be the wife you desire, and you have realized that covering my bosom won't solve the problem. You think I played an unkind joke on you, which I did not, but your conclusion is the same: I am not the sort of woman you wished to marry."

"Do you have to be the person most talked about in any room?"

Yasmin shook her head. "Perhaps we should break our engagement, Giles."

He stood a step closer and said, fiercely, "No. I want to marry you."

She double knotted the cord of her dressing gown. "*I* want to marry someone who will defend me from criticism. Who won't be ashamed of me."

"I am not—"

"You are," she said, cutting him off. "I would guess that you listened to your sister's opinion of my gown. Do you know that she was the one who added Napoleon's hat to the list of scavenger hunt items? Silvester asked one of his sisters. I am the only person in London who could produce such a hat, which Lydia knew."

"I see." A touch of red appeared high on Giles's cheeks.

"You gave her that weapon by telling her I owned the hat." Anger drained away, leaving Yasmin in a pit of despair. She'd made a terrible mistake, nearly as bad as her relationship with Hippolyte. "I believe I will retire to the country for the rest of the Season," she said, making up her mind on the spot. "You and Lydia can finish the Season together. I would be grateful not to be in her vicinity."

"You can't leave London!"

For once, Giles's eyes were unguarded. Yasmin knew that look: desire. Lust. The mere sight of it made her tired.

"This decision shouldn't be made when we are both overwrought," he said, exhibiting the nimble ability to shift arguments that made him so successful in the House of Lords. "You cannot go to the country immediately. You accepted the Prince Regent's invitation to a reception tomorrow."

Yasmin sighed. "Those receptions are dreadful crushes. His Majesty won't notice if I don't attend."

"Your grandfather is looking forward to bringing you to court, albeit not to one of the queen's drawing rooms. I shall be there, since Lydia and Lord Pettigrew will be introduced to His Majesty as a betrothed couple. We can talk there, Yasmin. You can't simply leave for the country without speaking to me."

Yasmin knew full well that her grandfather would dig in his heels at the idea of departing London before the Regent's reception. His Grace was determined to prove that England's monarchs were more intelligent and forgiving than those of France. Or at least, than Empress Joséphine had been.

Why, why had she fallen in love with a man who wanted her but didn't like her? Why had she been so stupid? An idea struck her, and she blurted it out. "Do you think I agreed to marry you because it's not enough to be my mother's daughter and have a scandal in my past? You said I dress to flout society's opinion that I'm a strumpet. Did I promise to marry you in order to punish myself?" Her voice shook.

Giles's arms wrapped around her, pulling her against his warm, naked body. "No, Yasmin. No."

A sob pressed the back of her throat, but she fought against it, stepping backward, pulling free of his embrace. "Don't worry. I have no intention of making a scene."

"Yasmin!"

"I do hope that you manage to convince Lord Pettigrew to walk up the aisle."

Giles flinched.

"It will probably be as good a marriage as any," Yasmin said dryly. "I don't hold out much hope for fidelity." She wished she had snatched back the words but it was too late.

His eyes hardened. "My sister will be loyal to her husband. She has always been loyal to family. Don't you see? She played that trick with Napoleon's hat because she is convinced that you are the wrong wife for me. Convinced that you will sully the family name, but even more, that you will make me unhappy. She's just trying to protect me."

"It must be nice."

"What?"

"To have a sibling to defend oneself." Yasmin managed a faint smile. "We can look forward to marvelous Christmases."

"Once we are married, Lydia will behave."

"Actually, I intend to rethink our betrothal while in the country," Yasmin said. "I deserve someone who will love me as I am." She was proud of her assertive, calm tone.

Did Giles pale? No.

She couldn't fool herself that he looked particularly distressed, perhaps no more distressed than any man whose mistress decides to leave his side.

"Please don't do that. Don't leave London."

"Tell me it won't be easier for you if I am nowhere to be seen? If men aren't clustering around me and asking me to dance?"

"Easier for me?"

Yasmin folded her arms over her breasts. "Easier for you. You needn't lean against the walls and rage inwardly about your uncouth fiancée flirting with men."

His jaw tightened, but he came out with the truth. "Perhaps."

"Marvelous," Yasmin said, hearing the flatness in her own voice. "We are in agreement, then."

"I don't want you to go."

"You have had rather too much of what you *want*, Giles. You'll likely have your scandalous countess back in the fall. I don't think my grandfather would agree to a broken engagement, given the rashness of our behavior under his roof."

"My reluctant countess," Giles said, his lips twisting.

"That too. I would be grateful if you would leave now." She walked over to the door and stood there, waiting for him to dress.

Giles pulled on his clothes, walked to her, and stopped. After a long moment, he bowed over her hand.

"I look forward to seeing you tomorrow at Carlton House."

After his footsteps went down the stairs, Yasmin sank to the floor, her back against the door.

CHAPTER TWENTY-SEVEN

THE PRINCE REGENT'S RECEPTION
CARLTON HOUSE

Thankfully, Yasmin did not have to wear hoops to Carlton House, as she would if she attended one of the queen's drawing rooms. Instead, she put on a favorite gown she had last worn at the French court, cream colored with magnificent gold trim and a high-standing Medici collar, adorned by the Portbellow diamonds.

Her grandfather looked every inch a duke in a dark violet coat studded with emeralds, his wide cuffs thick with embroidery.

"We shall be the most elegant personages in the room," he observed with satisfaction. "I gather from my correspondence that Lord Pettigrew will introduce his fiancée to the Regent this evening. Let's hope the sour-faced puss hasn't learned that you left the ball with her brother last night."

"We must remain far away from her," Yasmin said, taking his arm.

He patted her hand. "Away from your fiancé too, I suspect?"

Yasmin swallowed a lump in her throat. Her

grandfather had easily agreed over breakfast to eschew the rest of the Season and retire to the country. He truly cared for her. "I think it would be best."

"The two of you are like a Shakespeare play," His Grace observed. "Beatrice and Benedict, wasn't it? The couple who fought so much?"

Yasmin smiled wryly. "My English isn't good enough for Shakespeare. We are certainly not Romeo and Juliet."

"Pooh!" the duke retorted. "Those two young fools didn't love each other. When your grandmother died, did I contemplate suicide? Absolutely not!"

"Yet you loved her, didn't you?" Yasmin asked.

"Exactly why I wouldn't follow her," he said gruffly. "If I had drunk poison, who would keep her memory alive? Your mother has never shown much interest in either of us. I had to stay in this world or you, for one, would have known nothing of your own grandmother."

Yasmin rubbed her cheek against his shoulder. "I shall always remember you, Grandfather. I wish I'd known the duchess as well."

"Yes, well," His Grace said. "No need to mourn my death yet. Once you marry that irascible earl of yours, you'll need me to keep the peace."

"We will always need you," Yasmin promised. "*If* I marry the earl."

"Pooh!" her grandfather said, chuckling. "The two of you blaze like the sun at high noon, but you'll be true to one another. He loves you. I can see it in his eyes."

Yasmin's heart thumped. "He doesn't show it."

The duke laughed. "Yes, he does!"

Carlton House, home to the Prince Regent, did not compare to Versailles, but it was lavishly elegant in an English fashion. The Prince Regent had positioned himself in the spacious entry, greeting guests before dispatching them to the ballroom on the floor above. To either side of him, a double marble staircase turned this way and that, twisting around a glittering chandelier that hung from the pale green ceiling far above.

Yasmin had been unable to summon up much excitement about meeting a member of the British royal family, and meeting the Prince of Wales didn't change her mind. The Regent's bosom was as large as hers, and his cheeks were veined and red. He leaned in until she could smell brandy on his breath and informed her that he adored Frenchwomen.

"Made his admiration clear, didn't he?" her grandfather said after they murmured farewell and started up one of the flights of stairs. "I reckon you could outdo your mother and take a future king rather than a mere emperor, if you wished."

"Grandfather!"

"A joke in poor taste. I apologize, my dear. The Regent's a lustful fellow but easily as tiresome as Napoleon. You don't want him."

"For many reasons," Yasmin observed.

"There's a beautiful library here," her grandfather told her, escorting her up the steps. "Not that Prinny uses it much. I hear that he had that lady novelist, Jane Otter, to visit."

"Jane Austen," Yasmin corrected him. She felt wretchedly nervous about seeing Giles. To her dismay, the ballroom was crowded, but not so much that she didn't instantly register the earl and Lydia on the other side of the chamber.

"Come along, Granddaughter," the duke said, marching toward them.

"We were going to avoid Lydia!" Yasmin hissed.

"That was your suggestion, not mine. A future countess does not scurry around corners to avoid a bad-tempered lass, not to mention her irritable brother."

Yasmin sighed, but truly, she did want to see Giles before she and her grandfather left for the country. If they ever married, they would have to agree to make up quarrels before going to bed, because she was unable to sleep while angry at him.

They emerged from a crowd of people . . .

And walked into a nightmare.

Bowing over Lydia's hand was Hippolyte Charles.

He looked just the same. The luxurious black mustaches that he had groomed so lovingly still curled slightly; his handsome profile was just as chiseled, his bottom lip just as red.

Yasmin froze, but her grandfather muttered

something under his breath and swept her forward.

"Good evening, Lady Lydia," he said. "Lilford, Pettigrew." He put up his lorgnette and stared at Hippolyte. His lack of greeting was marked.

Hippolyte, meanwhile, was staring at Yasmin with an openly assessing look. Her stomach clenched.

She raised her chin and dropped into a curtsy without looking at Giles. "Good evening, Lady Lydia, Lord Lilford, Lord Pettigrew . . . Monsieur Charles."

"Oh, you know Monsieur Charles," Lydia exclaimed. "Of course, you are both French." To her credit, she didn't scowl at Yasmin. The royal greeting must have gone well; her eyes were shining, and she was holding hands with Lord Pettigrew.

"We have met," Yasmin said.

"More than that, *chère amie*," Hippolyte crooned, stooping into a deep, flourishing bow. "I ventured to this country for one reason, a reason of the heart: to find you, my long-lost love."

"That label is neither appropriate nor truthful," Yasmin said flatly. Her heart was pounding so hard that she felt ill. Giles's shoulders stiffened. All around them, with the honed instincts of hunting dogs, English nobility stopped talking and melted into an audience.

"But, *chérie*, you wished nothing more than to be my wife," Hippolyte said. He treated all those listening to a lavish smile. "I still have all your letters, your billet-doux. So passionate for such a young lady! Lady Yasmin won my heart, oh, these many years ago. I longed to marry her, but her father cruelly ripped us apart."

"Quite Romeo and Juliet," Yasmin's grandfather said sardonically. "I must have been under a misunderstanding. I always heard that it was Empress Joséphine whom you loved, if the word applies."

A trace of irritation crossed Hippolyte's face. "You must be my darling Yasmin's grandfather," he said, dropping into another bow.

"Surely, you know my name?" His Grace responded sweetly. "I thought you would have recognized the connection years ago, when your debts led to me confiscating the estate that the deluded empress had bestowed upon you. In gratitude for personal services, as I understand it."

Hippolyte's gaze turned cold. He hadn't realized.

"It makes me wonder how you can afford the clothing you wear," the duke added. "But on closer inspection I see that they are not precisely à la mode."

"You too were part of the conspiracy to drag us apart!" Hippolyte cried, ignoring the duke's sartorial criticism. He cast a glance at the eager audience surrounding them. "Imagine, if you will, the exquisite Lady Yasmin, at the age of sixteen, a rosebud, untouched by—"

"Enough," Yasmin said, surprised by the cutting tone in her own voice. "You are a blackguard, Monsieur Charles, and I can only say that my father was correct to reject your proposal of marriage."

"Given we had enjoyed each other for a week," Hippolyte retorted, "most in the French court thought he was foolish."

Whispers arose in a sharp wave like wind rattling through dry cornstalks.

"*I* was the foolish one," Yasmin said, head high. She glanced at the audience around them, though she couldn't bring herself to look at Giles. "I was sixteen years old, desperately in love. I believed this man when he brought me before an abbé, a priest, who pretended to marry us."

"Alas, one's first passions are inevitably horrifying in retrospect," her grandfather said contemptuously. "One can only hope those repellent mustaches were not in evidence years ago, but one fears they were."

Hippolyte opened his mouth, but Giles stepped forward. Without a word, his fist crashed into Hippolyte's jaw. The man swayed; Giles struck him another solid blow.

The Frenchman fell backward like a felled pine, ladies screaming as they leaped out of the way.

Giles prodded him with his foot, and then jerked his chin at one of the footmen. "Remove this rubbish."

The Prince Regent barreled up. "All the excitement happened when I was downstairs!" he squealed. Looking down, he made a childish pout. "Oh, it's that Frenchman. Who is he again?"

A cacophony of excited voices answered him,

but Lady Dunlap's rose above the rest. "One of Lady Yasmin's former lovers."

"Your Majesty, his name is Hippolyte Charles," Yasmin said.

"Well, get rid of him," the Regent cried, waving his hands at the footmen. "Hideous mustaches, *hideous.* I'm sure you can do much better." His smirk was a masterful invitation.

"Thank you," Yasmin said. She felt as if she had turned to ice.

Her grandfather took her arm. "Would you like to leave, my dear?"

"No," she said calmly. Her eyes met Giles.

He bowed. "Lady Yasmin, may I request the honor of your hand in this waltz?"

Her throat closed, and she couldn't answer, but she took his hand. Head high, she allowed Giles to sweep her into the waltz.

She only stumbled once, on meeting Lord Wade's gleaming eyes. He looked like a vulture, waiting to swoop down on carrion. *She* was the carrion: ruined now that English gentlepersons had encountered her past. Vague gossip was one thing, but now they knew she was no lady. She had been ruined since the age of sixteen.

After a few minutes of dead silence, Giles cleared his throat and said, "Would you like me to kill him?"

"What?"

"I could challenge Charles to a duel," Giles said. "He wouldn't put up much of a fight."

"No!"

"I thought you'd say that."

Yasmin struggled to come up with something to say. "If I had been carrying a child, my father intended to force Hippolyte to marry me and then stab him directly afterward."

"Had you been my daughter, I would have done that whether a child was involved or not," Giles said, his voice perfectly even.

"Yes, well, my father is . . . didn't see it that way."

"Are you still planning to retire to the country tomorrow?"

Yasmin gave him an incredulous look. "Yes!" She was trying to decide how many dances she had to endure in order to make it clear that she wasn't running away.

Before she could run away.

And perhaps never return.

His jaw flexed. "Am I to understand that you don't wish me to visit?"

"Why would you?"

"That is petty and unworthy of you."

Yasmin took a sharp breath. "You're right. I'm being childish. Yet there's no need for a lengthy discussion. I have moved from being scandalous to being a fallen woman, in the Biblical parlance. The Countess of Lilford can perhaps have a marred reputation, but she cannot be a trollop."

"Please do not use that word in relation to yourself. May I pay you a visit tonight?"

"No, oh, God, no," Yasmin cried, the raw note in

her voice surprising herself. "Please, Giles. I want to go home and leave for the country tomorrow without another scene. Please. I'm *begging* you."

"You may be carrying our child."

Yasmin gasped, but thankfully, the music was loud enough to prevent eavesdropping. "As I told you, we are not a fertile family," she said in a low voice. "My mother managed it only once, as did my grandmother. In that unlikely event, I will certainly let you know. I will send a letter."

Giles's brows were drawn together, his mouth tight, but the waltz ended.

Jake Addison stepped forward. "My dance, I believe."

"I will write to you," Giles said urgently.

"Very well," Yasmin said. Jake led her directly into a quadrille, which ended in front of Silvester, who swept her into a waltz, followed by Lord Pettigrew in a country dance, then her grandfather in a Scotch reel.

"I think we can leave now," His Grace said as they processed together under an arch of dancers holding hands over their heads, none of them meeting Yasmin's eyes. "Nine days' wonder, my dear. By next Season, they'll have forgotten all about it."

It was not true, but she loved him for saying it. "I would very much like to go home."

They were close to the entrance to the ballroom, so her grandfather simply turned and guided her out the door.

In the carriage, he handed her a handkerchief, but she didn't need one.

"I used to cry so much as a girl," Yasmin told him, managing a wry smile. "But these days I simply walk through it."

"As do I," her grandfather said. "As do I. That might be the definition of maturity, dear."

CHAPTER TWENTY-EIGHT

Ten days later

Dear Giles, if you don't mind the informal address,

I am writing to let you know that my grandfather and I have safely arrived at Portbellow House. However, we have decided to make a prolonged visit to the Duke and Duchess of Trent's country house in Norfolk.

I received your letter, with its kind assurance that you have no intention of breaking your promise to marry me. We both know that is a gentlemanly impulse, but a poor one. The Countess of Lilford, as you have told me many times, should be aligned with virtue. My answer is no. Please consider yourself free of any obligations.

I shall always think of you fondly.

With all best wishes,
Yasmin

A week later

Lydia was a woman who prided herself on decisiveness. She had steered her brother away from a disastrous marriage, and she was growing hopeful that he finally understood how suitable her friend Blanche would be as his wife. The other night, he had talked to Blanche for at least ten minutes about her canaries, and didn't complain on the way home.

Giles wasn't very communicative, but that was her brother. If Lydia hadn't known he was a brilliant debater in the House of Lords, she would never have believed it. No matter how she tried to coach him in the kind of light conversation that would attract a young lady, he just sat at dinner, silent as a stone.

He'd become even worse after the debacle at the Prince Regent's ball.

Since then, he was about as cheerful as a tombstone, which was incredibly childish. Frankly, no end of people had informed him over the last two years that Lady Yasmin was a loose woman. It shouldn't have come as such a shock.

Everyone pitied her for being taken advantage of at such a young age, but facts were facts.

One couldn't pretend the episode never happened. Ruined women were . . . well . . . ruined. Full stop. The episode had made her shudder to see how close *she* had come to a similar fate, though of course her brother would have forced Edwin Turing to marry her, whereas Lady Yasmin's father unaccountably did not.

When she had a daughter, she wouldn't allow her out of her sight.

"Do you have the mail?" Lydia called, seeing a footman with a silver tray piled high. "I'll take that, if you please."

Most of the missives would be for her, people sending congratulations and invitations. She and Lord Pettigrew would marry in just over two months. Her gown was finished, her jointure papers signed. More importantly, she'd learned how to handle her future husband. He didn't like fuss or raised voices, which she privately thought was cowardly but made him easy to manage.

Quickly, she sorted through the mail. One made her eyes narrow as fury turned her cheeks hot. The woman was *writing* to her brother. Lady Yasmin hadn't given up. It wasn't enough that she had distracted Giles from making a decent match for the second Season in a row.

Yasmin must be desperately keeping Giles on a string, tied to her immoral petticoats. She was probably inviting him to the country; Lydia had heard a rumor that she had joined the Duke and Duchess of Trent.

The duke's guests would go from his country house to Mrs. Addison's, then on to another estate, perhaps the Duke of Portbellow's. Yasmin would spend the summer traipsing from one house to another, likely enjoying any number of dalliances.

Giles would be destroyed if he married a woman with such light morals. Destroyed.

He didn't understand what infidelity did to a man. Lydia was certain that her father's suicide stemmed not from his theft—committed years before, after all—but from their mother's flagrant disloyalty.

She crushed the letter into her pocket. "Your correspondence!" she cried, tripping into the study where Giles was working.

She watched as he looked rapidly through the mail and then set the bundle to the side. He was looking for a letter from Yasmin, she realized, with a sick feeling. Her brother turned back to his work without saying a word.

"Did you hear about the house party being thrown by the Duke and Duchess of Trent?" Lydia asked gaily, leaning against his desk.

"We cannot leave London, Lydia. I am needed here. Moreover, your wedding rapidly approaches."

"Oh, I didn't mean that! For one thing, I haven't been invited."

"I have," her brother remarked, still not looking up from the letter he was writing.

Lydia leaned over suspiciously, but saw it was addressed to some lord or other.

"I wouldn't want to go," she said, keeping her voice sprightly. "I hear that all sorts of scandalous activities are going on. Birds of Paradise and opera singers."

Giles carefully put his quill back in the stand. "Lydia, you are a grown woman who is going to be married. You have to stop lying." His eyes were hard as stones.

Heat surged into Lydia's cheeks. "I'm not lying! People are chattering about the party."

"Whether Blanche is chattering or not, you know what she is saying isn't true, so do not repeat it."

Lydia straightened abruptly. "It's nice to know that my elder brother has no faith in me!"

Giles looked up again. "Faith has to be earned, Lydia. I gather that you dislike the duchess, but repeating unpleasant gossip about one of the leaders of society only harms you. If she learns of it, she will never invite you or Lord Pettigrew to future events, let alone one of her house parties."

"I don't dislike the American duchess." Lydia was conscious of a queasy feeling in the pit of her stomach. Perhaps a touch of guilt. "In fact, Lord Pettigrew offered her husband one of his puppies."

"In that case, I assume that you made up a story about Her Grace's party in order to tarnish the reputation of her close friend Lady Yasmin."

"I didn't make it up!"

But she had.

Still, all was fair when it came to protecting one's buffleheaded brother, surely? Giles the Guileless, unable to recognize the machinations of a designing woman. Just look at how trusting he had been as Lydia's chaperone. She could do— and had done—precisely as she wished.

Giles flicked a glance at her, and Lydia saw

very clearly that her brother didn't believe her, which hurt. Though she deserved it.

Fine.

Yasmin's name wouldn't cross her lips again, but she wouldn't merely give in and leave her brother to a sorry fate either.

"Good afternoon," she said, turning around.

She hunted down their butler in his pantry, polishing some silver. "Duckworthy, from now on, please deliver all the mail to me first. My brother tells me that several letters addressed to me have ended up on his desk."

"Aye, my lady," the butler said with complete indifference.

Another week

Dear Giles,

You haven't answered my letter . . . Perhaps foolishly, I am hoping that we can still be friends. I intend to return to society, you see, and brave it out. I have experience in that. You didn't ask, but I find I would like to tell you about Hippolyte.

Monsieur Charles was so dashing to a silly sixteen-year-old. Most people in the court ignored me, since my mother was engaged in an affaire *with Napoleon; Empress Joséphine was livid. It made Hippolyte's attentions all the more potent.*

I was as stupid as you can imagine, treasuring every whispered compliment and clandestine letter. I foolishly accepted his assurances that he could not court me openly, or even dance with me, because of my mother, or so he said.

After a few months, he lured me into an elopement, arranging for a ceremony with a false priest. He kept me in a cottage for a week before laughingly telling my parents what he had done. He offered to marry me if they gave him an estate.

But I gather his most important mission was to communicate Empress Joséphine's contemptuous congratulations.

She knew, you see. She more than knew: she planned it. She loathed my mother for seducing Napoleon, and Hippolyte was a weapon close to hand. They had been lovers, which everyone but myself knew. My ruination was the perfect revenge for an angry empress.

The two of them laughed openly about how easily I'd been seduced. I thought I outgrew the pain, but I didn't. It affected my attitude toward intimacy. My clothing is provocative because I cannot give in to how gossips characterize me. Still, inside, I have always felt disgusted by the memory of my own behavior.

You taught me not to be ashamed, and I will always be grateful.

I don't have much more to say than that. I wanted you to know that although I was a silly girl, I was outgunned, as they say.

All best wishes,
Yasmin

Two weeks later

Dear Giles,

I haven't heard anything from you, likely because
you agree with the wisdom of my first letter. Or
because you are busy. I read the account of your
fiery speech in Lords. Bravo!
    My grandfather's new puppy has been deliv-
ered. He has named him Puck, after the mischievous Shakespeare character. He got hold of one of
His Grace's favorite velvet slippers . . .

And a week later . . .

Dear Giles,

I have decided to ignore the fact that you are not
writing to me. I am used to embarrassing myself,
after all. The French court believed I would quietly fade out of society after that dreadful thing
happened with Hippolyte. I keep imagining that
perhaps my letters are going astray, so in case
they are, I told you in an earlier letter about how
silly I was at sixteen. Yet I insisted on returning to French society two years later. I could not
allow that malicious creature, Hippolyte, to ruin
my entire life.
    The scandal followed me here, along with the
lascivious gazes, the pinches, and the rest of it.

But at least I held my head high. I suppose that's why I'm still writing to you. I am too stubborn to accept it when people turn their back.

We had a conversation at dinner last night that made me think of you . . .

Another week, two letters, another week . . .

Dear Giles,

My grandfather and I have been invited to Cleo and Jake's country house, so we will travel there tomorrow.

My grandfather's correspondents tell him that Lydia and her betrothed are celebrated everywhere. I'm sure you know of the attention paid to her wedding gown in the gossip columns. I also read that you are certain to marry Lady Stella, having danced with her twice at a ball.

I have been thinking about my first letter, the one in which I told you that I would not marry you. Your silence seems to agree with me. Certainly, I am not what you wish for in a countess. In my own defense, I am faithful and principled. I have integrity, and Hippolyte is the only man whom I allowed to take advantage of me. Before you.

I'm forcing myself to write this final letter, to tell you that I've changed my mind about our marriage, and I hope you will at least consider it.

For years, I have never wanted to kiss anyone,

until I met you. In fact, the very idea was repellent. My revulsion stemmed from the aftermath of that dreadful affaire, *the way people in the French court characterized me as a grisette, a* bonne amie *looking for another man.*

Yet from the moment I saw you, I wanted to kiss you.

The truth is that I have fallen in love with you.

I am hopeful that you might come to love me as I am. That you chose a woman who is undignified because that person—me—will make you happy. I know my reputation is wretched. But couldn't we overcome the scandal together?

Please write me back. I have penned this letter eleven times and crumpled it each time. I am going to force myself to send this to you.

In all sincerity,
Yasmin

LYDIA DID NOT like getting up early. But in the service of her family, she forced herself downstairs at the crack of dawn to sift through the mail waiting to be handed over to the post. Sure enough, her brother—her poor, besotted brother—was writing to Yasmin every night. One day he wrote to her *twice*.

The woman wrote to him as well, not as frequently, but regularly. A day came when a letter from Yasmin appeared on the entry table after luncheon; luckily, Lydia noticed it in passing. That Frenchified handwriting caught her attention.

The return address was for Mr. Addison, so apparently, Yasmin had moved on to another house party.

"My dear brother," Lydia said at dinner that night, "so many people are asking me whether you have a *tendre* for Lady Stella. Surely, you feel, as I do, that the lady is principled and intelligent. Her spectacles are strangely flattering."

Giles looked at her over his roast beef. "I like her."

Excellent.

"Do you like her more than you like Blanche?" she asked boldly.

"Yes."

With that, Lydia gave up her hope of seeing Blanche as a countess. Stella would do. If only Lydia could be certain that Giles's attachment to Yasmin had been fleeting and died from not seeing her. Not to mention not hearing from her.

Yet he kept writing the woman every night.

Lydia found it pitiful. Her brother had no dignity. Yasmin never responded! Well, she had responded, but he didn't know that.

As far as he knew, Yasmin had turned to another man.

Giles's persistence was beginning to pose a problem, given Lydia's upcoming nuptials. She and Rupert would travel to Belgium on their wedding trip, tracking a rumor of excellent bloodhounds bred to high standards. She was looking forward to being Lady Pettigrew, a future marchioness.

If only she didn't have to worry about her brother sending more pitiable letters, once she wasn't there to confiscate them.

Just when she was considering that she might have to bribe Duckworthy, Giles missed a day. She crept down the stairs in the early morning and discovered the salver in the entry held a few letters to peers . . . and nothing for Lady Yasmin.

Another day passed without a letter, and then a third.

The morning before her wedding day, fortune turned in her favor. She and Giles were seated at breakfast, and Lydia was devouring *The Morning Post*'s gossip column, which not only detailed her wedding gown but claimed, untruthfully, that she would arrive at St. Paul's in a coach drawn by four white horses. Without question, crowds of Londoners would cluster around the church door, hoping the groom would toss coins.

"Goodness me," Lydia said, clearing her throat. "I know that I have been rather unkind to Lady Yasmin, but I must be the first to offer my congratulations. It says here that she has agreed to become a duchess."

Her brother didn't look up, but she saw a pulse beating in his forehead. "Indeed?" he said flatly.

Another person might have thought that he

had lost interest in the woman, but Lydia knew Giles. His lips had tightened. In fact, he looked so forbidding that she actually felt a bit nervous. But after all, she was merely noting what was written in the newspaper.

"Here," she said, handing over the sheet. "You can read it for yourself. I have a hundred things to do before tomorrow morning!" And with that, she left.

The next morning, she confiscated one final letter addressed to Yasmin, her last-ditch effort to save her brother from a terrible marriage.

There is only so much you can do for a person. She pitied Giles; she truly did. She had done her best, and she would marry Rupert with a clear conscience. Her father would have been proud of her efforts. The late earl may have been weak and light-fingered as a youth, but he would have hated to see his son repeat his marital mistakes.

The next morning, she walked slowly down the aisle of St. Paul's Cathedral, her hand tucked under her brother's elbow. She caught sight of two girls who had tormented her at school and sailed past them with a bright smile.

She would be a marchioness, whereas neither of them had found a husband. No one had murmured a word about her father's thefts in months, and no one had discovered that she was fathered by a footman.

When she was Lady Pettigrew, no one would even wonder about her birth.

At the end of the aisle, Rupert turned around to meet her, his brown eyes rather anxious. He had a strange likeness to a basset hound, but she smiled at him, anyway.

He was a sweet man, and they both liked dogs, and that would be good enough.

CHAPTER TWENTY-NINE

A broken heart is a stark kind of pain. In Yasmin's case, it didn't make her burst into gales of tears, or write ranting letters, or have the slightest impulse to tell anyone.

After his first letter, Giles had never written again. Of course, he was busy. Likely, he was irritated at her. Perhaps he hated her. Unquestionably, he agreed with her first letter, breaking off their engagement.

It felt as if a shard of glass lodged deeper in her heart as the days went by. She'd walk around a corner and discover Cleo in her husband's arms. The shard would shift, sending pain streaking through her chest. She had been certain Giles would respond to her letter about Hippolyte, but every day that passed without mail, the shard gouged again.

Finally, she wrote him a last letter . . . *that* letter. The one saying she loved him.

She didn't send it through the post, because she kept worrying that perhaps her other letters had been lost in the post. Instead, she dispatched one of Jake's grooms all the way to London. He reported that he had handed the letter to the Earl of Lilford's butler, who promised it would be waiting when His Lordship returned from Parliament.

Days passed, a week . . .

Giles didn't write back.

How could he not respond, after she put her heart on the page? She had other things she needed to tell him.

But she faltered at the idea of writing into that silent void.

After all, Giles wasn't injured or dead. The papers reported near daily on his oratorial prowess, when they weren't detailing his blooming romance with Lady Stella or simply mentioning him escorting his sister to this or that event.

One night she dreamed that he was tossing her unread letters into a ditch. The next night she dreamed that he galloped away, leaving her on a dusty road, and when she looked down, she was holding a little girl by the hand.

Her father had maintained dignity in the face of his wife's lust for an emperor. Yasmin could do the same while her betrothal was besieged by the bespeckled, befreckled Lady Stella.

That was not fair to the lady. She herself had broken off their betrothal before Lady Stella and Giles were linked in the press. Still, she would write no more letters. Dignity would bring her through. Or at least, that's what she told herself in the middle of the night.

Every morning, she woke convinced that Giles was not in love with Stella. Far more likely, once

Yasmin was out of sight, and desire waned, he turned back to his work and forgot about her.

Then night would fall, and with it came fear and shame. Giles had decided she was too scandalous, too frivolous, too stupid to marry. She had slept with him before marriage. He had never bothered to buy her an engagement ring. His sister hated her.

Undeniable facts made Yasmin feel defenseless and vulnerable. Desired, but not respected. Fairness made her admit there wasn't much about her to respect. Likely Hippolyte told everyone in London how lustful she'd been.

Shame squirmed in her stomach and made her feel more nauseated than the babe she was carrying was already doing.

"Why hasn't your earl paid us any visits?" her grandfather grumbled over breakfast. "And why aren't you eating your toast? You love toast. Shall I ask for kippers?"

Yasmin felt herself turning pale. "No!" she gasped.

Her grandfather narrowed his eyes. "Shall I ask for some ale?"

"Absolutely not." She felt a little dizzy, meeting his eyes.

Cleo walked into the room, tossing a laughing rejoinder over her shoulder at her husband.

"The fiancé of yours hasn't sloped off, has he?" the duke asked. "Just when you need him?"

"I don't need anyone," Yasmin said lightly. "I have you, Grandfather."

His Grace reached his hand across the table and took hers. "You do have me."

Yasmin managed a wobbly smile.

Cleo said, "I agree with your grandfather: Where is that fiancé of yours?"

"It's a secret betrothal," Yasmin said uncomfortably.

"If I were engaged to you, I would shout it from the rooftops," Jake Addison said, grunting when his wife poked him in the side. "That is, of course, if I hadn't already married my delightful wife."

Yasmin fiddled with her fork. She had thought that perhaps if she wrote to Giles saying that she loved him, he would answer. In that case, she wouldn't have to inform him that they *had* to marry because of the babe. It was so mortifying.

She and Giles could no longer break the engagement; she was carrying a child.

Yasmin shook her head. Across the table, Jake was piling scrambled eggs scattered with chives on his plate. The odor was revolting. "If you'll forgive me," she gasped, jumping to her feet.

She was barely in her room before she fell on her knees before the chamber pot. She didn't realize Cleo had followed her until her friend draped a cool, damp cloth on the back of her neck.

Yasmin bit back a sob. "I peed in that pot last night." She started sobbing. "Now I cast up my accounts on top, which is revolting. I almost never cry!"

Cleo curled an arm around her waist and pulled her to her feet. "Goodness me, you're tall.

Almost as tall as I am, aren't you? Come over here." She led Yasmin to an armchair and pushed her into it without ceremony.

Turning away, she dropped another linen cloth in the basin and wrung it out. "For your forehead. Now, where's your fiancé?"

"In London," Yasmin said, her voice breaking. "I wrote him a letter breaking off our engagement before I knew I was carrying a child. Since then, I've written letters that he hasn't answered. I had the groom deliver a letter to his house, but he didn't answer that either."

"Well, spit!" Cleo exclaimed.

Yasmin blinked.

"Vastly improper American slang that Merry taught me," Cleo explained. "I don't know Lilford terribly well, but this isn't characteristic behavior, is it?"

Yasmin shook her head. "I wrote one letter that I would give anything to take back," she blurted out. "Two, actually. First, I broke off our engagement. Then I . . . I told him how I felt about him. Now I'm so humiliated. Of course, I put him on the spot, and he wouldn't have liked that."

"Do you love him?"

Yasmin nodded. "I just wish I hadn't told him."

"Does he know of the babe?"

"No." She took a deep breath. "I hoped he would marry me for a better reason."

"I shall send *my* husband to fetch *your* future husband," Cleo said, dusting her hands together. "Lilford has no choice about marriage now that you're carrying a child. His lordship can explain his correspondence failures in person."

Pure humiliation made tears press on Yasmin's eyes again. "Your husband has more important things to do."

"He will understand," Cleo said. "Happy marriages require conversation. Misunderstandings cannot be allowed to fester."

"Giles is tremendously busy in the House of Lords. He puts things . . . me . . . out of his mind when he's working."

Cleo frowned.

"He divides his life into boxes," Yasmin said, knowing how foolish it sounded. "I suspect my box is stored in a far corner. The attic, perhaps."

A flash of pity crossed Cleo's face. "No wife should be in a box *or* an attic," she said, adding, "Parliament adjourned a week ago. What's more, you wrote him that important letter. Two of them. He should be here."

"What if Giles refuses to accompany your husband?" Yasmin asked, swallowing back tears.

"No one refuses Jake Addison," his wife said with satisfaction. "It's the American side of him. You'll have the father of that babe at our front door in no time."

Embarrassment was a cold lump in Yasmin's stomach. Her fiancé had to be fetched, like a recalcitrant schoolboy. "I'll have to tell Giles about the baby." A sob forced its way out of her chest. "I don't know why I'm so emotional. I never cry." She snatched up a handkerchief Cleo offered.

"The baby does it," Cleo said. "Merry told me that when she was carrying her first, she came across a dying heifer with a newborn calf and cried for two days."

Yasmin's eyes widened. "Its mother had died?"

"Merry fed it with a bottle!" Cleo said hastily. And then got up to fetch another handkerchief.

CHAPTER THIRTY

Giles saw his sister and her new husband off for their wedding trip with a rush of relief. It wasn't just that Lydia was safely married. Yasmin's silence was driving him mad.

If she thought he would allow her to break their engagement, she was wrong. He would sue her for breach of promise. He was compelled to find her, to keep her. Even if, as he thought in his worst moments, she had chosen another man.

His trunk had been loaded on his traveling coach since dawn.

Bidding farewell to guests at the marriage breakfast following the ceremony was an excruciating exercise in patience. He didn't encourage chattering; he had Duckworthy bring outer garments to the entry long before people might have expected to depart.

He was saying goodbye to a set of distant cousins when he realized that one man remained.

He wasn't a guest.

Jake Addison was leaning against the door to Giles's library, arms crossed over his broad chest.

Giles stilled. Jake had the promise of violence in his eyes.

"May I be of service?" Giles asked. He had no fear of Jake. In fact, he would welcome an opportunity to box him. It would be a fair match; they were both burly men. These days he felt buffeted by rage and happy to make use of it.

"Yes. You can come with me."

"I'm sorry, but I have somewhere I must be."

"You can postpone it, or I can knock you unconscious and throw you in my carriage."

"Are you out of your mind?" Giles asked in disbelief. "I don't care to fight you, but you couldn't knock me unconscious."

The American's eyes narrowed.

Giles didn't bother to flex his muscles. "Why are you here? Where do you want to take me?"

"Where's your fiancée?" Jake replied insolently.

Fury spilled through Giles's limbs like acid. "My fiancée." He spoke through his teeth. "Why do you ask? She's with friends."

"Are you sure?" Insolence shone from Jake's eyes.

"Are you her messenger boy, then?"

Jake's fist curled. "Do you want to be knocked down in your own entry?"

"You could try." Duckworthy was hovering at the back of the entry, gaping at the two of them. Giles looked to his butler. "Has the traveling coach been brought around?"

"Yes, my lord. Your trunk is strapped to the

back. Your valet is just packing a few last necessities."

"Perhaps you're not the fool I thought," Jake allowed. "She's at my house. You might as well come with me. Your coach can follow more slowly. I'm in a chaise with a good team, and can be home by tonight."

Giles froze. "Is Yasmin ill?" His heart twisted. "Is something wrong with her?"

"No," Jake said. "Though given your patent disregard for her well-being, I'm surprised you give a damn."

The Earl of Lilford had never impulsively attacked any man other than Hippolyte Charles, even those who infuriated him in the House of Lords. His sister was the impetuous one in the family; he considered himself a measured, thoughtful, boring man.

Now his mind turned black with rage. He launched himself at Addison without a thought more than the wish to do grave injury, to knock that smirk off the American's face. His fist rounded into the man's cheekbone at the same moment that Jake's fist caught him in the chest. The force of blows rocked them both back. But rather than square up for another round, the American started laughing, deep peals of laughter coming from his chest.

Giles dropped his hands. The man was cracked. "Where the hell is my valet!" Giles barked at Duckworthy.

The butler scurried through the green baize door at the back of the entry.

"I'll take it that you do give a damn," Jake said, gingerly feeling around his eyes. "Damn it, you've given me a black eye."

"She's my *fiancée*," Giles snarled.

"My wife and I exchange letters daily when I'm away," Jake said.

Giles felt a torrent of rage followed by bitter shame. Yasmin didn't care to write him back. She didn't love him the way Cleo did her husband. The feeling backed up in his throat like sour milk. "My fiancée is not comfortable writing in the English language," he managed.

Addison straightened up. "You are ignoring her letters because they're written in her mother tongue? You plan to marry her, you pigheaded man. Bloody well learn French!"

Giles's chest tightened as if steel bands were around it. "She doesn't write to me in French either," he said curtly.

"The devil she doesn't! She's stayed up at night writing letters to you. Don't try to feed me a cock-and-bull story about not receiving them, because one of my grooms brought a letter to this very door and gave it to your butler."

Shock swept through Giles. He literally couldn't understand the words at first, his mind picking through them and trying to put them into reasonable sense. "She didn't."

"She did." Jake peered into the entry mirror,

pressing on his eye bone. "My wife isn't going to be happy with you. You'll be lucky if she doesn't take out your spleen with a hatpin once she sees my eye. She wields it like a weapon."

Giles ignored him.

Yasmin had written to him. Letters, to him. A letter sent by a groom so it didn't go astray. It made no sense.

"Duckworthy!"

His butler popped from the back like a startled hare.

Giles's voice emerged in a bellow, rather than a measured query. "Did one of Mr. Addison's grooms deliver a letter, addressed to me?"

"Why, yes, he did," Duckworthy said nervously, licking his lips. "Around two weeks ago, I'd say, wouldn't you?"

"I wouldn't say because I never saw it," Giles said. "What in the bloody hell happened to that letter?"

The butler's eyes nearly popped out of his head. "Nothing happened to it, my lord. Nothing at all. Why, I put it right here, where all your letters go." He pointed a shaking hand at the silver salver on the entry table.

"I never saw it." Giles took a step closer to Duckworthy.

"Not the butler," Jake said behind his back. "He's too thin. One blow from those mitts of yours, and the man will land in the next county."

Duckworthy audibly gulped. "I told the groom

that it would be right there when you returned from the House of Lords. That's what I do with letters that arrive by messenger, my lord."

Jake Addison strolled forward. "Someone took that letter," he said, looking interested. "What about the others?" he asked the butler. "Lady Yasmin wrote quite a few letters. I gather that Lilford here didn't receive them."

"Any mail that came I . . . I . . ." Duckworthy's eyes bulged again.

"Yes?" The word snapped from Giles's throat, gritty and enraged.

He saw it now. He knew—

"I delivered the morning mail to Lady Lydia so that she could remove her own mail before the rest was delivered to His Lordship," the butler squeaked.

The truth settled in Giles's gut like burning lava. His sister had taken his letters. Blithely taken his correspondence, not giving a damn that he was—

He turned his head to Jake. "Are you here because my fiancée did not receive any correspondence from me?"

"Yup. No letters for weeks as I understand it. I suppose your sister intercepted yours as well?"

"I frank my correspondence at night to save time and place it here, in the entry," Giles said dully.

"The mail is picked up the next morning," Duckworthy agreed, nodding madly.

"I suppose the girl skulked around, made sure

that she pinched your letters before the post took them. Rum thing to do, trying to ruin her brother's engagement."

Rage slid away, followed by sadness. Giles couldn't blame this on Lydia's impulsiveness. Week after week, she had actively tried to destroy the most important relationship of his life. Yet the scenario made sense. Lydia used to sleep late until a few months ago, when she began waking early. When he commented, she said that she was practicing to be a good wife.

Smiling at him over the breakfast table after having stolen his and Yasmin's letters.

"Lydia didn't know we were betrothed," he told Jake.

"Not good enough," he retorted, his eyes disdainful. "Spiteful thing to do."

Would Lydia have destroyed the letters? Without another word, Giles brushed past Duckworthy, standing white-faced at the newel post, and bounded up the stairs.

His valet passed him on the way down. "I am ready, my lord. I added a few more pressed neck scarves to your trunk."

Jake was at Giles's heels. "Your master will be traveling with me."

"You can follow in the coach," Giles told the valet over his shoulder. He strode down the corridor and pushed open the door to his sister's room without ceremony. A maid was on her knees, gathering ribbons and lace that would be sent to the bride's new home.

It was a large room, wallpapered in a cloying pink that Lydia said flattered her skin. The bed was topped with a carved giltwood corona hung with white brocade trimmed with rosy pompoms. All of her furniture was gilt as well, most of it imported from Italy, as was the corona.

Jake walked in the door after him and gave a low whistle. "Fit for a princess."

Giles looked about slowly, hands on his hips. Since it was summer, the fireplace looked unused.

"If I was pilfering mail, I'd burn it," Jake said, following his gaze. "Wouldn't want the evidence left behind, would I?"

"Did Lady Lydia regularly ask for a fire at night?" Giles barked at the maid, who had straightened, gaping at him over a handful of ribbons.

"No, my lord. I don't think so."

Giles jerked his head. "Ask Duckworthy."

"Immediately, sir," she said, bobbing a curtsy before she trotted out of the room.

"Mattress?" Jake asked, going to the bed. Giles joined him, and they flipped the heavy horsehair mattress onto its side. Nothing underneath either.

"It would be a large bundle, if she kept all the letters I wrote," Giles said.

"Wrote to Yasmin regularly, did you?" The American wandered over to Lydia's dressing table and began opening the drawers.

"Every day."

"That will cheer her up," Jake said. "Not that Yasmin is one to wear her heart on her sleeve, but she's been looking peaky."

Rage throbbed in Giles's veins. He tipped up the sofa, but there was nothing under it.

His sister had a waist-high bookcase on one side of the room, filled mostly with novels in three-book sets. Giles grabbed a bound volume with gold-leaf edges and riffled through the pages.

"No letters here." He dropped the book on the floor and took another one. Jake joined him, and for five minutes the only sounds in the room were ruffled pages and the gentle thump of rejected books.

"Wait!" Jake said. "Look at the bottom row. Perhaps the letters are behind." The books were perfectly lined up to the edge of the shelf, whereas on the upper shelves they were pushed in, allowing room for the ceramic sheep that Lydia collected. Jake crouched down and swept the row of books out at once. They fell to the floor with a puff of dust and flurry of pages, leaving an empty shelf.

"She had a commode. Where is it?" Giles strode over to the bed and found Lydia's wooden stepstool shoved against the wall. He hauled it out and opened the step that concealed a commode, but the hidden chamber pot was missing. "Where's the chamber pot?"

"Likely, she preferred to visit the privy instead," Jake said. He had checked the remaining books and was stacking them in short towers.

"I don't have a water closet on this floor, only downstairs."

"And you count yourself friends with my wife?

Tsk, tsk. We have her commodes on every level. If my wife had her way, there'd be a water closet attached to every bedchamber."

"I could imagine Lydia throwing Yasmin's letters into a chamber pot. That would amuse her."

"Charming," Jake said, looking behind the drapes. "If the letters were stuffed in the commode or the chamber pot, for that matter, her maid would have found them."

Giles's curse was met with a wry smile. "Time to leave," Jake continued. "My wife gets tetchy if I'm not home before dark. You can explain yourself and your purloined letters in person."

Giles cast one last look around the room. Would Lydia, his own sister, actually burn his letters? And if so, *how*? He looked at the bed again, then stepped onto the stool positioned beside it and looked on top of the gilt corona.

There they were.

Letters spilled across the white brocade that topped the bed, some in Yasmin's looping hand and others in his. From the look of it, Lydia had flipped letters onto the top of the bed.

Two minutes later, a footman was brushing letters to the ground with a broom.

"I apologize, my lord," Duckworthy said, his voice quavering. "I'd have never imagined that Lady Lydia would do such a thing. I've known her since she was a little girl. I'm sure she didn't mean to cause harm."

Giles didn't agree, but he did know that Lydia wouldn't have spent much time considering the ethics of the situation, any more than his mother used to when launching her lawsuits. Lydia wanted to win, and that meant eliminating Yasmin by any means possible.

He heaved a basket filled with crumpled, dusty letters into Addison's chaise.

Jake settled into the corner. "Having enraged my wife a time or two, I have some advice to offer."

The last thing Giles wanted was advice. But he was in the man's vehicle. "Yes?"

"On your knees," Jake said flatly. "On. Your. Knees. Your bloody sister stole Yasmin's letters, but you didn't follow your fiancée to the country when you didn't hear from her, did you? You wrote more letters, but you didn't get in a fast carriage to see if she'd been taken ill."

"I knew she wasn't ill."

"How?"

"My sister read the gossip columns aloud at breakfast. Yasmin was often mentioned."

"Most of the news is made up from whole cloth," Jake pointed out. "One of our guests—not knowing of your secret betrothal—told the dinner table the other night that you were stitching up a marriage with Lady Stella. I don't suppose that made Yasmin very happy."

"I didn't let myself think of Yasmin being ill," Giles said, the truth wrenched out of him. "I thought she wanted to break our engagement, that she might have chosen another man. I had to keep my sister's betrothal afloat, so I planned to join her the moment Lydia married."

They were silent for a few minutes.

"I feel sorry for Pettigrew," Jake said.

"She likes him." It was a lame excuse, and Giles knew it. "They both like dogs."

"It was his choice," Jake said. "More the fool he. Still, you've got a steep hill ahead of you. My point is that Yasmin should matter more than your dignity."

"I see." He did.

"Don't read her letters now," Jake suggested. "Do it together."

The carriage jolted on. Jake braced himself in a corner and went to sleep with the ease of a man who often spent days on the road. Giles stayed awake, allowing himself to recognize the cold feeling he felt as terror, stark terror.

He fully expected a wheel to come off. A milk cart to cross the road. A horse to go lame. Instead, Jake's carriage pulled into an inn and smoothly changed to a fresh team. He and Jake used the necessary, then climbed back into the carriage, devouring the roast chicken handed over by the innkeeper.

Jake entertained them both by telling the story of how the Duke of Trent managed to marry his brother's fiancée. Giles nodded here and there, watching the mile posts flash by. His heart was thumping a rhythm that spelled out the name of his betrothed.

The name of the woman he loved.

CHAPTER THIRTY-ONE

When Jake Addison's carriage bowled through the tall gates that surrounded his country estate, Yasmin was in the drawing room alone. Cleo was working in her study upstairs.

She was seated at the window, practicing a crochet stitch that made it easier to create strings adorned with scraps of silk. One of Merry's sons wanted a kite with twelve tails. It would never take flight, in her opinion, but that wasn't relevant.

Her host's chaise was a sleek green vehicle built for speed. She saw it coming from far away as it swept down the long avenue lined by elms. She watched Giles climb from the carriage, shake himself, and stride into the house.

She began trembling and put her crochet work to the side.

Giles walked into the room carrying a covered basket. He pushed the door shut behind him without a word. He was pale, his eyes tight and shadowed, his jaw hard, a pulse beating in his forehead.

Yasmin didn't smile, an errant bolt of pride flaring up her backbone. "I see that your right hand has not been amputated," she said, because a lady needs to claim some self-respect. "I thought perhaps injury had prevented you from answering my letters."

Giles walked across the room to her, dropped the basket, and stood, looking down at her. "Good evening, Yasmin." Courteous as always. Remote, polite, solicitous.

Even if he had chosen Lady Stella, he would have to change his mind, given the child Yasmin carried. A knot twisted in her stomach. Yasmin opened her mouth to give him the bad news, but he snatched her to her feet and kissed her hard.

"What?" she breathed, and he took advantage, deepening the kiss until her heart thudded in her chest. One hand curled around the back of her head, holding her in place, apparently not realizing she was clinging to him. It was wildly erotic and endearing at the same time.

By the time Giles drew away, Yasmin's mind was reeling. He was not going to marry Stella. They still had fierce, sweet desire between them. Surely that was enough.

It would have to be enough, given the babe.

The thought made her drop onto the window seat again. "We must talk." She curled her fingers, realizing her hand was visibly trembling.

Giles sat down and picked up the basket, putting it between them and flipping open the hinged top. Yasmin's mouth fell open. It was full of letters: dusty, crumpled letters mostly franked with the Earl of Lilford's seal.

"Unsent?" she whispered. She raised her eyes, flabbergasted. "What on earth?"

His Adam's apple bobbed as he swallowed. "Lydia." Giles's voice was even but she could hear grating fury beneath the word.

Yasmin blinked. *"What?"*

"My sister stole our correspondence."

Yasmin reached out and turned over some letters. "You wrote all of these?"

"I wrote to you every day, though you never answered. I thought you'd left me, but I kept writing. I wanted to come to you, but I had to stay in London with Lydia."

She stared down at the letters and then back up at Giles, stunned.

His mouth twisted, and he caught up her hands. "Did you think I didn't care?"

"I thought perhaps you wanted a better . . . a different wife." She swallowed hard around the knot in her throat. "Or you didn't have time to write. You were too busy."

Giles didn't care for her as much as Yasmin would like him to . . . but marriage could take care of that, couldn't it? He might fall in love with her in time.

Learn to love her.

The way your mother loved you? a small voice in the back of her mind inquired. *Or your father, who blithely bid you farewell, not knowing if he'd see you again?*

Yasmin took a deep breath. Suddenly she remembered the letter in which she bared her heart. The one that she had lain awake wishing that she hadn't sent. She riffled through the pile, pouncing on a thicker one in her handwriting. "I'll keep this one."

His brows drew together. "Why?"

"Because I wish to." She tried to stuff it in her pocket, but it wouldn't fit, so she tucked it down her bodice instead. Giles's eyes rested on her breasts. Her neckline wasn't terribly low but her breasts were overflowing a bodice that used to fit. "There are no men here to gawk at me," she said defensively. "I'm not creating a scandal."

"I was wrong to try to ask you to dress differently," Giles said abruptly. "You are exquisite in whatever you wear, and it's none of my business." He stopped. "I was just so damned jealous, Yasmin. I started to feel as if I was losing my mind."

Yasmin's throat ached so she cleared it. "You quite naturally want your countess to be dignified and proper."

"No," he said flatly. "I just want my countess to be you. *You*, whatever you wear. I don't want you to blanket yourself in fabric. I want you to be yourself, to dress as you wish. You're perfect just as you are."

A little spark of joy made itself known, but Yasmin reminded herself that they had to talk about several things, including the baby. She looked down at the basket, trying to figure out how to discuss love without sounding wretchedly childish.

The basket was full of letters. Surely that was a good sign? "Why did Lydia do it?" Yasmin asked, turning over a couple. "I know she didn't like me but this is . . ."

"You will never see her again. Ever."

Yasmin sighed. "She's your sister, Giles."

His jaw set. "Did my silence make you unhappy, Yasmin?"

She found one of her letters, avoiding his eyes. "Yes."

"I lay awake at night, tormenting myself by imagining you turning away from me. At breakfast, she read aloud newspaper accounts pairing you with other men."

Yasmin bit her lip. "I thought you had forgotten about me when I wasn't there. Or that you had realized Lady Stella would make a better countess which, to be fair, she surely would."

Giles lunged to his feet and drew his hand through his hair. "I can't keep you separate from my working life, Yasmin!" His voice was a growl. "I can't stop thinking of you, day or night. I didn't know if you were safe or happy. If you hated me or had injured yourself. The last weeks were endless."

"Then why?" she asked, but her voice quavered.

"Why didn't I come to you? Why didn't I drop Lydia with a chaperone and find you, wherever you were? Jake Addison would have done it. He as much as charged me with being an idiot."

Yasmin knew the answer to his questions.

Jake was in love with Cleo, and that made all the difference.

"Our marriage won't be the same as theirs," she said, clearing her throat. "After I broke off our engagement—"

He wheeled about. "You broke off our engagement?"

Yasmin fidgeted. "In a letter."

"I never received it. Presumably, it's in the basket."

He crouched down in front of her. "I want you to care." The words sounded as if they were wrenched from his chest.

"I do care. I—I do. Why didn't you come find me?" Despite herself, her voice had a thread of anguish.

"It would have meant that I had to admit to *feeling*." His jaw flexed. "I'm damned jealous of any man near you, Yasmin. It was easier when I couldn't see you across the room. But I couldn't—I couldn't bear the—" He stopped and started over, the most eloquent man in the House of Lords floundering.

"You were jealous," Yasmin prompted.

"Jealousy is a terrible emotion, not behooving a gentleman, a primitive, stupid instinct. My father was a complete gentleman. He loved me and Lydia, though we were likely fathered by different men. I never heard him say a cross word to my mother. I will not be as civilized. We will quite likely argue." His gaze was unnervingly direct.

"Your father didn't care about your mother, did he, Giles?"

"He was very fond of her."

"Not loving, though."

His lashes flicked. "Perhaps not."

"That allowed him to be so gentlemanly. If you sleep with Lady Stella," she said with a gasp, "I shall do something terrible."

He was still crouched before her. "I have dreamed of dismembering Silvester, whom I've known since childhood," Giles said flatly. "That is one reason why I didn't come find you, Yasmin."

"Didn't you want to be *with* me?" She sounded pathetic.

"Of course I want you."

Her heart sank. "I do know that."

"Because I *love* you," he said grimly. "Damn it to hell."

After a moment of shock, a shaky smile crossed her lips. "Earls don't curse. I have it on the best authority."

"I'm no authority." He shifted forward and went to his knees, wrapping his arms around her waist. "I can't bear the idea of being apart from you ever again. I mean to tell you that I love you, morning and night and in between."

"Are you sure?" she asked, the meaning of his words slowly filtering into her mind.

"Marry me. Please marry me. I want to wed

you next Season with pomp and circumstance and the whole of polite society in the cathedral."

Yasmin felt a surge of happiness so intense that it felt as if her skin prickled. "No."

His eyes turned bleak, and she realized how much power she had over Giles. Over the man she loved most in the world.

"You don't love me?"

"I love you. I'm in love with you." She leaned forward, and their lips met.

She held his face in her hands, kissing him fiercely.

"Will you make love to me?" His voice was hoarse.

At her joyous nod, he moved the basket to the floor, stood up, and pulled up her skirts.

"Giles! I thought you meant in a bedchamber!"

"May I?"

She laughed.

A rip signaled silk smalls torn apart. Yasmin almost came with the first rough swipe of his thumb. She was wet and ready, had been from the moment he strode into the room. Shameful—but she refused to accept that emotion.

"God, I missed you," Giles groaned out. He sat down, pulled her on top of him. "All right?"

Yasmin giggled. "I love it when my oh, so proper earl loses his head."

Kissing her, he held her up and thrust inside, filling her so suddenly that she winced.

Instantly, he stilled. "Not good?"

"Wait," Yasmin gasped. "A minute. I need to—I need a minute. What if someone comes in?"

"They would have no idea," Giles said into her ear. "Look down, Yasmin."

Her satin overskirt had billowed around them, falling from the window seat to the floor.

"Not that Jake's butler would ever allow someone to enter this room." A rumble of amusement went through his voice. "He's no fool."

She took a deep breath. The feeling of being uncomfortably full was easing. She wiggled.

He drew out the letter stuck in her bodice. "May I read this someday?"

Yasmin gave him a mischievous smile. "Perhaps."

Giles tossed it into the basket and yanked down her bodice. His mouth bent to her breast, and she sighed, wrapping a hand around the back of his neck. Then her eyes widened as he effortlessly lifted her in the air until only the very end of his thick cock was still inside.

"Yes?" he asked hoarsely.

Yasmin nodded and gasped when he let her body slide down at the same moment he thrust up. Slowly, he began to rhythmically flex beneath her, his hips rising over and over until she had to clench her teeth to stop cries flying into the air.

"You feel so good," he grunted, his hands holding her hips tightly. "I love making love to you like this." He lifted her again and let their bodies slide back together so she felt every inch of him.

Sweat was prickling on Yasmin's back and behind her knees. She was clinging to his shoulders, allowing every thrust to jolt pleasure through her body, chasing a wanton heat that was spreading through her legs. "Like what?" she breathed. "Oh, please, go faster."

"No." Giles leaned in and nipped her earlobe with his teeth. "Slow is best."

Yasmin clenched him intimately, as hard as she could.

"Vixen," he breathed.

"Hmmm." Rather than wait for him, she wedged her knees beside his legs and rose up, high enough to let their bodies separate. Then she laughed at the expression on his face, reached under her skirts, and caught him unerringly in her hand. He was smooth and wet and hot to the touch.

She rubbed him over her folds, which felt so good that she threw back her head and groaned before she slowly, slowly, slid downward, gasping when she had taken him fully. "My earl is so puritanical in public," she whispered, her breath shuddering. "Wild in private. Though this is arguably public."

"Look there, Yasmin," Giles said, nodding to the right.

She turned her head and caught sight of the two of them in the huge gilt mirror that hung over the mantel. Though the glass was hazy with age, she could see her outline, breasts free of her bodice, nipples standing out cherry colored in the glass, hair falling down her back.

Giles was looking at her from under heavy lids, his hands spread on her back. As she watched, he thrust upward again. She let out a groan, her head tipping toward him, her hands tightening on his shoulders to keep her balance.

"Watch," he whispered.

Yasmin shook her head. "No."

He stopped moving. "Why?" His tone wasn't condemnatory, just curious.

"We *are* in public," she gasped. "The mirror makes it more so."

His hips circled, making her take a quick breath. "When we're married, I'll take you in every room, in front of every mirror."

"I prefer a bed," Yasmin breathed.

Giles's hands gripped her hips, raising her enough to free their bodies from each other. Then he set her on her feet, allowing her skirts to fall to her slippers. With a few swift motions, he buttoned the fall on his breeches and stuffed his shirt back into his waistband.

Yasmin blinked at him, her mind fogged. Giles scooped her into his arms, striding through the room.

"No!" she said urgently, pulling her bodice up. "Everyone will know. The footmen will know!"

"You are mine," Giles said evenly, looking down at her.

"Not yet!"

Slowly, he placed her on her feet. "I don't care what servants think."

She pulled open the door. Footmen were always

stationed in the entry, but there was no one to be seen. Giles caught her around the waist. "May I carry you upstairs in the absence of witnesses?"

Yasmin turned into his arms. Her body was throbbing, and she knew her cheeks were crimson. She wanted nothing more than to go to her bedchamber and fall backward onto her bed, drawing his delicious weight down on top of her.

She snuggled close and put her cheek against his chest. His heart was pounding hard. Desire surged through her, but at the same time . . .

They had to talk.

"Yasmin," Giles said, his voice taut as a violin string. "Please, may I take you upstairs? Or in a carriage? In the library? The back garden?"

That startled a giggle from her. "It's beginning to rain!"

"I would make love to you in the rain."

"Everyone would see us from the back windows."

"I wouldn't care. I would pull a blanket over us."

The expression on his face made her heart thunder and her worries ease away. When Giles looked at her like that, with need and desire and affection in his eyes, she would do anything for him.

She raised her mouth. "Kiss me."

His mouth descended on hers, a desperate edge making her tremble. She didn't protest when he swung her into his arms, when he walked up the stairs still kissing her. Walked down the corridor until she pointed at a door.

It slammed behind them, and Giles placed her

gently on the bed. He stripped off his clothing, then eased up her skirts and deftly unclothed her. She held out her arms, but he grinned and lowered his head between her legs. "I dreamed of this."

One rough swipe of his tongue, and Yasmin let out a startled gasp that turned into a moan. She was already swollen and wet, so when he licked her again, rubbing her with his thumb, she fell into an orgasm that was almost frightening in its heat and ferocity. She was lying back, dazed from her body's convulsions, when Giles nudged her higher on the bed, brushed a kiss on her lips, and whispered, "Yes?"

"You'd have to do all the work," Yasmin breathed. "I don't think I can move again."

He—the man who rarely smiled—let out a crack of laughter. "That would be my privilege."

She turned her head and caught sight of the two of them in the glass over her dressing table, Giles driving into her, his hair rumpled, his powerful shoulders flexing. The sight sent a bolt of heat through her tired body.

Compromise. Marriage was about compromise.

And in return? *This.* This was worth anything.

"Look," she whispered hoarsely.

Giles turned his head to the glass and laughed. But he didn't bother to look again, instead gazing into her eyes, caressing her breasts, making her tremble, and then sob with pleasure.

Afterward, he lay beside her on his stomach.

His broad back glistened with sweat. "I like mirrors," Yasmin told him dreamily, "as long as they are in our bedchamber, not the drawing room."

"Mirrors," he repeated, his voice hoarse. One hand moved slowly to her chest. "I like breasts. Your breasts." A thumb rubbed over her nipple.

"I couldn't possibly. Get away from me!" Giggling, she rolled over onto her stomach, knowing he would pounce on her.

She waited until they had kissed, and kissed again, and kissed once more before she whispered, "I'm having your baby, so we cannot wait to marry until next Season."

Giles lurched backward so fast that he nearly fell to the floor. "A baby!" His voice was shocked, hoarse.

Yasmin sat up, anxiety thrumming through her. "I told you that my mother wasn't very fertile but it seems that I am quite different. Do you . . . Do you mind?"

The joy shining from Giles's eyes answered her question, transforming his somber face entirely.

For the first time, Yasmin glimpsed the man whom their children would call Father: a man who smiled easily and laughed on occasion, a man who was far prouder of his family than his title. Who would never consider reputation more important than love.

Later, they lay on the bed side by side, reading letters. Aloud.

First Giles ordered them by date. "I wrote far more than you did," he said with satisfaction.

When they reached her letter describing how Hippolyte Charles had seduced her at sixteen in an act of revenge, Giles pushed the letters aside and rolled onto her, holding her as tightly as he could. "I *will* kill him."

Yasmin chortled and gave his shoulder a little nip. "He's left the country for Spain. That's what Grandfather heard."

"I'm so sorry, Yasmin."

She couldn't feel sorry, not anymore. "If Hippolyte hadn't seduced me, I never would have traveled to England."

"That's true."

"If I never traveled to England"—she reached out and grabbed the thickest letter—"I wouldn't have written this."

Giles's eyes were still dark with anger, but he said, "There is one more of mine that was written before that one. We must read them in order."

Dear Yasmin,

You haven't answered any of my letters, and I am afraid that you have decided to throw me over. At the same time, I know you. You are not a woman who would hop from my bed to Silvester's, no matter what the gossip columns say. You are funny, and wise, and perhaps afraid of your own sensuality.

I am afraid of myself too. I've lost the control I pride myself on. Did you realize that if you kick a man in the right place, you can rupture his spleen?

I'm not sure what the organ does, but I lie awake at night and imagine that I'd done that to Hippolyte Charles, rather than merely knocking him out.

You were sixteen, Yasmin. A baby, in anyone's eyes. Where was your father? Why did no one revenge you?

I cannot bear thinking of you, innocent and naïve, tricked by that revolting man, who has to be twenty years older than you.

You may not be reading my letters. If you open this one, I want you to know that my respect for you has only deepened after learning of his seduction. You were taken advantage of, yet did not allow him to steal you, the essential you, the joyful you. You did not allow his evil intentions to define you.

I suspect you already know what I want to say next. It took me a while to realize it.

I'm in love with you, Yasmin.

I am madly in love with you, and if you don't marry me, I shan't marry at all, because you are the only person I will ever love so much.

Except perhaps our children.

With every wish for your happiness,
Giles

There was silence in the room after he stopped reading. When they finally stopped kissing, Yasmin asked, "What day did you write this letter, Giles?"

"May twelfth."

She pressed another kiss on his lips. "You were indeed ahead of me, then." She rolled to the side and shook open her letter, dated May thirteenth.

When she had finished reading aloud, Yasmin decided that no one else in the world had seen that smile on the Earl of Lilford's face, and perhaps no one would, at least until their first child was born.

They pushed the remaining letters to the side so they could make love again. Over tea and toast, delivered discreetly to their door, they read aloud the remaining letters.

"They smell so dusty," Yasmin said, wrinkling her nose. "These days, any strong odor makes me nauseated, Giles. It's a dreadful side effect of carrying a child."

"I sympathize. Occasionally, the Thames reeks so that I cannot bear to go near it."

"What about linseed oil?"

"Putrid," he said with a shudder.

Yasmin rolled onto her side and propped herself upon on an elbow. "I have been thinking about your nose, Giles."

"It's not as pretty as yours," he said, leaning in to nuzzle her.

"Your father couldn't bear linseed oil, and his father couldn't either, and neither can you." She waited until his eyes registered what she was saying. Then she brushed a kiss on his mouth. "Not that you weren't already the earl, but it seems the title came to you along with a nobleman's nose."

"I love you," Giles said hoarsely.

"I love you too," Yasmin said somewhat drowsily. "There is one thing left in the basket."

"Another letter? I thought your summary of the Corn Laws was very learned, Giles, but I am tired."

He held up the basket.

Yasmin reached her hand into the basket but instead of a folded paper, she pulled out a box. It held a ring with an exquisite pink jewel surrounded by a halo of diamonds. "Oh, Giles," she breathed. "I . . . I had hoped to have an engagement ring someday." She managed a watery smile. "I love it. I've never seen anything so beautiful."

"I wanted to put one on your finger the day after we met," Giles said. "It took time for the jeweler, Rumfeld, to find me just the right pink sapphire."

She touched the stone wonderingly. "It's the most beautiful sapphire I've ever seen, Giles. I thought sapphires were blue or green."

"A few, a very few, are pink, giddy, and exquisite," he said, sliding it on her finger. "They are rare and beyond price, just like you, Mina."

"I never cry!" Yasmin said, her voice wavering.

But every time she looked at her hand, her eyes flooded with tears.

Giles's arms wrapped around her. "Next week, a wedding ring?"

"Yes," Yasmin said happily. She leaned back

against his shoulder and held up her hand so the pink sapphire caught the light.

"You see?" Giles asked.

"See what?"

"The stone laughs. It twinkles."

She pulled his head down to hers. The evidence was incontrovertible: her grumpy earl was the most romantic man she'd ever known.

EPILOGUE

The Queen's Drawing Rooms, St. James's Palace
On the Occasion of the visit of the French
Ambassador
October 14, 1816

René-Eustache, Marquis d'Osmond, had been appointed French ambassador to England last November, yet this was his first visit to the country. He had lived in Switzerland during Napoleon's shameful ascendancy.

Waiting to be presented to the Queen by the former ambassador, he was surprised to find that he felt slightly intimated by the grandeur of the English court. Who would have imagined it?

As he watched, a group of ladies caused Her Majesty to dissolve into gusts of laughter. Entranced, the Queen paid no attention to the fact that such an august personage as himself was waiting.

René spun the corners of his waxed mustaches, considering the dynamics of the court. Given His Majesty's indisposition, the English queen was powerful. He only recognized one of the women, the Duchess of Trent, famous for being originally from America. The ladies clearly had the Queen's ear.

"Pay attention!" the man next to him hissed.

René frowned at the Comte de Ségur, the former ambassador. Ségur would introduce him to the queen and then make his way back to the court of King Louis XVIII.

An exquisite woman had entered from a side door, thus avoiding the throngs of peers waiting behind René. She had the face of a naughty angel, albeit with such dignity as befit royalty. At least six ostrich plumes nodded on her head, yet she carried herself with such grace that she made the style—antiquated to French eyes but required by the English queen—positively elegant.

Her Majesty and her ladies instantly beckoned to her. Aiming a charmingly apologetic smile at those waiting, the lady made her way to the throne and dropped into a deep curtsy.

"Who is she?" René asked.

"The Countess of Lilford," Ségur breathed. "Her husband is formidable in the House of Lords. They haven't been married long, but people say she is likely to become the most powerful woman in the kingdom after royalty, of course."

"I see," René said, watching with sharp eyes as the countess rose from her deep curtsy, and was tapped on her shoulder by the Queen's fan, as if Her Majesty was knighting her. Women were often the true power behind the throne, and a wise ambassador did not ignore such matters.

"Lady Lilford is half French and grew up

around the Napoleonic court," Ségur continued under his breath. "There was some sort of
scandal—wasn't there always in that gathering
of appalling reprobates?—and she traveled to England to live with her grandfather, a *duc*, as I understand it. Yes, there he is."

They watched as a distinguished gentleman
dressed with the flair of a French *duc* bowed over
the queen's hand.

"The countess speaks French, oh so exqui-
sitely," Ségur said, kissing the tips of his gloves.
"Those diamonds she wears are incredible. By all
accounts, she inherited two fortunes. You must
find her good side, marquis, or you will get nowhere in English society."

"It will be a pleasure," René acknowledged.
The queen was smiling up at the countess in a
manner that suggested the lady was a favorite.

"Be careful around her husband. He has a fierce
temper, that one, and is monstrously jealous."

René nodded.

"The most recent gossip is that the earl's sister, Lady Lydia, ran away with another man after
only a few months of marriage. Lady Lilford has
requested that no one gossip of the matter, and
strangely enough, I believe that English society
has obeyed her. I hear nothing."

Society was such that a woman of such intelligence, birth, and beauty, combined with a powerful husband, would naturally rise to the top and
command the field as a general might a battle.

René watched as the lady swept another curtsy

before the queen, and then backed away, holding her grandfather's arm. He actually drew in a breath as she passed. Her court dress was designed with such flare that her *modiste* was obviously of French origin. Other ladies wore gowns as wide as doorways, but the countess had struck a balance between English tradition and French elegance.

"I heard that this will be her last visit to the court in some time, as she is in a delicate condition," Ségur said. "Once she returns to London, you must pay her a call immediately. Whatever you do, do not admit that your brother sided with Napoleon."

René winced. "Do not say that so loudly! My brother is deeply regretful of his foolishness."

"Yes, I expect he is," Ségur murmured.

SECOND EPILOGUE

"I don't like pain."

"I know, darling."

"I don't care for that endearment!" Yasmin bent over with a grunt. "Ow!"

Giles bent with her, one strong arm supporting her. "You *are* my darling."

"*Merde!*" Yasmin cried.

Her husband turned her against his chest, her belly a hard mound between them. His voice was as close to a croon as a well-bred English aristocrat could manage. "Darling, dearest, sweetest Mina."

Yasmin's belly contracted again, pain shooting down her legs. Sweat was rolling down her neck.

"Her Ladyship may be more comfortable lying down," their midwife suggested from the other side of the room, where Giles had banished her.

"No," Yasmin gasped. She felt like walking, so walking was what she intended to do. She took a step and another step, looking down just in time to see that she'd peed all over her feet. "Merry warned me this would happen," she gasped.

Giles began pulling up her wet nightgown, looking entirely unperturbed.

"This is just the beginning," Yasmin said, panting because she could feel another wave of pain coming. "Childbirth is revolting, and babies are even worse. You're going to rue the day that we got married. It's all going to be so . . . so disgusting."

"I will never regret a moment," Giles said, throwing away her wet nightgown and accepting a towel. He crouched at her feet, drying off her legs, smiling up at her. He smiled now. Not all the time, and rarely in public, but he did smile.

"Merde, merde, merde!" Yasmin said vehemently. "This is too painf—" Her voice broke off with a deep grunt.

"I know that sound, my lord. On the bed!" the midwife cried, pointing.

Yasmin made it to the toweling when her body was gripped in a fierce contraction.

Giles lunged forward and barely caught his son and heir as Benjamin propelled into the world. "Bloody hell," he said, dumbfounded, looking at the slippery little creature in his hands.

Yasmin's hair was damp with sweat, her face exhausted from pain, but she erupted into a bellow of laughter. "How the mighty are fallen. The first words the future earl hears are blasphemous!"

Giles looked down at the wide eyes blinking at him. "He's so beautiful, Yasmin."

"From here," his wife said with a dose of French

practicality, "he looks very odd." She reached out her hands.

"One moment, my lady," the midwife said.

A few hours later, the three of them sat on the earl's huge bed, a bed that had seen the births and deaths of five generations of Earls of Lilford.

The baby's parents hung over the fifth earl's squashed little face with that stunned, blissful look that lucky new parents have, no matter their title, their blue blood, their money, or lack thereof.

After a while, when it was clear that their son and heir was giving up on nursing and had fallen asleep, Yasmin asked, "Did you see the wardrobe that Lydia sent for Benjamin?"

"No," Giles said. He was holding one of his son's tiny feet. "Did you ever imagine that a human could be so tiny and yet perfectly formed?"

His wife elbowed him. "She's really trying, Giles. Your sister went to the Emporium and had Mrs. Quimby make her very first baby clothing. Our son is going to be the most fashionable baby in the kingdom."

He didn't answer, so Yasmin said, "You'll have to get over it, love, because soon Lydia will have a baby, which means that Benjamin will have a cousin." Yasmin smiled down at her baby. "You're such a lucky, lucky baby."

He *was* lucky. In his parents' eyes shone the most important promises they would make in life: that they would always love him, and that they would always love each other.

"He's so perfect," Yasmin whispered, a finger stroking down Benjamin's cheek.

"Just like his mother," Giles said, his voice deep with certainty. "I have never been so happy in my life. I'm frightened, Yasmin."

She turned her head and brushed a kiss on his mouth, and then said, with utter certainty, "There's no need to be frightened because we're here. Your family is here."

AN AUTHOR'S NOTE ABOUT FICTION AND TRUTH—AND LOVE

If you are a Jane Austen enthusiast, you may have recognized the inspiration behind the scene in which Lydia briefly transforms into Lady Catherine de Bourgh, horrified at the idea of Elizabeth accepting a second proposal of marriage from Darcy. It was great fun borrowing some of Her Ladyship's sour rhetoric, but I do want to note that Lydia's complicated unhappiness does not align with Lady Catherine's personality in any other way, given Lady Catherine de Bourgh's utter conviction of her worth and station in life. I chose that scene as a counterpoint in a novel that argues that worth has nothing to do with birthright.

The inspiration offered by Hippolyte Charles was more truth than fiction. I inserted my characters into a historical melodrama of lovers and spouses that circled around Napoleon Bonaparte. Early in his marriage to Joséphine, the lady had a much-publicized *affaire* with Hippolyte Charles, a volunteer in the French Army blessed with charm and extraordinary mustaches. Joséphine gave Hippolyte the funds to buy the Cassan estate, but in all fairness, there is no evidence that she revenged herself against her husband's many mistresses. I gave Napoleon an English mistress—Yasmin's mother, Mabel—who would have come between his historical *affaires* with Pauline Foures and the Countess Maria Walewka.

I also want to note that although there has been a small fruit-and-veg market at Covent Garden since the 1650s, the market as I describe it didn't come into being for another thirty years when an Act of Parliament cleared up the brothels and a neo-classical building was erected to cover the market. I have dear memories of wandering the area while studying for a master's degree at Oxford. I had little money, but I could not resist a pair of over-the-knee green suede boots, which I wore a year later when asked to dinner by a handsome Italian graduate student, whom I later married.

So for me, Covent Garden is a very lucky and romantic place.

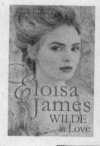

Do you love historical fiction?

Want the chance to hear news about your favourite
authors (and the chance to win free books)?

Suzanne Allain
Mary Balogh
Lenora Bell
Charlotte Betts
Manda Collins
Joanna Courtney
Grace Burrowes
Evie Dunmore
Lynne Francis
Pamela Hart
Elizabeth Hoyt
Eloisa James
Lisa Kleypas
Jayne Ann Krentz
Sarah MacLean
Terri Nixon
Julia Quinn

Then visit the Piatkus website
www.yourswithlove.co.uk

And follow us on Facebook and Instagram
www.facebook.com/yourswithlovex | @yourswithlovex

PIATKUS